MW00580837

PRIOR CONVICTIONS

SOUTHWEST LIFE AND LETTERS

*A series designed to publish outstanding new fiction and
nonfiction about Texas and the American Southwest and to
present classic works of the region in handsome
new editions.*

GENERAL EDITORS

*Suzanne Comer, Southern Methodist University Press;
Tom Pilkington, Tarleton State University.*

PRIOR CONVICTIONS

Stories from the Sixties

✝

DAVE HICKEY

SOUTHERN METHODIST UNIVERSITY PRESS

Dallas

First edition, 1989
Requests for permission to reproduce material
from this work should be sent to:

Permissions
Southern Methodist University Press
Box 415
Dallas, Texas 75275

LIBRARY OF CONGRESS CATALOGING-IN-PUBLICATION DATA

Hickey, Dave, 1940–
Prior convictions / Dave Hickey.—1st ed.
p.   cm.   —(Southwest life and letters)
ISBN 0-87074-286-8
1. Texas—Fiction.   I. Title.   II. Series.
PS3558.I226P75   1989
813'.54—dc19   88-43253
CIP

This book is for Mary Jane,
without whom none of this
And not a day goes by

CONTENTS

The Closed Season

1

I'm Bound to Follow the Longhorn Cows

18

The Passion of Saint Darrell

33

A Winter's Tale

52

The Authentic Life and Death of Smiley Logan

74

An Essay on Style

92

Garland Marlinberg and the City of God

112

Three Days in a South Texas Spring

125

Proof through the Night

AN ESSAY ON MORALS

161

Tell them I said something.

    —PANCHO VILLA'S LAST WORDS

THE CLOSED SEASON

That dream I had while Virgil and I were down in Edmunds County wasn't so unusual. Once I dreamed that we were honky-tonking down on Lower Main Street when we ran into Pa. He invited both of us into the Rustic Lounge and bought us a Lone Star beer. Then I dreamed that I found Pa laid up in the Osteopathic Hospital where he was dying of cancer; but I only had that cancer dream once, when I was trying to quit cigarettes. I dreamed all the time that Pa was still alive, though, that he showed up at the house—not the new house, but the old house over in South Fort Worth where we lived before Pa started doing well. I would come into the kitchen and Pa would be leaning against the icebox grinning while Mom cussed him for leaving her alone.

I sat on the steps of the old house at sunup, smoking a cigarette and enjoying the first cool bite of autumn. When Pa had added the second story, he had had to put the steps on the outside, and those were the steps I sat on, in this dream, under the big chinaberry tree, looking at the new asphalt-shingled houses across the Santa Fe tracks. Behind those neat, square white houses, the morning sky spangled like the scrubbed bottom of a brass pan, and the grass in the yard sparkled like green glass. I had to squint my eyes against the light; then I saw Pa standing in front of me, or I thought I saw him, because shafts of light slanted around his head, over his shoulders and between his legs. I could make out the shiny toes of his alligator boots against the sparkling green grass. Yellow chinaberry leaves tilted on the grass. The smell of cottonseed was on the air.

"Hidey, squirt," Pa said.

"Hi, Pa! Let me tell Mom you're here."

"No need to upset your mother," he said, waving his hand. "She's doing just fine without me. I came to see you, squirt."

"But we all thought you were dead, Pa, and Mom had all your clothes altered to fit Virgil and me—"

Pa laughed. No, he said, he wasn't dead but if Mom came out, he might as well be. He tousled my hair like he used to when I was a kid, and said he hadn't come all the way from Amarillo to argue whether he was dead or not. I felt a fool for mentioning Pa's clothes since at that very minute I had on his old Levi jacket.

"I wonder if you still have my old .410, Gordon?" Pa said.

I couldn't look at him or close my eyes against the glaring light, so I stared down at the step. The planks had weathered; black and gray grains ran through them. Pa asked about the shotgun again; his voice was sharp this time.

"You shot yourself with it, Pa," I said, but he went on to say that the reason he wanted the shotgun was because he and George and Flickey—two of his old air force buddies—wanted to fly up to South Dakota and do some hunting. Pa said he had himself a new airplane, a sweet little Jetstream.

"You shot yourself with it, Pa," I said again. "Mom threw it in the Trinity."

"Well, you're not much help, squirt," Pa said, sticking his thumbs in his gabardine slacks. "I just thought I'd drop by and see if you still had it. That was a fine piece of machinery, Gordon. It deserved to be taken care of."

He stopped me when I stood up and put his arm around my shoulders. Next to my cheek, I could see the black hair curling on his tanned forearm and the yellow cigarette stains on his manicured fingers. Then I looked up into his face and it was Pa all right; his eyes were blue as petunias. There was the mole he cut when he shaved, right next to his left nostril. I have a mole there too, but I use an electric razor.

"Come on, squirt," Pa said. "Don't walk away from me. Virgil wouldn't." I really did love him, but I ran like a scalded cat into the street. The street might have been running with quicksilver.

It didn't make any difference to me, in this dream, where Pa lived. He could live in Amarillo and fly anywhere he wanted to with George and Flickey, but I ran toward the street until Virgil was pulling on my ankle. We were hunting down in South Texas, so Pa couldn't have the shotgun anyway. But what the hell, I thought, I can use one of Virgil's guns. Old Virgil had some nice guns: he is also gettin' some nice tail, I'll bet, off Mildred Ranserhoff. But what the hell, I thought, then I couldn't think what the hell what because Virgil's hand was cold and hard on my ankle. Cold air rushed in under the blanket.

"You're freezing my ass, Virgil," I said.

"Well, you better get your frozen ass out of the sack if you're hunting with me," Virgil said, looming over me in the darkness. He pushed his long, stringy cowlick off his forehead and grinned at me.

"I have to use one of your shotguns, Virgil, I—"

"I know it, dumb-butt," Virgil said, dropping my leg.

Without turning on the light, Virgil stuck his feet in his old combat boots and clumped to the door. Every time his left foot hit the floor, his right shoulder dipped from an old rodeo injury. In his white longhandles and those combat boots, he looked more comical than usual. Three years ago, he got pitched off a bronc out at Fort Stockton. Instead of going to a doctor like any sane man, Virgil packed his shoulder up in ether and ice and won the day-money the next afternoon. According to Virgil, Absorbine Senior cures any disease of man or beast, but his shoulder never did heal right, though he kept it taped up and rubbed down with Absorbine for nearly a month. He keeps pretty much away from rodeoing now—which is all right with Mom.

"I'll fix some breakfast," he said, going through the door. "Since you probably couldn't if you had to."

When Virgil closed the door, I pulled the blanket back over my shoulder and snuggled down into the little nest of warmth I'd made for myself. It was damn cold for this time of the year. My breath fogged in the air, billowing out across the pillow, and I lay there, half awake, and wondered what Mom would do if

she knew I was out hunting with Virgil. I remembered the night
she threw Pa's guns off the Forest Park bridge. She stood on the
bridge with her hair up in curlers, with the cold wind flapping
her blue housecoat around her ankles, and dropped the guns
over one by one while I waited in the car. I heard Virgil throw
some kindling into the stove, and the heavy thuds as he threw
some ash logs in on top of the kindling. It was a comfortable
sound, so I closed my eyes and slept a little more, dreaming
a crazy dream about Virgil and me riding horses, chasing this
other horse. Then the kitchen door slammed and, still holding
the blanket to my shoulder, I rolled over toward the window.

The moon was down but there was no sign of the dawn; the sky
was black and the air was cold and clear. My breath fogged on the
pane so I stuck two fingers out from under the blanket to clear it,
my fingers squeaking on the cold glass. The gravel road running
down to the creek, the barn beside the road and the limestone
bluff beyond the creek glowed white in the darkness, while along
the crest of the bluff a few scraggly trees were blacker than the
sky full of stars. It was still as death out there—until Virgil came
striding across my field of vision, looking a little silly since he had
thrown his big sheepskin coat on over his longhandles. His legs
looked white and skinny between the big coat and the unlaced
combat boots.

Virgil trudged up the rise to the water tower and started fooling around with a knob on the pipe. Finally he walked away
from the tower, kicking around in the weeds until he found a
two-by-four. He picked up the piece of board and swung it like
a baseball bat. There wasn't a sound. I could see Virgil's breath
trailing in the clear air; I could see the arc of the board as it hit
the pipe, and Virgil's lips moving as he cussed it, all in silence.
It made me feel so cut off, so lonesome and alone, that I rolled
over and stared at the dark ceiling until Virgil yelled from the
kitchen for me to come get it before he threw it out and spit in
the skillet. I had to run across that cold room and put on my
hat and shirt before I could even light a cigarette. By then I had
my blood moving, so I pulled on my Levi's and boots quickly

and went clumping down the dark hall. The sound of my boots echoing in the hall made me happy. By the time I grabbed the cold knob of the kitchen door and pulled it open, the lonesome feeling was gone. Virgil turned bacon in the skillet. I could smell the sizzling meat as the light and heat rushed around me. In that bright kitchen with the cabinets trimmed in red, with yellow curtains shutting out the dark morning, all that dreaming seemed pretty silly to me. Virgil turned around with the skillet in his hand and told me to get my ass in there and close the door.

The day before, while Virgil and I were driving down from Fort Worth, the Mexican caretaker had hauled a pickup-load of groceries and whiskey out from Randall Springs, so for breakfast we had eggs sunnyside, Canadian bacon, thick toast and milk with ice in it. Afterward we had black coffee from Neiman-Marcus mugs with the Ranserhoff brand on them, and Virgil started to roll a cigarette. I lit a ready-made and watched Virgil's skinny face wrinkle and relax while he worked the tobacco around in the paper. I thought that if the truth were told, I favored Pa a lot more in the face than Virgil did. But inside, it was probably different.

"Your boss has a nice layout here," I said.

"Mmmmm," Virgil said. He licked the paper and fitted the cigarette together. "Mil Ranserhoff's a damn good woman," he said when he was done.

"You like her, huh?" I said. "You could find people in Fort Worth who don't."

"I could find people in Fort Worth who don't like *you*, squirt," Virgil said.

"Don't call me squirt, huh?" I said.

"Mil's damn good with horses, squirt. She just keeps me around 'cause she has them stashed all over the hot-damn state." He put the cigarette neatly in front of him on the table and walked to the cabinet. "Yeah, I like her fine," he said, "regardless of what Mom says."

Mildred Ranserhoff is a hard, blond-headed old girl of about forty who likes whiskey and horses better than people, with the possible exception of Virgil. And what Mom said was that Mildred was a rich tramp and that it killed her soul to go to a party and see her own son standing around in his rough-out boots drinking sidecars— but it went a little deeper than that.

After Virgil got hurt out at Fort Stockton he went to work for Stanley Bracker training quarter horses. Mom didn't think training quarter horses was a very respectable profession, but Stanley was a friend of the family and training horses beat the hell out of rodeoing. Pa had redesigned two DC-3s for the Bracker oil operation and hunted some with Stanley; then when Pa died, Stanley started taking Mom around to the parties, mostly out of politeness, I guess. So as long as Virgil worked for Stanley, she pretty much let him alone. Then there was the run-in over Stanley's Triple-A Rocket Bar colt.

It happened one afternoon while Stanley and Mom were out at the stables. Stanley was about half-tight and showing off his horses, but he made the mistake of running that nice little colt around for a while and putting him up wet. Virgil flipped. He told Stanley that if he was gonna be careless with four thousand dollars worth of horse, there wasn't any reason for him, Virgil, to stay around there. Virgil cussed him out good and proper while old Stan hung his head and shuffled his boots in the dust. You'd have thought they caught him eating his soup with his salad fork. Stanley ended up apologizing all over the place but Virgil quit him anyway and went to work for Mildred Ranserhoff. Well, that tore it with Mom. It was bad enough quitting Stanley, but going to work for Mildred, who has a rough reputation to say the least, really ripped the sheet. Of course Virgil, not being a social butterfly of any kind, didn't really understand. He was just going where they treated horses right.

As it turned out, he was going where they treated Virgil all right, too. Just the week before out at Mildred's stable, he mentioned he'd like to shoot some dove and Mildred walked over to her desk, opened the drawer and tossed him the keys to the ranch house. Then she sat down and called the Mexican about food and whiskey. So last Friday, for some reason, Virgil called me. I answered the phone in the hall on my way to class.

"Hey, squirt," he said. "How'dja like to go dove hunting?"

Mom was in the living room playing bridge with some of her friends, so I lowered my voice and asked where.

"Edmunds County. Mildred's got a place down there that hasn't been hunted in five years. Also seems the local law is in somebody's back pocket."

"Damn right," I said. "Damn right I do."

I told Mom we were going to a horse show.

Virgil scratched a kitchen match under the table and lifted the yellow-blue flame carefully to his cigarette, his blue eyes crossing a little as he did. After taking a long drag that turned a half-inch of cigarette into ash, he pulled the cigarette from his lips, balanced the ash for a few seconds, then flicked it into the remains of his yellow eggs.

"You ever heard of an ashtray?" I said.

"I prefer the plate, Miz Vanderbilt," Virgil said. "I'm just a crude country boy, not up on citified ways."

He grinned, showing me the gold tooth nestled in the side of his mouth which he got much the same way he got his shoulder. I asked him how he got off calling me citified since we grew up in the same damn house, and Virgil said that everybody who went to college was a citified bastard unless they went to Texas Tech or Sul Ross. I told him that Mildred Ranserhoff probably went to Vassar, and he said that was an altogether different thing. He pushed the dirty plate away, though, and dragged the ashtray over with one finger.

I had to admit, then, that I liked Virgil for all his faults. His worst fault had been his talent for starting a fight at home when we were kids, and then walking out. It was a real gift. Virgil could get everybody in the house cussing and screaming and slamming doors, then walk out the door, climb in his pickup and go off to drink some beer. Sis always locked herself in her room, so that left me to take the crap that was being dealt out. It was a fine talent, though, and I think Pa envied it as much as I did. In fact, Pa probably preferred Virgil to me on most counts, though he never let on.

When Virgil had finished his cigarette, he slid his chair back and stood up, stretching and scratching his stomach. "You clear the table, Miz Vanderbilt," he said. "I'll fetch the weapons."

While he fiddled with the combination on the window box, I scraped and stacked the dishes and the skillet. I had rinsed the dishes off with icy water and decided they were pretty well washed when Virgil asked me if I knew about the time he ran into Pa in New York City.

"No," I said.

"Well, hell," he said, opening the window box and taking out two shotguns in soft leather cases. "It was my first trip to the big city, and my first and last time riding in the Madison Square Garden. Let me tell you, squirt, I wasn't nowhere *near* those old boys' class, never was. At the time of course I said I was getting beat in the hat, but I was getting beat in the saddle and that's for sure. Man, Jimmy *Shoulders* was in that rodeo. Anyway, the day after the show closed I was stove up and broke and sitting around Rockefeller Center looking at the pretty girls when who should come striding by in a silk suit with a big-titted blond on his arm, but Pa. He taken one look at me, and I taken one look at that blond, and he loaned me fifty bucks. The idea was that every time I thought about that blond, I put a big steak in my mouth."

"That's more than he ever loaned me," I said.

"Well, you never caught him in New York City with a blond," Virgil said with a sly grin. "But you know what I did with that money?"

"I guess, knowing you, that you got pretty well drunked up."

"Hell, I wasn't even that smart." I finished wiping off the table with the dishrag and Virgil laid the guns down. "I caught the first subway down to Green Witch Village and got this artist down there on Bleecker Street to do this chalk portrait of me in my riding clothes, number and all. Then I got my boots polished and tipped the boy two dollars. I finally ended up hitchhiking back to Texas and not eating for three days. Pa was dead when I got back."

"He would have got a kick out of it," I said. "He used to tell me if you were gonna spend money sensibly there wasn't any reason to work for it."

"I still have me a pretty good picture, though, or had a pretty good picture. I gave it to Mildred, for Christmas." He untied the strings and reached into the first gun case. Grabbing the end of the stock with one hand, he slipped the leather cover off a Winchester pump with a carved walnut stock. "When was the last time you were out?" Virgil said. "Three years?" He laid the Winchester down and picked up the other case.

"Closer to four. I'm glad you asked me, Virgil."

"What did you tell Mom?"

"I told her we were going to a horse show."

"You know you shouldn't let yourself get bitched at Mom. She's got a right."

"I know she's got a right," I said. "That's a nice gun."

"You damn right it's a nice gun, honcho," Virgil said, balancing the second gun on his palm. It was a Browning automatic, one of those fancy gas-operated, Belgian-made models. Virgil hiked it up under his arm and walked to the cabinet; he took down six boxes of shells and slapped them down on the table.

"We goin' to war, Virgil?" I said.

"Toss me that rag under the sink, will you?"

Virgil wiped the excess oil off the Browning and laid it on the table and I watched it resting there, dark against the white enamel tabletop. I remembered Pa telling me that a good shotgun was the most beautiful piece of machinery in the world, and it had a strange effect on me, watching that gun resting on the table. I remembered things that had happened so long ago that there were no words for them—things that had happened even before I was born. Watching that beautiful Browning, glowing bluey gray and dull walnut against the white table, I felt older and stronger and a little scared—as if everything that had happened since I had been hunting last hadn't happened, had been a dream. Then I noticed Virgil watching me, so I picked up the automatic. It was lighter than I remembered and finer. I ran my hand along the cool walnut stock, then slapped it into my shoulder. The stock was cut for Virgil but it felt fine. I sighted on a pair of antlers over the sink, then looked over the stock at Virgil, who was wiping the oil from the pump mechanism of the Winchester, his forehead wrinkled in concentration.

"I forgot what a thing I used to have for guns," I said, pulling the stock away from my cheek and dropping it from my shoulder.

"It gets in your blood," Virgil said, not looking up. "Calf-ropin's like that for me. Can't look at a calf without gettin' an itchy rope-hand." Putting down the Winchester on the drain-board, he grabbed his Levi's off the stove, where he'd hung them up to warm. He hopped around on one foot while he stuck the other into the jeans.

"You have trouble with the water this morning?"

"Naw, you just got to bang the rust loose."

"We're not gonna get arrested for this, are we?" I said as I walked to the door to get my big coat.

"This is South Texas, old boy," Virgil said. "Everything's squared away."

"Well, let's get moving."

"We're good as gone."

Virgil slipped what was left of a bottle of Wild Turkey bourbon into one of the pockets of his sheepskin coat; then we stood across the table from one another slipping shells into our pockets. When the boxes were empty, Virgil picked up the Browning automatic.

"Gordy, why don't you use the pump? It's a safer gun and I wouldn't want you to . . ."

"Okay, okay," I said. "Jus' so it shoot."

"It shoot, all right," Virgil said, but I had already grabbed the pump and walked out into the cold, dim morning.

The chill would fade when the sun hit the air but as Virgil guided the jeep down the yellow ruts the cold was quick and dry. The rims of my eyes stung, and my nostrils and the tops of my ears above the collar of the coat. I pulled the collar up higher as we passed the barn and turned down toward the foot of the limestone bluff. Above the bluff the sky was gray and overcast, and the bluff itself was the same raw color as the clouds.

Virgil drove with both hands on the wheel.

"Little brother?" he said.

"Yeah, Virgil."

"You can use the automatic if you want to."

"Forget it. I couldn't hit anything with a howitzer."

"Well, I'd just as soon use the Winchester. I know you can shoot, for God's sake. You used to shoot circles around me."

"It's all right. I'll use the pump."

"Well, it don't make no nevermind to me," Virgil said, then added, "if you can say that."

"If you can say what?"

"It don't make no nevermind," Virgil said. "That's not good English, is it?"

"Hell, Virgil, it's as good as anything," I said. "Anyway, two years at TCU doesn't make me any kind of authority."

"Well, use whatever gun you want to."

"I'd just as soon use the pump."

"Suit yourself," Virgil said, looking straight ahead at the road.

A breeze lifted out of the grass and slid along the slope. The breeze was still cold, but there was a taste of warm in it—only a taste. We were driving through the taller grass along the creek bank. A few scrub oak overhung the road, and through their bare branches I saw the clouds begin to move like a herd of dirty sheep. The humps and billows of gray slid down the sky toward the bluff that loomed above us now.

"Say, Gordy," Virgil said, "will you do something for me?"

"Sure, what do you want?"

"Well, acknowledgin' the fact that you aren't any kind of authority, I want you to correct me when I say something stupid like 'don't make no nevermind' and all that crap. Whenever I say something really stupid."

"You talk all right, Virgil."

"Hell I do. Not all the time. Sometimes I say something stupid around Mil, that's Mrs. Ranserhoff, and I feel like a fool."

"Okay," I said. "I'll correct you when it's really bad."

Virgil never once looked at me. Tall grass slapped against the side of the jeep, and looking back over my shoulder I could see the slate-green roof of the barn. The grass we had driven through was darker than the rest of the grass on the slope. Virgil was saying, "What I really ought to do, little brother, is to get some dogs. Good hunting dogs and learn to train 'em. Anybody as good with horses as I am ought to be able to train a hound."

"I read in the barbershop the other day that poodles used to be good hunting dogs before the ladies got hold of them," I said.

"That so?" Virgil said. "You know old George Simmons' wife has a poodle that's dyed pink. We ought to sneak over there some evening and steal the little beggar, teach him how to hunt. You know, we'd wash that goddamn dye out and teach him to hunt birds." Virgil grinned. "I bet that little pink peckerwood would have the time of his life."

"He might that," I said.

"Here's the ford," Virgil said. "This creek is called Indian Creek, don't ask me why." He edged the jeep into the dull brown water. As we moved deeper, a brown swell rolled before us and the floating weeds on the far bank rose and fell. At the deepest part of the creek, Virgil pushed the shift lever down into four-wheel low and gunned the motor. "Hang on!" he yelled. We reared out of the water in a flume of spray and bounced onto the steep road that ran up the bluff. A rabbit broke cover and scampered along in front of us. After about fifteen yards the rabbit veered off into the brush and almost fell over his own feet. We followed the yellow-gray ruts up a narrow arroyo until we were about fifty feet from the top; then Virgil stopped.

Another arroyo came running in from the northeast, and on the delta of high ground between the two arroyos, a barbed-wire fence petered out. The dirt had washed from underneath the last fence post and it hung off the incline at a crazy angle, held up by the tangled wire. Resting his arm on top of the windshield, Virgil pointed upward.

"Fence up there runs a good two mile," he said. "If you take that side and I take this one, there's a chance we won't kill each other if we fire away from the fence."

We didn't speak for a while. I leaned against the spare tire slipping shells into the breech of the Winchester while Virgil sat on the hood and loaded the Browning. Down below, the creek riffled through some high rocks, and above us the wind shushed through the grass on the plateau. The shaggy clouds were sliding faster now.

"Looks as if it's gonna fair off," I said.

"Yeah," Virgil said, sliding off the hood. "You can still use this gun if you want to."

I just waved my hand and waded into the tall grass at the mouth of the little arroyo. In a minute Virgil was out of sight and I was alone. At the head of the arroyo a scrap of morning blue broke through the clouds; it turned gray and then there was some more blue off to the left. I could hear Virgil crashing brush as he moved up the other arroyo. For some reason I had pumped the Winchester twice, and two red shells lay in the damp grass. I reinserted the shells and stood with my feet apart, resting the butt of the stock into my hipbone; then I slapped the stock into my shoulder, sighting on the tops of the windswept scrub oaks along the crest of the bluff. There was sun up there, and a few remaining leaves winked gold and green. This was the way Pa used to shoot when he was showing off at the gun club. Virgil and I would sit on the ground outside the box while Pa stood on the line with the stock into his hip and his black hair flaring

in the wind. "Pull!" he'd shout, yanking the gun to his shoulder
and firing in the same movement. The pigeon didn't break, it
disappeared. Virgil and I would tell Pa what a fine shot he was
and Pa would smile and wink. He always did things the hard
way, but he was a damn fine shot.

I picked my way through the cenizo and around the occasional patch of prickly pear that grew along the arroyo. My sweat
chilled on my forehead and I wished to hell Virgil was walking with me, but it was just like him, leaving me alone. It was a
Vernon family trait, leaving people alone, except for Mom and
she tended in the other direction, and I was in my same old fix.
Pa was four years dead, and nothing had changed. I was in the
thick of a family fight, just like always, with Pa yanking on my
butt and Mom yanking on my head, and Virgil, that son of a
bitch, squatting off in the corner with a silly grin on his face. I
was so mad at Virgil for leaving me alone that if he'd walked up,
I might have shot him.

Then I tripped over a root and landed with my hand square
in a patch of nettle. This revived me proper, so I climbed on
up the arroyo, scratching my palm and thinking about Pa. It
was funny, I could only remember him doing two things: having
dinner in the old house with the chinaberry trees and fooling
with guns. Sometimes after dinner he climbed the stairs to my
room with an armload of guns. We would clean them together
and he would tell me about being a boy in Orange, Texas, and
how much he hated cotton farming. That was how he got to
flying, as a crop duster in a little Piper after the war. Then he
and two of his hard-drinking air force buddies went into the——
airplane business. They ended up redesigning old multi-engine
jobs into posh executive planes, and coining the money. It was
about this time we sold the old house with the chinaberry trees,
moved to the west side, and Mom started in on us to call him
"Dad" instead of "Pa." My little sis changed but Virgil and I
never could. So, finally, there seemed to be two men living in
the house. One was "Dad" and the other was "Pa." Pa took us
hunting or out to the gun club and Dad flew to New York and

Washington and down to South America where some of the big honchos down there were his best customers.

When I was a kid, I was never sure that the fellow in the narrow gray suit was Pa. It was, though; they buried him in a narrow gray suit and a South American general, who was in town at the time, came to the funeral in a private limousine. After the service he gave Virgil and me one of his medals and told us that Pa was "muy simpático." I hadn't thought about all these things for a long time. In some ways they were all thought out for me since they didn't explain anything. So I thought about that blond in New York, which didn't explain anything either, and nearly stepped on a blue jay. The jay clattered, burst in an explosion of blue feathers right past my face. My hand jerked on the Winchester so hard that I nearly fell down again, but suddenly I was at the head of the arroyo.

Rolling country spread away from me in the sun which shone through two gray ranks of clouds. The light, falling at a sharp angle, washed the prairie grass on the ridges bright yellow and left the coulees full of shadows. Starting to walk, I spotted the fence about thirty yards to my right. The muzzle of the Winchester watched the tangled sod in front of me, but I kept losing my balance and weaving. The slightest ridge or dip in the sod threw me off balance; stale coffee rose up in my throat, my stomach gathered into a fist, and I sweated like a hog. It took every bit of concentration I had just to put one foot in front of the other. A whole flight of dove could have broken and I would have never known because I was watching the grass at my feet. The grass was brown at the top and darker green down on the body, then yellow and purplish red down next to the sod, like veins. I stopped and looked around but Virgil was no place to be seen and I felt naked and alone under the sky. It had been stupid for us to split up when we could have hunted just as well together, but here I was. So I tried to think about Virgil and Mildred Ranserhoff and Virgil asking me, of all people, to tutor his English, but the thoughts slipped right out of my mind. It was like grabbing minnows in a bucket. All I could think about was that goddamn lonesome prairie, and the effort it took to walk.

There was a lone hackberry about fifty yards to my left and I started moving toward it. The idea of getting under that hackberry really appealed to me. I glanced around from time to time, pretending to myself that I was hunting, but that just reminded me of the Winchester in my hands and the shells in the magazine. When I reached the hackberry I leaned against the rough bark. I just leaned there taking deep breaths while sweat ran down the side of my nose. I was so damn glad to be underneath something. Three little ants crawled out of the bark onto the shoulder of my coat, but I let them be. A scudding cloud covered the sun and the gold drained away from the ridges. I was sweating something terrible now, so I unbuttoned my coat and sat down in the soft damp grass with my back against the tree. With both hands I held Virgil's shotgun upright between my knees. For no reason I tried to hold as still as possible. I tried not to move at all, to blank every little thought out of my mind, but there were thoughts that I couldn't understand and couldn't stop. They swirled just below the surface, like black bass in a dark pond, and I couldn't stop them. I sat there and watched my knuckles whiten on the breech of the Winchester. I hooked one thumb in the trigger guard, but other than moving those three bones in my thumb, I held perfectly still. I even held my eyes still, gazing past the gun at the gray country. The gun seemed to disappear when I focused my eyes on the prairie. The prairie spread as far as I could see into the pale blue horizon, but I dropped my eyes. The butt of the stock slid an inch or two toward the damp heels of my boots. It was the damnedest thing, since I was holding so still, to see that fine carved walnut stock slide smoothly through the grass, and the smooth deep muzzle lower toward my face. Until my thumb had moved, I didn't realize that I had taken the safety off. It was probably an old reflex, but no, I knew exactly what that guy sitting under the hackberry was doing. He was trying to keep as quiet as possible, but the blood kept gushing and pumping through his wrists so it was impossible to keep completely quiet. So he thought about blood: about his blood, and his pa's and his brother's. Then he realized that his blood was thinking.

For a second, when the shot rang out, and for two or three seconds longer, while the noise echoed around me, I didn't know whether I was alive or dead. Then slowly, so slowly that if you had been watching me you probably couldn't tell, I pulled the muzzle of the Winchester away from my forehead. I heard Virgil calling, something about birds, but his voice died and everything was quiet again. Off to my right I saw the birds, two bandtails, skimming over the top of the grass. If I didn't want to take a chance of hitting Virgil, I would have to fire with the birds going away at an angle. I scrambled to my feet, bringing up the gun. The birds, coming fast and staying close together, began to climb. A piece of sun broke under the clouds and their fluttering brown bodies were burned against the light. Giving the first bird a slight lead, I squeezed the trigger. The shot hurt my ears and knocked me back a step, but I didn't fall on my ass.

I hadn't led him quite enough. The second bird, though, was caught full. It was knocked about two feet along the path of the shot, then it fell like a rock. The lead bird bucked in its flight. It lifted its wings two or three more times, and then started to cut a clean arc toward the ground with one wing swinging behind it like a free rudder. Watching those birds fall, I knew I had killed one hell of a lot more than two pigeons. I had killed my pa—not finally, maybe, not forever, I knew, but for that rising moment at least, I had really fucking *done it* and I felt so light I could have flown. Virgil ran toward me, holding the automatic out from his body. He came up smiling and panting with his gold tooth glinting in the sun, and grabbed me around the shoulders.

"You shoot good, old boy," he said, shaking me like a rag doll.

"Shoot well," I said.

"Huh?"

"The right way to say it is 'You shoot well,'" I said.

I'M BOUND TO FOLLOW
THE LONGHORN COWS

I'm bound to follow the longhorn cows until I get too old;
It's well to work for wages, boys, I get my pay in gold.
My girl must cheer up courage and choose some other one,
For I'm bound to follow the longhorn cows until my race is run.

—A COWBOY SONG

When the white sun had spun into the pupil of the sky, as it
hung at the top of its trajectory between the two horizons and
then began to fall into early afternoon, the old man found himself trapped in a bathtub of tepid water on the second floor
of his ancient house. He flailed about for a few moments and
then he became quiet and listened to the long winds shushing
through the empty corridors and rooms of his house, which was
Victorian in design, having two stories, an attic, a storm cellar,
spires, lightning rods, weather vanes, cupolas, traceries and an
occasional leaded window. It rested on the plain like a child's
block dropped on an immense crazy quilt patched with green
and yellow, an old house, but the interior had been completely
modernized, and the bathroom in which the old man sat was
paneled with cool blue tile.

He had seen ninety summers, as the Comanches, who were
gone now, would say, and he was the only person in the surrounding country who was older than the house. On the old
man's first birthday his father had driven four stakes into a
bald ridge on the prairie, and begun to lay the foundation, and
the old man had grown up with the house. It was part of all
his memories, the nucleus of his childhood, the point of de-

parture and the point of return for the many journeys of his youth and manhood, for, during his first half-century, the old man had been a rambler and a heller. But, unfortunately, unlike his house, the old man could not be modernized, except by the use of what he called "contraptions": his false teeth, his electric wheelchair.

He was just a shriveled man with gray eyes whose sight was still keen, with a yellowish white mustache drooping below a swollen pockmarked nose that still smelled well enough. He had only a few fringes of white hair on his head, and there was more growing out of his ears than around them, but his hearing was still better than most since he knew what to listen for. He still had the use of his senses, but ninety is an age when senses can be a burden, for your body no longer responds to them. It would have been a blessing if the old man had been a little deaf, or a little blind; then he could not hear the hooves clopping beside the stable, or see the Mexican cowboys ride out toward the pasture where the white-faced cattle dipped their heads slowly in the heat.

At the age of sixty-five he had lost his teeth and his virility, and hadn't mourned his teeth for an hour; he put them in a bottle on his desk. At the age of eighty his right arm was crippled with arthritis, and at the age of eighty-six his legs gave out. They refused once and forever to clench a horse's side, or even to support his weight, though he was a small man. When this happened his son, who was born when the old man was fifty, bought an electric wheelchair for his father and, after several interviews, hired a pretty blond nurse with heavy breasts and a slow smile to care for him. For the next four years the old man spent most of his time resting on a couch in his second-floor bedroom, watching his land, watching the seasons and the sun change its face. Sometimes the nurse, whose name was Roberta May Kuykendall, would read the newspaper to him, and once a week she bathed him.

Roberta May had left the old man's face covered with a lather of soap and it dried into a crust in the first few minutes, while he sat there, immobile, not knowing what to do. Finally he decided to remove the soap by lifting his knees and sliding down into the clear water. His buoyant heels and buttocks leisurely rose and fell as he let the water creep over his chin and climb in a prickly line across his cheeks. He lifted his good arm and freed the dried soap by rubbing his sand-grained face. His skin felt better, but the taste of soap still hung about his gums. Roberta May had let one soapy finger slip into the old man's mouth as she fell. He sucked his saliva into a cud and spat vehemently into the bath water.

Roberta May lay where she had fallen. She had been scrubbing the old man's neck when her eyes had widened. Her hand jumped, a soapy finger slipped into the old man's mouth, and she had collapsed. She sat for a moment shaking convulsively. Then she had cried something in surprise and fallen back, her head striking the tile like a clay jar. And she had died, so quickly it wasn't even sad, sprawled on the blue tile with her blue eyes looking upward, her skirt caught up around her thighs, and one white arm extended so that the hand rested on a crumpled pile of clothes.

The clothes belonged to the old man's son. As Roberta May had wheeled him down the hall they had met him coming out of the bath. "I have to fly to Dallas, Pa. I'll see you tomorrow afternoon," he had said and run down the steps three at a time. Now his jeans, his denim work shirt and his wide-brimmed straw hat lay in a little pile between the toilet and the bathtub, and the girl's hand seemed to be pointing to them. A scrap of a breeze lifted Roberta May's skirt, revealing another inch of her thigh.

The bathroom curtains billowed white above the old man's head, and the smell of alfalfa, incredibly sweet, swam into his nostrils, only to be cut by the lingering fumes of the soap. The alfalfa wind died quickly, like a breath sucked in, and becalmed the curtains. The old man heard the starched linen crackle faintly as it collapsed. Then he became aware of grasshoppers clicking in the hot grass of the lawn. Outside the window the lawn sloped down to a barbed-wire fence where the hayfields

and pastures began and continued into the horizon, but the
sill was two feet above the old man's head. All he could see by
looking upward was a rectangle of blue sky.

It irritated him to be able to move with such relative freedom
in the buoyancy of the water, and yet not be able to climb out of
the tub and into the wheelchair, which stood by the bathroom
door, but he knew he couldn't. He pulled in his lower lip and
clamped it with his gum. Before him the pale image of his body
undulated on the surface of the water. His legs were thin and
hairless, and the skin on his ankles and thighs had a yellowish
cast; his narrow chest was covered with white hair that bristled
in patches out of the water, creating little patterns of surface
tension. His body, which in its time had mounted many good
horses, and many women as good as Berta May, was just a stringy
bag of flesh. He glanced at Roberta May Kuykendall's nylon-
sheathed legs, and then slowly looked away.

Just a few minutes before she died, they had heard the Estansas' Chevrolet clatter by the house, had heard Manuel's special
honk which he gave every Saturday when he and Señora Estansa
headed for town.

"I can tell you two Mesicans gonna be drunk tonight," the old
man had said.

"Oh, Mr. Cotton," Roberta May had said, "now how do you
know that?"

"I tell you, punkin'. I done a little cowboyin' in my time, and
whenever I got to town, it sure wasn't for no tea party."

"Mr. Cotton, I bet you were a wild one."

"That I was, in my way. I drank a little whiskey, and chased
me a few girls might' near as pretty as you." He had winked at
her. "I ain't gonna tell you if I caught 'em or not."

Roberta May had laughed as she bent over and scrubbed
the old man's neck. He looked down the V of her blouse and
watched her hanging breasts quiver as she laughed. What a
sweet hussy you would have been, he thought, and cast a furtive
glance down into the water, where everything was still. And if
the old man had ever cried, which he hadn't, he would have

then; he would have clenched his fists and let the hateful tears, squeezed like vinegar from his clenched eyelids, crash down over his cheekbones; he would have dropped his toothless jaws and howled, then or any of a thousand times when Roberta May with her soft hands was bathing him or changing his clothes. He would watch her narrowly as she went about her business, as a newly broken horse will watch the wrangler approaching with the bridle dangling from one hand, trailing in the dust. He would decide that she was teasing him, that she was flaunting herself, but closeted in the back of his mind he marked a secret calendar from Saturday to Saturday, when he was bathed by Roberta May Kuykendall who bent forward so casually. Then he would try to convince himself that it was a good thing, nature's law, that old men and young girls could not get together, but he was never completely successful, and now the heart beneath those breasts had stopped, the valves had sucked closed, stopping the surge of blood that flushed her cheeks and made little patterns of red on her neck, and the darkness in her veins, where her blood eddied into stillness, had closed around her sight. She had fallen very heavily, not at all as a girl should fall, onto the blue tile, with her blond hair sprayed around her head . . .

And so he sat there for a long time, not thinking anything, knowing all along that the day was Saturday and that the Estansas had gone to town to get drunk, that his son was relaxing in flight somewhere between Sonora and Dallas, in the blue air, and that he, like some goddamned relic, had been left in Roberta May's care and that she was stiffening on the chilly tile, but not formulating these thoughts in his mind, not admitting their consequences, until the room began to fill with golden light that poured through the bright window like water from a sluice. It was only then, when he knew the sun was falling, that he accepted the fact that the tub was a prison. Its slick white sides described his boundaries and confined him. He, who owned three hundred sections, who had ridden to Montana and back, might as well have been in a life raft in the middle of a golden ocean, or in a coffin.

But deep in his marrow it was not fear that the old man felt, it was inconvenience; the habits of his last four years, the last fifteen hundred days, plucked at him more urgently than any terror. More than anything on God's green earth he wanted, desired even, to be on his couch by the window, dry, in soft pajamas, his knees covered with a Navajo blanket. He wanted Roberta May to rise up and read him the newspaper while he watched the prairie change colors, or he wanted his son to come into the room and talk to him, a little dully, about a new cattle deal, or oil deal, or the prospects for the cotton crop. His warm bedroom was twenty steps away from the bathtub. Behind the blue-tiled wall, one door down the upstairs hall, his couch was being warmed by the falling sunlight, the Navajo blanket folded at its foot. He shivered.

It startled him for a moment because he thought he was afraid of dying there, ending his century in the bathtub, but it just irritated him. The whole idea filled him with indignation: to have to spend the night in the bathtub! He wasn't afraid, but he was very nearly mad. He lifted his good hand and tugged at his mustache, twisting the damp hairs and poking the end into his mouth. "Crap!" he said aloud.

Then, when he dropped his hand, making a little splash, he realized that the water had become chilled. Three hours. With a little effort he lifted his left leg, watched it appear like a continent bursting from the sea, draining, and with his toe he turned on the hot water faucet. The burst of water burned his heel and so, maneuvering his foot, he turned on the cold faucet and settled back to enjoy the warm surge of water around his feet and up his legs, the tingling when it reached his crotch.

When the edge of the water's surface began to sting like the touch of a hot razor, he turned off the water, and no sooner had the last drop pinged into the tub than a muffling silence settled around him. It pressed against his eardrums and drew sweat from his bald scalp. But the silence, in itself, wouldn't have bothered him, for he had spent a large portion of his life in silence. It was the noiselessness, the noiselessness of an empty house, and different from the silence of the High Plains. Out there there were distances in the silence, crystalline depths; it had size, magnitude, but it didn't make a man, or a man on a horse anyway, feel small. Somehow the two feet between the stirrup and the ground put a man's head among the stars, if he was young, and made the silence right. But in the house, where the silence was cut into dusty cubes, divided into a thousand little silences . . .

He grasped the side of the tub, pulled himself into a sitting position, and to the golden room, the dead girl and the cavernous house he shouted:

"I'm big and I'm bold, boys, and I was big and bold when I was but nine days old. I'm the meanest son of a bitch north, south, east and west of Sonora, Texus. I've rode everything with hair on it and a few things that was too tough to grow any hair. I've rode bull moose on the prod, she-grizzlies and long bolts of lightning. I got nine rows of jaw teeth and holes bored for more, and whenever I get hungry, I eat stick dynamite cut with alkali, and when I get thirsty, I can drink a risin' creek after a goose-downer plumb dry and still have a thirst for a little Texas whiskey cut with cyanide. Why, when I'm cold and lonesome, I nestle down in a den of rattlers 'cause they make me feel so nice and warm!"

He took a long breath and continued at the top of his lungs. "And when I'm tired, I pillow my head on the Big Horn Mountains, and stretch out from the upper Gray Bull River clean over to the Crazy Woman Fork. I set my boots in Montana and my hat in Colorada. My bed tarp covers half of Texus and all of Old Mesico. The Grand Canyon ain't nothin' but my bean hole. But boys, there's one thing for sure and certain, and if you want to know, I'll tell ya: that I'm a long way short of being the Daddy of 'em all. 'Cause he's full growed. And as any fool can plainly see, why, boys, I ain't nothin' but a youngun!"

Ho! Drunk in Tascosa or Abilene with your hands behind you holding to the bar, bellied out and hell-raisin', stinkin' of two weeks' sweat, bad whiskey, Bull Durham and cow dung, with a whole skillet of mountain oysters under your belt . . . The echoes of his voice wandered for a few moments down the halls and into some of the empty rooms of the old house; then, one after another, like pebbles falling into a stream, they dropped into silence. (Shards and flecks of the yellow light glittered in Roberta May's eyes.) There was the silence again, but the old man felt better for having shouted.

He had composed that brag, and a lot more of it he couldn't remember, when he was a boy, seventeen, nineteen, he couldn't remember now, but when he had followed the last of the big herds up the trail through the Indian Territory into Wyoming and Montana. It was something to do while you rode in the drag and chewed on the cloud of dust that billowed from the herd of long-striding cattle who walked steadily with their heads down and their wide horns dipping rhythmically. But most of all it passed the time on night watch after the herd had been thrown off the trail. The old man could remember himself, young Jerry Cotton, sitting in the saddle, there in the tall darkness, feeling his pony breathing, its barrel expanding and contracting regularly between his thighs, listening to the sleeping cattle snort and bluster in their dreams of new grass. There was nothing to do but lean on the saddle horn and compose brags, or rather compile them, adding an occasional flourish of your own, putting them in the order in which the words fell right. It was the kind of thing to do in silence. Or he could count the stars which hung like diamonds on fire around his head. (And he counted the stars so often, and in such detail, that he used to tell his wife: "Judy, I got so I could tell you the date, tomorrow's weather and who your grandmother was, just by looking at the stars." And she would always ask him what if it was cloudy? "Then I could only tell you tomorrow's weather and let you worry about the date and your grandmother, which you ought to know anyway.") Or he could sing songs, which he did, in a thin voice that was a little unsteady, but good enough for himself and the cattle. In his prime he had known eighty-five verses to "The Texas Rangers," some of which he had composed himself.

And so, as the surface of the water grew placid around him,

old Jerome Cotton shuttled these memories through his mind, selecting the ones he liked and discarding those he didn't (and also those dealing with women, in respect for, or at least because of, Roberta May, whose feet, encased in sandals, stood up awkwardly at the ends of her exposed legs). He reflected that he liked these memories, but he was not such a damn fool as to say that there was anything good about those days except that they were the days when he was a young bull and on the prod. He had sold his Longhorns and bought white-faced cattle when they produced more beef, and when the railroads came, and hadn't wept one tear for the old rangy cattle who could live on anything and tasted like it. He and Judith had nearly starved when the drought came and the Depression on top of it. He had taken Mr. Roosevelt's money, gladly. When the oil came, he found some, more or less on his property, a good deal of it, and when irrigation was practical he irrigated and planted cotton and alfalfa, but by then George was running the land. His son, though, being his son, didn't get too excited about leaving land fallow and taking Mr. Truman's money or, though he was a Republican, Mr. Eisenhower's or Mr. Kennedy's either.

Whenever some old coot would get to talking around the table about the "good old days," Jerome Cotton would lean forward out of his wheelchair and say: "I'll tell you what, sir, there is not one good thing about eatin' dust all day and gettin' rained on at night unless you're young." But by damned if you were young . . .

✝

It became dark in a moment, as it always does when the air is clear, and a square of moonlight appeared on the door opposite the window as if a switch had been snapped. The wreath of white hair around the back of his skull dripped onto his neck, and little droplets traced cold paths down onto his narrow shoulders. He slid again down into the tepid water and, resting his chin on his shoulder, watched the square of moonlight on the door until he

could perceive it moving downward toward Roberta May, who
was stretched in the shadows.

It was an exercise in patience. It kept his mind off his stomach,
which was tightening painfully, excreting unusable acid, waiting for food, wanting food. He watched the square moving and
finally he thought about food: enchiladas covered with cheese,
frijoles, tortillas with steam rising from them, which you picked
up gingerly, smeared with butter, salted, poured hot sauce on,
folded, bent so the sauce would not run out and stuffed into
your mouth while they were still hot. There was an art to folding
tortillas, you had to do it quickly or the thin circles of cornmeal
would cool, and dexterously, or the hot sauce would pour into
your lap. And when the sauce burned your throat, when you
could feel it burning all the way down to your stomach . . . He
could see Señora Estansa silhouetted in the kitchen door holding a big plate of enchiladas and chili con queso . . . His chin fell
forward into the water and awakened him. It frightened him a
little that he had fallen asleep, so he reached up with his toe and
flipped the handle which let the water out of the tub.

This amused him for a few minutes: listening to the gurgling
water and watching his dark body appear like islands growing
out of a sea of mercury. But then he felt his weight returning to
press him into the bottom of the tub. His head became hard to
manage; it seemed to roll erratically on his white shoulders, and
his good arm, when he reached up to pull three towels from the
rack above his head, was as heavy as a log. But he laboriously
dried himself and the inside of the tub as well as possible. His
elbows and knees made thumping and clanging noises as they
collided awkwardly with the porcelain, sometimes causing little
pinches of pain and making red flowers bloom and fade before
his eyes. But as he worked in the darkness he was not altogether
unhappy; he enjoyed being without his contraptions, controlling
what he did, even if it was only drying a bathtub from which he
might never escape, in which he might wake up dead. "This is a
hell of a thing for a man ninety years old!" he said to the dark,

and a hilarious vision of himself being buried in the tub built itself before his eyes: there he was, arms folded, in a blue suit, resting in the tub. He chuckled.

When the tub was as dry as he could get it, he folded a towel and placed it beneath his head. As he closed his eyes he reflected that the towel was a damn sight softer than some saddles. But it was no good. There is no one in the world, he realized, as naked as a naked man in a damp empty bathtub, and there is no place which is more uncomfortable to sleep in when you are naked. His shoulder began to ache, as did his arthritic arm. His hipbone was thrust cruelly against the stone-hard bottom of the tub. But worst of all, his manhood—his "gentleman," his granny had called it (*It ain't no gentleman now*, he thought. *Wouldn't stand up for nobody.*)—lay damply against his leg. When he rolled over, if it touched the porcelain, he awoke with a start; if he rolled the other way it became uncomfortably wedged between his legs. *If he could only get out!* He grasped the side of the tub with both hands and, with a wrenching movement, began to lift the dead weight of his body. Flares of pain pulsed through his bad arm and the flowers returned whirling before his eyes. But he was almost up, he had almost raised himself high enough to flop forward out of the tub, when he saw poor dead Roberta May Kuykendall, and his bad arm slipped. He fell, striking his chin on the edge of the tub and slithering and squeaking back into its dark maw. He curled in the bottom of the tub with his eyes closed and his breath coming in cries. He knew the side of his chin would be black with a bruise in the morning. On the other side of the white wall, Roberta May rested with her pale face framed in the moonlight, lips slightly parted. Her hair flared out to one side, as if windblown, and her eyes flickered in the silver light.

In an hour he moved: he held his bad arm to his side and rolled over onto his back; then, with his toes, he turned on the water full force and closed the drain. The roar of the water laughed in his ears; it laughed down the halls of the empty house and out into the climbing night. The water was fine; it brought heat, buoyancy, freedom, everything a man could want. He arranged a wet towel around his neck so he would not drown himself, turned off the water and relaxed. Involuntarily he glanced at Roberta May. The moonlight had moved again and now it fell across her breasts. Only her chin and her half-smiling mouth were visible above the V of her blouse. Her brassiere held her breasts upright and they flowed together on her bare neck. But the old man pushed thoughts of the dead girl behind curtains in his ancient mind. Before he went to sleep, he lowered his chin and quenched his thirst, then he leaned his head back comfortably, his "gentleman" floating blessedly free . . .

In his dream the old man was a part of a story which he hadn't believed when he had heard it. Marsh, who had had his nose cut off, squatted just inside the circle of light thrown by the bitter-smelling mesquite fire and spoke with a Colorado twang. "By God it was raining catfish and nigger babies, and we was so drunk you would have had to sober us up to kill us . . ." They were all drunk and running through the back streets of Tascosa in the rain. Jerome Cotton could feel the deep mud gurgling over the instep of his boot every time he took a step. They ran past bright windows, whose light bled in this vision like yellow paint. There were four or two of them running together, and he could see Marsh's noseless profile rising and falling beside him as they ran through the downpour. Finally, after hours it seemed, he realized that they were looking for a special whore.

Suddenly Marsh, without saying a word, dodged into a lighted doorway, and Jerry followed. He burst into dryness and light just in time to see Marsh draw his pistol and shoot a Mexican who was climbing out of a high window. (*I don't believe this story,* the old man thought, but the Mexican fell with a splash outside the window.) Then Marsh, the two nostrils on his face bubbling because he had a cold, turned the pistol on the whore who was curled on the bed staring at them. She was a tall black-headed woman, slightly pretty. Marsh lowered the barrel of his pistol, as if he were shooting a bottle off a fence post, and shot her.

"You want her in here or out in the street?"

"Out in the street," Jerome Cotton heard himself say in a young voice.

"Good enough," Marsh said, and slung the whore over his shoulder and carried her into the rain. Jerome Cotton heard the splash as Marsh threw her into the mud; it seemed to come from down on the river . . .

But then it was daylight, dry beautiful daylight, and they were on the trail. He was sitting on his pony on a grassy slope overlooking the Platte River; its wide sandy bed twined away into green distance. Down on the river the boys were trying to free about ten head of cattle who were being sucked into a bed of quicksand. He noticed one particular steer who was caught near the bank. A cowboy had waded out and slipped a rope around one of the steer's hind legs. The rope was tied to the saddle horn of another cowboy who was trying to pull the steer free, and the steer was bawling to the sky. In a moment there was a sucking noise as the leg to which the rope was tied popped up out of the sand and lay at an odd angle in the water. The man on the horse continued to pull but he couldn't free the other three legs. Two men were with the steer in the water now.

Jerry Cotton took off his hat and swatted a fly. There was a nice breeze and it was a pretty day. He seemed to be hearing the shouts of the cowboys and the bawling of the cattle from a great distance. When he looked again down into the riverbed, the boys had tied the rope that was attached to the steer to the chuckwagon, and the grubspoiler was trying to drive the team up the slope and out of the riverbed. There was a clatter of harness and a shout from the cookie as the wagon shot forward. Young Jerry Cotton had to look very closely to see that the steer's hind leg was bouncing behind the wagon trailing water and blood.

The old man was awake during the last few seconds of this dream but he didn't open his eyes; he let the phantasma play themselves out on the back of his eyelids until the team and the driver disappeared behind a melting bluff, but still he did not open his eyes. He knew that the room was lit by the gray gallows-light that crept like smoke before the dawn. He lowered his chin and took some of the bitter water into his mouth and spat it out. He had relieved himself during the night. His face itched with its damp morning bristle, which Roberta May would —which Roberta May *used to* shave with his electric razor. Still without opening his eyes, he raised his foot and let the polluted water out of the tub; then, feeling with his feet, he turned on the faucets, admitting fresh water. The water crackled like new fire as it spattered on the porcelain. "Just like a goddamn goldfish," he mumbled to himself, but he drank great quantities of the new water.

He opened his eyes, looking straight ahead. His hands were grotesquely shriveled, and his entire floating body was logged and puckered. The old man felt that if he grasped his arthritic arm tightly, he could slide the skin right off the bone. All of his joints ached and hunger sent pains sliding up under his ribs. Ninety years old, he thought, and found the dangling tip of his mustache with his tongue and sucked on it. To avoid looking at the girl he closed his eyes again and waited for the sunlight; Sunday morning . . .

But even after the light shone dark red through the blood vessels in his eyelids, and an occasional flash fell through his lashes like dawn through a forest, the old man kept his eyes clenched against it. He lifted his hand from the water and pressed two fingers into his eye sockets until they hurt. But finally he had to; it became, in the darkness of his morning thoughts, a test of courage. He opened his eyes and deliberately looked at the body stretched on the tile. He stared at her for a moment and then, strangely, the vision liquified. He blinked his eyes fiercely to clear his vision only to discover that there were tears in them. Children, women, cowards and men in pain may cry, but the old man who had nearly turned a century wept.

He wept because during the night some immodest wind had blown her skirt completely up, exposing her legs, her blue garters and her blue panties; wept for the silliest thing: a heart sewn on the panties just above the left leg, and *Saturday* embroidered just below it. He wept because he had desired her so overtly and called her the names of his frustration. But most of all, and this is why he wept and didn't cry, the tears topped his lower lids and streamed down because she was dead. His own life had only been a furious explosion of days, a mad clock that ran the seasons round, a flash in the eye of time. What a flicker hers must have been, who had touched and seen and tasted only one year for his five. And he wept because he was ashamed and brave enough, or old enough, to be.

But he didn't weep for long at all with his forehead pressed to the side of the tub. The sobbing in his throat relaxed. His eyes dried quickly as he stared down into the turquoise water. He was ninety years old, and it seemed to him a little sacrilegious for a man ninety years old to weep for very long, and a little silly for anyone to be weeping in a bathtub where he was preserved like a snake in a fruit jar; too much weeping renounces too many things. And so he raised his head and looked at the girl again, giving her the respect which, perhaps, is due the dead. He looked at her closely and dispassionately, wishing the body could be taken to a funeral home, noticing again her hand which seemed to be pointing to his son's clothing which lay between the toilet and the bathtub. With his good hand the old man reached over . . .

✝

George Cotton arrived from Dallas in the late afternoon. He entered the front door and called and when he heard the muffled answer he ran up the stairs three at a time. He threw open the bathroom door and saw his father sitting in the bathtub pulling at his mustache, wearing the wide-brimmed hat he had left on the floor.

"You take care of that poor dead girl," his father said.

"Here, Pa, let me get you out of that tub," George Cotton said, and he started to step over Roberta May Kuykendall.

"You get that girl," his father said. "I just may never get out."

THE PASSION OF

SAINT DARRELL

You tell me that Bonosus, like a true son of the Fish, makes for watery
places. For myself, I am still foul with my ancient stains, and like the
basilisk and scorpion I seek out any place that is dry. Bonosus today
treads the serpent's head beneath his heel; I am still food for the
creeping monster who by God's decree devours the earth.

—ST. JEROME

Darrell Boylan's roommate, Kevin Lloyd, was a little vain about
his powers of persuasion, so he probably couldn't have told you,
as he leaned in the phone booth on the second floor of the Kappa
Sigma house pleading urgently with Cynthia Winslow, whether
he was most anxious to win her company or to win his plea. He
was, however, working as hard as he could at translating that
anxiety, whatever its source, into what he hoped was an irresist-
ible boyish exuberance as he argued that she should duck out of
her party and go driving with him because life was short, youth
was fleeting and there was no damn telling what Khrushchev
would do to fuck up the fall semester *this* year.

He didn't have to remind her what had happened last year,
when it seemed like Khrushchev was just *waiting,* you know, until
rush parties were over and classes were underway and everybody was looking forward to some serious beer-drinking and
fast-dancing to get himself caught trying to smuggle atomic mis-
siles into Cuba, thus precipitating a thermonuclear confronta-
tion whose queasy miasma had glued everyone to a television set
for a couple of weeks—waiting to be blasted into Silly Putty. Ultimately (Kevin Lloyd was sure she remembered) this had soured

the entire fall party-season. Cynthia Winslow wondered at this
point if Kevin Lloyd remembered what a really nice suit the
president had been wearing the night he announced the Block-
ade on TV?

Outside, the September evening was warm and clear. Small
groups of freshman women were beginning to make their way
down the purple sidewalks toward sorority houses where the
sisters (with the momentary exception of Cynthia Winslow) prepared to greet them singing. Two blocks away, along Fraternity
Row, young men in madras shirts, khaki-twill slacks and Foot Joy
loafers (without socks) sat on twilit porches, sipping beer from
cold cans and watching their brothers toss footballs back and
forth in lazy arcs against the lipstick-red sunset.

Across the street from Fraternity Row, the western faces of
empty classroom buildings glowed like coals in the sunset's
reflection. Blue-green shadows bloomed beneath their eastern
walls and stretched out as well behind the orderly trees and
hedges. A heavy, grapefruit moon hung in purple twilight
over the campus like a giant party balloon, and it was—if
you were willing to disregard the nagging spectre of imminent
atomic cataclysm—a perfect setting, quintessentially American
and plangently Arcadian.

Unfortunately, it was becoming increasingly clear to Kevin
Lloyd (as he stood with the receiver wedged between his ear and
shoulder, tugging his left cuff the correct three-eighths-inch out
of the sleeve of his tweed jacket), this was exactly what Cynthia
Winslow was willing to do. Disregard the nagging spectre. And
himself along with it.

"Cynthia, my love, my perfect treasure, my one true flower . . ."

"Kevin, it's the first night of rush. I *have* to be at this party . . ."

". . . while Western Civilization, all life as we know it on this
planet, teeters on the brink of oblivion . . ."

". . . *somebody* has to keep up appearances!" She said this in
what Kevin Lloyd recognized as her mother's voice. "Now *you*,"
she said, "you and those . . . circus animals you live with may be

ready to give yourselves over to Bacchanalian despair, but *I* come from sterner stock. Pioneer stock! Church people! I have things to do, Kevin. There are young ladies to be pledged, credentials to be validated, an entire closet of party dresses to be utilized . . ."

Kevin Lloyd knew that he'd been outflanked—the "twilight of Western Civilization" argument turned deftly against him—and found himself more impressed than disappointed. He was rapidly considering his options for honorable retreat when the door of the phone booth flew open and, in the instant before the icy water struck, he saw, through the fingers of sparkling liquid leaping out of the pail, the smiling face of his roommate, The Good Saint Darrell.

The pail of water drenched him and a gale of laughter followed in its wake. Percival David "P. D." Simms and Gregory "Fatty" Falstaff reeled around the hall, arms clasped about their bellies, Fatty bouncing from wall to wall like a three-rail billiard shot. Darrell Boylan collapsed with mirth, hanging his arms back over the stairwell banister and laughing until his face was flushed dark red. Boylan would nearly regain his breath, then raise his eyes and glimpse Kevin Lloyd dripping in the telephone booth and collapse in choking laughter again.

Kevin Lloyd raised his hand to cover the receiver. Cold water ran down his forearm inside his sleeve. "Sons of bitches!" he shouted. More laughter.

"Kevin?"

"I'll have to call you back. Boylan just drowned me out."

"He what?"

"I'll have to call you back."

"Goodbye, Kevin. I'm going to my party." There was a dial tone.

"Sons of bitches," Kevin Lloyd said again, this time through his teeth. Exercising some control, he gently replaced the receiver and stalked off down the hall, leaving puddles behind him on the parquet floor. Once in his room, he stripped off the sodden jacket, threw it on Darrell Boylan's bed, took a can of mentholated shaving cream from the bureau and headed back into the hall.

"You shoulda *seen* your face!" Darrell Boylan was curled on the wet floor outside the telephone booth, still convulsed with laughter.

Kevin Lloyd pressed the button and covered him with a pale green cloud of shaving foam. Darrell Boylan continued to laugh and Percival David Simms, standing smugly to one side adjusting his beige cashmere sweater, snickered, so Kevin Lloyd covered *him* with a blizzard of shaving foam.

"Goddammit, god *damn* it!" P. D. shrieked. He turned to flee and was greeted by a new pailful of cold water. This new deluge, which also wet down two pledges coming up the stairs, came courtesy of Fatty Falstaff, "The Great One," who now stood grinning with a plastic pail dangling from his big fist. Kevin Lloyd sprayed Fatty with shaving foam, and was in turn sprayed by one of the newly damp pledges, quick to take advantage of the specially sanctioned equality between actives and pledges which existed only during water fights and intramural athletics. In less than a minute roughly fifteen brothers and pledges were actively engaged, whooping, dodging and sliding on the wet floor.

"Water fight! Water fight in *progress!*" shouted Darrell Boylan, scrambling down the hall toward the shower room with a wastebasket in tow.

The term "water fight," as should be apparent by now, was a general one, applicable only in that all of the weapons involved were liquid. Often it was water, of course, in pails, wastebaskets and garbage cans, but more often it was pressurized cans of shaving cream, or spray deodorant. Warm beer was also a weapon of choice and, on one memorable occasion, a two-gallon jar of industrial-strength thousand island salad dressing had been introduced into the action. These battles always raged out of control in firecracker chains of random skirmishes up and down the walnut-paneled halls of the second floor, with no definable sides or tactics except to get everyone as wet as possible.

In this manner scores of major and minor grievances were

avenged and others perpetrated. On this particular evening the courtly and circumspect Neil Osmond Carver, president of the fraternity, was hurled, fully clothed, into the shower and a visiting brother from Texas Technological University was spattered with shaving cream as he ventured up the stairs to ask if he could use the telephone.

The Good Saint Darrell, like some Viking marauder, ran amok. Having kicked the screen off one of the windows over the front door, he doused two brothers attempting to escape by that route with a wastebasket full of hot soapy water and was still standing by the window, grinning and happy, when his victims counterattacked and he was forced to defenestrate into an adjacent gardenia bush below. He landed heavily in the bush, paused for a moment, breathing deeply and listening to the shouts and laughter coming from the house, then began to pick his way out of the slick-leaved branches. Having extricated himself, he stood barefoot on the cold grass of the lawn and, looking into the remains of the long, late evening, was overcome by one of those visions of congruence and loveliness to which he had inadvertently testified in Religion 342 the previous spring.

It had been hot in the classroom and Professor Everett Greenspan had been lecturing on the social consequences of the ecstatic aspects of early twentieth-century Methodism when, apropos of nothing, Darrell Boylan had blurted out, "*I* have visions of beauty!" The class had fallen silent; Professor Greenspan had cleared his throat noisily and, two rows over, a guy had actually written something down in his notebook. Darrell Boylan imagined it said *Boylan hz visions!??*

Now, behind the black, silhouetted buildings, the day was just a white line at the base of a violet sky, empty except for a single scrap of cloud with a fringe of flame. The air around him was dark and cool. Stars blossomed over his head in clusters and as he turned to look down the Row, the houses flamed with rectangles of golden light that spilled evenly across the clipped lawns and flickered on the new cars parked along the street. Darrell Boylan didn't own a car; didn't want one. His father had offered to buy him a turquoise and white Mercury Monterrey, but he had begged off with the excuse that cars were too much trouble. Still, the sight of them, lined along the Row, glistening like sleek jewels, was lovely indeed.

A Pontiac convertible slid to a stop in front of the house and Dicky McPhail, who now played defensive back for the hapless Dallas Cowboys, stepped out and started up the walk. He saw Darrell Boylan in the semi-darkness.

"That you, Boylan?"

"Hi, Dicky."

"You feel Christian enough for a little poker?"

"Not tonight."

"Jesus, you look like hell. What is it? Water fight?"

Darrell Boylan grinned and looked down at himself. The sweat suit he was wearing was soaking wet and flecked with pale green shaving foam.

"Damn," said Dicky McPhail.

"We can't all be scholar athletes," Darrell Boylan said.

Shaking his head, McPhail walked back to his car, which was double-parked.

"See ya, Boylan."

"See ya, Dicky."

Dicky McPhail's convertible was not even around the corner before Darrell Boylan had scampered around to the back of the house and was connecting the hose. He attached the spray nozzle and threw the hose up over the rail of the outside balcony; then he turned on the water, ran up the outside stairs and grabbed the hose, which was bucking like a snake. Once he had it under control, he dragged it into the upstairs hall, adjusting the nozzle for maximum power.

"Ultimate weapon!" he shouted. "Ultimate weapon!" And began to spray everyone without fear or favor.

Darrell Boylan did indeed have the ultimate weapon and, as is so often the case with ultimate weapons, it stopped the war. In her apartment on the first floor Mrs. Wanda Gleeson Johnson sat at her mirror putting up her hair. She had been a house-mother for eleven years so she was oblivious to the shouts and thumps coming from the floor above. Also she had her FM radio tuned at substantial volume to Mantovani ("It Ain't Necessarily So"). Then, above the shouting and the "singing strings," she heard a cracking, slushing sound and turned on her cushioned stool just in time to see a steady stream of chalky water pour from the ceiling into the middle of her antique lace counterpane. Without hesitation Mrs. Wanda Gleeson Johnson grabbed her red-flowered housecoat, marched out of her apartment and up the stairs. Two steps below the second landing, she halted.

She didn't really have to say anything; the mere presence of "Miz Wanda" on the second floor was sufficient to quell any disturbance. The brothers who were only partially clad broke for cover. Darrell Boylan furtively ducked out the balcony door, tossed the gurgling hose over the rail and returned, gazing innocently about him. A silence materialized while Mrs. Gleeson Johnson surveyed the damage like a defeated general. The brothers, only mildly abashed, stood around.

"Now y'all have *ruined* this house. I have water coming through my ceiling!" She shook her head and looked down at the puddled floor, then raised her eyes to survey the foam-speckled walls. "And after it was so nice for rush."

"Sorry, Miz Johnson," said Percival David Simms. "I'll get some pledges. We'll get this place cleaned up. Send some down to your room too."

Mrs. Johnson cast an icy glance at Simms, whose blond hair and cashmere sweater were matted and mottled with shaving cream.

"I can take care of my own room, thank you. Except to re-plaster the ceiling. You worry about this mess up here." As she turned to descend, she said, "By the way, Mr. Simms, you look like a mangy merino."

A few minutes later Dicky McPhail reappeared—tentatively poking his head around the front door—having somehow sensed, wherever he was drinking beer, that the childishness was over. Dicky organized a poker game on the third floor, and a group of pledges forlornly began washing the shaving cream from the walls and drying the floor, crawling around on their hands and knees.

"Well, we started the year off with a bang, huh?"

"We, hell. You ruined that goddamn tweed jacket."

"It was *my* jacket."

"Yeah but *I* was in it, and you ruined *my* slacks and *my* cordovans. Look at these goddamn shoes. They'll never walk again."

"You shouldn't buy cheap shoes."

"I didn't buy them to swim in. Go read your Bible. Read that part about how hard it is for a rich man to get into heaven."

"That's a figurative usage."

"You better hope so, or you gon' be toastin' yo' tootsies. Throw me those cigarettes on the desk, will you. Under that paper."

It was after midnight, almost five hours after the water fight, and the house was quiet except for an occasional tinkle of notes from the piano downstairs, where Fatty Falstaff sat in the darkened living room drunkenly pecking at the white keys and mumbling, *"Louie, Lou-wee, Louie, Lou-way, we gotta go . . ."* Darrell Boylan sat at his desk wearing a pair of red-and-white-striped pajamas. After he had thrown the package of Camels to Kevin Lloyd, who was lying on his bed with his feet propped up on the footboard, he returned his attention to the *Concordance of the Holy Scriptures* from which he was making notes.

Kevin Lloyd lit a cigarette and turned to sit on the edge of the bed. He reached down and picked up the damp cordovans and, after removing the shoe trees, began to saddle-soap one of them, humming absently along with the piano, *"I sailed a ship . . . across da sea."*

Darrell Boylan closed the concordance and walked to the bureau. He opened a tube of medication and began to apply it to his acne-scarred cheeks, watching himself in the mirror as he did. Kevin Lloyd saddle-soaped the cordovans and watched him too.

"You a *ugly* bastard," he said.

"Right," Darrell Boylan said absently. He applied some medication to his chin and Kevin Lloyd wondered, as he often did, what the hell Boylan thought he was doing, living in this raunchy house at this snotty school. It mystified him. Early on, he had suspected his roommate of having ecclesiastical social ambitions, but he'd never been able to visualize Boylan standing solicitously at the door of some ritzy suburban church as the congregation filed out, shaking hands with rich old broads and pricing their jewelry while he dropped hints about the building fund.

Certainly, he thought, in your appearance-and-grooming area Boylan was about as far from the Fraternity Row norm as you could get, and although he met all the social requirements (his father owned a chain of grocery stores and shot in the low eighties), he met none of the temperamental ones. You would never *know*, for instance, that Boylan had bucks, and in this he differed even from the other unobtrusive gentry around the house. These guys dressed cheap and lived frugally but there was something in their sangfroid that said, I can afford to live this way. Boylan had no sangfroid; he was oblivious.

When they were pledges, four of Boylan's ties had been burned before the entire pledge class. The pledge trainer had squirted lighter fluid on them and burned them ceremonially in an ashtray, designating the little pyre a flaming monument to Pledge Boylan's taste in neckwear. Boylan had just grinned and watched them burn, unperturbed. He was the guy whose ties got burned. He was the only divinity student in a house renowned for its adolescent contempt for all human decency—and that was good enough for him. In fact, that was just great.

Kevin Lloyd wiped the excess soap from his shoes and watched his roommate working on his complexion. He sensed, if he did not know, that in most of the ways that counted, he and his roommate lacked common ground and he understood that this was probably why they were such great friends and accomplices. And why (since Kevin Lloyd was outwardly as typical as Darrell Boylan was atypical) Boylan was, among the brothers, the most popular member of the fraternity—accepted, liked and believed

in as only a black sheep (or, in this case, white sheep) could be.
To all of them he was something bizarre and strange, a symbol of sanity, a talisman, really, and as such, he was important,
valuable. He seemed to exist in a state which Kevin Lloyd would
later describe (when Darrell Boylan was gone, living in a dingy
apartment over a washateria) as a state of "bumptious euphoria."

"You had to know him six months," Kevin Lloyd would say,
"before you could convince yourself he wasn't a secret drinker.
But he wasn't. Never touched it—but never bitched at those who
did." Which was true; still, at parties Darrell Boylan would laugh
as loudly as the drunks at the dirty jokes he never told.

"He was always laughin'," Kevin Lloyd would say, and in his
official role as Keeper of the Legend he would tell how Boylan
would accompany them on their wild, four-hundred-mile for-
ays down the face of Texas and across the border to Mexico—a
living Saint Christopher, negotiating with law enforcement offi-
cers when it was necessary, driving when they were too drunk
to—how he would roam shouting through the streets with them
and sit with them in the cantinas of whorehouses where they
drank and fornicated and never flinch when someone pointed
at him and shouted, "He cherry! He cherry!" or pointed between
his legs and indicated a length as one would describe the length
of a fish.

"Mucho grande!" someone would shout, and someone at another table would answer, "Si! Good Saint Darrell es mucho
grande!" The dark-eyed whores would giggle and wink and
drape themselves around him, and Darrell Boylan, far from
home, would sit there, feet apart, his red face beaming, and
laugh too.

"Hey, roomie!" he would cry. "Look aheah. I'm a sultan."

"You're a eunuch, Boylan, and a goddamn hypocrite!"

"Wouldn't be fair to the girls," Boylan would say. "I got this
sex problem. Cain't get it down."

"How do you *know,* Good Saint Darrell?"

"My strength is as the strength of ten," he would say. "My heart
is pure."

"Pee-yure bullshit!" Kevin Lloyd would drawl, and Boylan would laugh and stay pure.

"How was your date tonight?" Darrell Boylan asked. He had finished applying the medication and returned to his desk, opening the concordance again.

"Thanks to you I didn't have one. I spent a delightful evening drinking beer with Fatty. I mean, what a depressing bastard. Didju know he was initiated in nineteen-fucking-*fifty*!"

"Fifty-three," Darrell Boylan said. "I looked it up."

"Anyway he flunks out, does four years in the army, goes home to work in his daddy's stock office till his old man, to his everlasting credit, figgers out Fatty is incompetent. So now he's back amongst us . . ."

"A believable scenario," Darrell Boylan said.

"I bet he's fucking *thirty*!" Kevin Lloyd said. "And I spent half the night hearing about this big water fight they had when he was a freshman." Kevin Lloyd closed the saddle soap and took some cordovan shoe polish out of his kit. "And you know what his major ambition in life is? You're gonna love this: he wants to manage a rock and roll band. Right. I'm not kidding. According to Fatty, the invention of the electric guitar is more important than the invention of the atom bomb! I mean, *It is the key to power!*"

"The road to hell," Darrell Boylan said, "is paved with good inventions."

Kevin Lloyd had to laugh, but then he said, "Couldn't we just once leave heaven and hell out of it? Perhaps reside, just momentarily, in the real world?"

"Could you just let me up, Lloyd?" Darrell Boylan said, grinning over his shoulder. "You wouldn't know the real world if it was curled up in your boot."

"Come on now, Dare. Don't be shy. What is it you're trying to say? Just spit it out."

"I am trying to say, Cisco, that you have about as much spiritual sensitivity as a bottle of Wild Root Cream Oil."

"Oh, Christ! He wants to have A-Bull-Session-about-Religion!" Kevin Lloyd adopted his Bull-Session-about-Religion voice. "Well, if you ask me, Darrell, like, God doesn't *really* have to be a *personage,* you know. I mean he could, you know, be a *spirit!* He could, you know, be like the objectification of our own, uh, *spiritual sensitivity!*"

"Lloyd, are you drunk?"

"Si, Pancho. That's why I drank ten beers."

"Whenever you're drunk you bug me about religion."

"Is that right."

"Yeah. You're the one who always brings up religion."

"Yeah, and that's what's so goddamn *sad,* Boylan. Why don't *you* ever bring up religion? You're the Bible-buster in this cell."

"Kevin, me lad, I believe in 'live and let live', and besides, I don't know if you've noticed this, but the brand of Jesus we peddle round this here country club ain't exactly what you'd call, uh, Eee-van-gelical."

"Boylan, I'm not talking about baptizing black babies on the Ivory Coast. I'm talking about your friends! Other white people. Don't you care about *me* . . . or poor old Fatty down there? Don't you care if we go to hell? We're your *pals,* for Christ's sake! How about me and poor old Fatty?"

"You and poor old Fatty," Darrell Boylan said, "are beyond all redemption."

"Like hell we are!" Kevin Lloyd cried, leaping up from the bed, in that instant not quite sure he was being funny. "You're the goddamn preacher! I'm the goddamn sinner! Why in the hell don't you save me?"

"How soon they forget," Darrell Boylan said, shaking his head. "When only hours before he has been the recipient of the Good Saint Darrell All-Purpose Total-Immersion Involuntary Baptism, which, judging by his present condition, obviously didn't take."

"Right," Kevin Lloyd said. He sat down again and began to polish his other shoe.

"Look, man," Darrell Boylan said, so firmly that Kevin Lloyd quickly looked up at him. "I would save you, okay? But I don't know how. Okay? That's why I'm going to school. And you can take this any way you want to, but I believe there's a God, and there's immortality if you live as a Christian. Okay?"

"Bull, Dare," Kevin Lloyd said quietly, looking back down at his shoe. "You don't believe that."

"I do too."

"Do not."

"Do too."

"Do not."

"Do *too*," Darrell Boylan said, his voice light again. "And furthermore," he said, lifting his finger into the air, "*I* believe that: *One Person Can Make a Difference*!"

"Yeah," Kevin Lloyd said, raising his finger as well, "but *usually* . . ."—he paused so they could complete the joke in unison —"usually it's a *Baaaad Person*!"

Kevin Lloyd slipped a cordovan onto his left foot and began buffing it. "Well now," he said after a moment. "Well now, Boylan, you just tell me this. Do you call it Christian driving all of us sinners down to Mexico? What's that? Leading by example? *Drivin'* us down the road to hell, which, I admit, is paved with good inventions. What's your plan? Are we supposed to realize how unpleasant a little piece of ass is and *convert*?"

Darrell Boylan closed his book with great ceremony, turned slowly and addressed his roommate with grave mock-solemnity:

"Well, isn't it a little unpleasant, big fella?"

Kevin Lloyd flopped back on the bed again, the unlaced cordovans on his bare feet. He held them up to the light to inspect the shine.

"Well, isn't it a little unpleasant?" Darrell Boylan said again. "Paying some poor woman to use her body?"

"No, it is *not* unpleasant, Boylan. Don't knock it if you haven't tried it."

"You get my share, Lloyd," Darrell Boylan said.

"Like hell. I hardly get my own."

"Well, *somebody's* getting my share."

"Half the rednecks in Fort Worth getting your share, Boylan."

Darrell Boylan picked up the heavy concordance. "Here, read this," he said, and pitched it underhand so it smacked onto Kevin Lloyd's naked stomach as he lay with his feet in the air. "It'll do you some good."

Kevin Lloyd bounced up, snatching the book before it fell to the floor, and tossed it back onto the long double-desk which was built into one wall of the room.

"Keep that on your own side of the goddamn desk," he said. "Jus' second . . ." He had risen too quickly and had to grab the back of a chair for support; then he lurched to the desk, snatched up a pencil and drew an irregular line bisecting the desk. "Just so you won't get any of your holiness on my sinful side of the desk. This is hell," he said, "and this is heaven." On one side of the line he wrote *Lloyd* and on the other side *Boylan.*

Darrell Boylan looked quizzically at him. "Are you serious, Lloyd?"

"Of course I'm not. I'm drunk." He grasped his chin with his hand. "That pencil's not very good." He left the room and Darrell Boylan stared at the line dividing the desk.

"This will be better," Kevin Lloyd said, kicking the door open before him. His arms were full of tempera paint and brushes the fraternity used to paint signs for school elections. He took a brush, dipped it into a jar of white paint and painted over the line he had drawn. "There, that *is* better."

"Well, what about the floor?" Darrell Boylan said. "What about if you get on my side of the floor?"

"That is a problem, Good Saint Darrell, that *is* a problem." He bent over and painted a line down the center of the room.

"Here, give me a brush. I'll help."

"Use the white paint," Kevin Lloyd said. "We want to be consistent."

And so they painted, dividing their room in the sleeping house. Even the piano had stopped now. They carefully divided the windows, the doors, the inside of the closet and even the doorknobs although the water-base paint didn't adhere very well to the brass plating.

Wherever room permitted, *Lloyd* was painted on one side of the line and *Boylan* on the other. Darrell Boylan climbed up on a chair and began to divide the ceiling.

"This is great," Darrell Boylan said. "I feel like one of those guys at Panmunjom."

"Want my full share of the goddamn ceiling."

"You got it. How about the light fixture?"

"Public domain," Kevin Lloyd said. "Shines on you and it shines on me. Now get down from there. We have to divide the hall."

"Right!"

They had painted their line halfway down the hall to the toilet when they discovered Fatty Falstaff.

"Passed out."

"What should we do with him?" Darrell Boylan said. He looked down at the sleeping form.

"Looks like a beached walrus."

"Shouldn't we put him in bed?"

"Hell, no," Kevin Lloyd said. "Let's divide him." He pulled Fatty's shirt out of his trousers and painted a stripe across his wide, quivering stomach. "At least I got the head."

"I got tails!"

Darrell Boylan giggled at his own joke and Kevin Lloyd looked up at him. Now which one of us, he thought, which one of us is drunk? He watched his roommate backing down the hall painting a white stripe on the floor between his feet.

"Get the hell off my side!"

Darrell Boylan jerked his foot up so quickly he nearly fell onto his knees.

In the toilet the paint would not adhere at all to the blue tile, so they had to settle for dividing the commodes. Kevin Lloyd painted a white stripe down a pale blue commode seat. "Both of us," he said, "demonstrably half-assed."

"A job well done," Darrell Boylan said after they had walked back to their room, each on his own side of the hall. Kevin Lloyd had opened the door without touching Boylan's side of the knob. They had undressed, and because the light switch was on Darrell Boylan's side of the room, he had turned off the light.

"A job really well done," Darrell Boylan said again, settling back in bed with a sigh.

"Yeah, we got 'er done, all right," Kevin Lloyd said. "Now you can doze off to the thought of all the poor starving people in the world. Whores too."

"And who the heck are you? Mahatma Gandhi?"

"Not me. I don't care a damn who's starving," Kevin Lloyd said to the darkness.

"I'd like a hamburger," Darrell Boylan said.

"Myself. Do you want to wake up a pledge?"

"Naw, let's go to sleep."

Kevin Lloyd awoke around noon on the next day and the room was awash with dusty, golden light. It puzzled him for a moment, this raw, bright light, and then he noticed that the curtains Darrell Boylan had brought with him were gone; his roommate's half of the closet was empty too except for the damp tweed coat, and his mattress was bare. Kevin Lloyd reached over and took a cigarette from the holder on the nightstand and lit it. He lay back in the bed, smoked the cigarette and stared at the ceiling, which had an irregular white line painted across it. When he had finished the cigarette, he crushed it out, got up and noticed that Darrell Boylan's Bible was still on the side of the desk designated *Boylan*. He slipped into the white coveralls he used to work on his car and stepped into the hall. A pledge wearing a sleeveless tee shirt was scrubbing the white tempera off the hall floor.

"Get in my room when you're finished with the hall," Kevin Lloyd told him, and walked downstairs. Four people were playing bridge in the den.

"Any of y'all seen Boylan this morning?"

"Yeah, he moved out," Neil Carver said. "Looks like you got the room to yourself. He said he was paid up."

"Is he going to be here for rush?"

"Said he wasn't."

"He gonna pay the fines for missing?" Kevin Lloyd said.

"Said he was going inactive, as of this morning. Go figger that bastard. I can't."

"He'll be back," Kevin Lloyd said. "He left his Bible. Got his name on it. In gold. Didju know his middle name was Arnold?"

"Darrell Arnold," Neil Carver said. "That's a cross to bear."

"'S not a cross I'd bear," Fatty Falstaff said glumly, gazing across the table at the dummy hand.

"*But who wants a cross-eyed bear?*" they all said, sotto voce, more or less in unison, completing the joke.

"I wish he'd woke me up," Kevin Lloyd said. "I coulda talked him out of it."

When Darrell Boylan's father heard the news, he recapped the fountain pen he had picked up when the telephone rang. He rose from his desk, walked to the bookcase that covered one wall of his office and selected a leatherbound volume entitled *The Complete Works of John Barleycorn.* He unscrewed the cap from the concealed flask and, after cleaning the dust from the lip with his thumb, tilted the spiggot on his lower teeth and let the amber liquor splash onto his tongue. He stood there with the whiskey burning his throat, head thrown back, eyes tightly closed, and felt as if he were falling through floors. The floor of his office gave way beneath his weight, dropping him into the office below, and when he tried to move, that floor gave way with a crunching of timbers, dropping him again, and again, and again, into the dusty basement.

He spent the first three days of his ten-day bender in the bar at Riverlawn Country Club. On the fourth morning Bruce Snyder, the club manager, met him on his way to the bar, delicately maneuvering his way through the club's golf museum.

"You drank us dry yesterday, Arnie," said the manager, smiling.

"I did?"

"Yeah, I'm afraid so, Arn. Sorry."

" 'S okay, Ron," Arnold Boylan said, letting one of his grainy eyelids droop into a sly Irish wink. "You ain't the only water hole in town." He clapped the manager on the shoulder and turned to walk back down the aisle of shining trophy cases and out into the sun-washed morning.

Bruce Snyder stuck his hands into his pockets and watched him go. He waited until Arnold Boylan had climbed back into his Oldsmobile and was, a little unsteadily, on his way before turning back. When he did, he discovered George, the black porter, standing behind his shoulder.

"Seems like about three years," George said.

"Three at least," Snyder said. "But he's sure off it now."

"He is that," George said. "He is that."

The police found him a week later drinking bourbon with beer chasers in a hillbilly joint called Loretta's down on lower Main Street. They took him home and his wife put him to bed.

"You needn't have worried, Mr. Boylan. It's really quite common among young men who study for the ministry. You know that as well as I. He's a sensitive boy. He's searching for, and must find on his own, a mature, living faith." The minister placed his hand on the bedpost and leaned forward confidentially. "In a way, you know, it's a sign of strength. The sign of a powerful, questing spirit. I myself went through such a phase."

Arnold Boylan said nothing. He did not like the minister. He did not like him at all.

"I even grew a beard," the minister said. "Can you imagine that? *Me*? With a *beard*?"

"He told me," Arnold Boylan said, looking at the ceiling. "He called me up and told me. That he had resigned his scholarship. That he didn't believe in God, and I could tell . . . he didn't give a damn what I thought about it. Not a damn. And it . . . well, it broke my will . . . my willpower, destroyed it. I counted on the boy, I guess."

"Now come on, Arnie, It's just a phase. He'll change. You've just got to believe he will. And be a better Christian for it." The minister touched Arnold Boylan softly on the back of his hand and rose from the bedside.

"No, he won't," Arnold Boylan said. He rolled onto his shoulder away from the room and, pulling the covers up around his neck, thought about whiskey.

A WINTER'S TALE

Once upon a time in West Texas there was a minister who had milky blue eyes beneath sandy lashes, a high forehead and thinning blond hair. He was a tall man, well over six feet, and he had a beautiful daughter. He had grown up in rural Illinois and graduated from a small Protestant seminary there, but he had spent his entire professional life preaching in the small towns of Texas. These towns were not Robert Winslow's towns, but they were the towns in which he preached the gospel—towns that grew like lichen on the coast, towns hacked out of chaparral, or scented pine, or stinking cedar, or (as at the time of this story) arbitrarily squared off on the empty prairie, where the night sky was black and the stars curved down to a circular horizon.

In this part of Texas there had never been any way to predict the weather, so no one really tried. There were no mountains to catch the rain or to buffer the wind and so channel the year's weather into a particular pattern. There were not even hills. Nor was there a substantial body of water, as in the coastal areas, to temper the air. There was only the plain and the wind that moved across it, raw and free.

Sometimes it came blasting up out of the furnace of Chihuahua; at others it swept down from the distant ranges of Saskatchewan, clear and cold, sucking the last morsel of warmth from the soil to dissipate in the blackness between the chilled stars. Sometimes it came heavy with rain, or dust or snow, and sometimes, in the worst times, with all three, and then the air was bitter with a dirty, wet cold. Always the wind dashed across the prairie like a startled colt, swerving this way and that according to its own whimsical logic, distributing bizarre weather without reason or restraint.

And so, in the year of this story, it came as no surprise to anyone when Indian Summer lasted until Christmas Eve. There had been a little frost in November, some freezing rain in early December, but other than that the small sun moved in its taciturn fashion across the dark blue sky, glinting on the flaming winter trees. (There were thirty of them, ranked at attention on either side of the main residential street like a gaunt, abandoned garrison.) Then, on Christmas Eve, the norther came sweeping down from the Dakotas, whistling across empty leagues of wind-bent grass.

The morning of Christmas Eve was bright and blue, warm enough for the hunters and fishermen camped around the man-made lake to chop wood and cook breakfast in their shirt-sleeves. Robert Winslow was able to sit in his study and read by window light. He browsed through his collection of Samuel Taylor Coleridge's table conversation. Having just returned from his morning coffee at Patti's Pantry down on the square, he was able to draw some rather sharp comparisons.

By eleven o'clock, however, the light was smothered by dirty running clouds, and by noon a hard, icy rain, angled by the wind, was pelting down, sending the hunters and fishermen scrambling for cover and scattering the loungers from their time-honored positions around the square, shouting to one another as they broke for shelter that a "blue-tailed bitch of a norther" was in the offing. A few of the newer people, peering out of front windows ringed with Christmas lights, made the old remark about Texas having no climate, just weather, and in this case the observation was justified. By 12:30 the rain was freezing on the streets and highways, coating the fence wire with ice, and by one o'clock it was snowing—a heavy, blinding snow that fell directly out of the low clouds and smothered the plains as the clouds had smothered the sky.

Rather than turning on his reading lamp, Robert Winslow had tossed the copy of *Table Talk* onto his desk and, sinking back into his leather chair, gazed around what until recently had been his solitary refuge from the world. The built-in bookshelves were empty now and already gathering dust and there were fade-marks on the wallpaper where his diplomas had hung alongside his color reproduction of Holman Hunt's *The Light of the World,* which was leaning against one of the yellow packing boxes that crowded the floor. Eventually he turned his gaze out the window and watched the falling snow and the rapidly whitening prairie upon which it fell.

When his wife opened the door, admitting a path of yellow light, he was sitting silently in the dark.

"Bobby? Are you in there?"

"Yes, dear, come on in if you want."

"May I turn on a light?"

"If you like, but close the door."

Emily Winslow tripped on the light and, closing the door behind her, walked over and stood beside his chair, bending forward confidentially.

"What's the matter, darlin'?"

"Oh. Just thinking I'm pretty much of a failure."

"Oh, come on now, Bobby, I thought we were bigger than that. To let somebody like that get you down. An uncivilized boor with a lot of dirty money and political ambi—"

"Tom Bagley does not, as you say, 'get me down'. I learned long ago how to deal with that kind. No, Tommy has nothing to do with it. Neither does our moving except in the most general sense. This goes deeper, I think."

"Well, what *does* it have to do with?" she said. "What on earth's the matter with you, Bobby?"

He looked up at her and smiled. "Nothing, probably. Just fragile, I guess. Must be the weather. You know, 'The hare limp'd trembling through the frozen grass . . .'"

Even as he said it, Robert Winslow felt a twinge at having made one of those "exter-scriptural illusions" Tom Bagley got so excited about and instantly reproved himself, not for the allusion, but for noticing it and flinching like a frightened puppy.

Emily Winslow patted him on the shoulder and shook her head. It was her "what am I gonna do with that man" gesture and it warmed him even as he realized, not for the first time in their twenty years, that however much shelter they offered one another, there remained a great deal they could not share. But it was just as well. And it was nice that she was still so young in spirit, that the gray streaks in her hair just matched her eyes and that the extra flesh on her face had given her an aura of maturity without stealing her beauty. She was a gentle, earthbound creature, he thought, and a splendid companion.

"Well, you just brood yourself out of whatever you've brooded yourself into. I'm going to fix some dinner."

"The light," he said.

She clicked the darkness back upon him, and the swirling snow and the naked prairie rose again into his vision. Robert Winslow couldn't tell her that he was frightened at the thought of spending the rest of his life in this blunt, foreign country where she felt so at home. And because it was her country, he couldn't tell her that he would stand in his pulpit sometimes, looking out across the clenched and unforgiving faces of his congregation, and feel all the warmth and blood sucked from his body by the incoherent, brutalized *need* in the creatures huddled before him. That he felt like the last soft man on this hard shoulder of the world—the last Victorian in this dingy century.

I need a high collar, he thought, *a frock coat . . . some table talk!*

He couldn't tell her that. So he watched the storm from the window of his darkened study. And so it was that, a little while later, he saw the small white MG encrusted with frozen mud and dirty icicles slide to the curb in front of his house—a tarpaulin-wrapped bundle tied to its luggage rack. Saw the two young men, scruffy, unshaven and obviously cold, clamber hurriedly out of it and, hands in pockets, shoulders hunched against the wind, come trotting rapidly across the snowy lawn toward his front door.

They were college friends of Robert Winslow's beautiful daughter, Cynthia, in flight from their campsite on the lake, and Robert Winslow made them welcome, insisting that they stay for dinner and spend the night. He helped them unload their car, and while they washed up and shaved with Robert Winslow's

razor, Emily Winslow stretched the meal she was preparing—
retrieving two extra pork chops from the freezer, another carton
of cottage cheese from the Frigidaire and a few more canned
peaches. There was already enough of her famous String Beans
with Mushrooms and Cheese Sauce, she decided, since she had
made extra for leftovers.

During their meal they talked about the storm, and Emily
Winslow said how sad it was they always had to work so hard during Christmas and Easter when Cynthia was home from school.
"But when you think about it," Robert Winslow said, "really,
we're in the Christmas and Easter *business*," and they all laughed
and admitted this was so. Then, after dinner, as Cynthia and
Mrs. Winslow set out into the snow, laden with brightly wrapped
food packages for needy families on the congregation's Christmas list, Robert Winslow and the young men retired to his dis-
mantled study. There, over coffee, they talked about books and
poetry and the untimely deaths of John Keats and Buddy Holly.

And that night, as Robert Winslow lay next to his sleeping wife
reviewing the evening in his head, cozy under the weight of blankets in a room filled with the ghostly ambience of streetlamps
reflected off the fallen snow, he heard the footsteps in the hall.
When he heard them, the first thing he felt was confusion, then
anger, then annoyance at the prospect of an awkward confronta-
tion in the darkened hallway; then he was overcome by a raging
sense of betrayal and self-ridicule as he admitted to himself that
up until that moment he had been enjoying the young men's visit
and pleasantly recalling their conversation. They had even, in a
rough-and-ready, West Texas sort of way, had some table talk;
and it had been refreshing, for once, to engage in a conversation
without the ironbound decorum of "pastor" and "flock" firmly
in place. If the young men could not see themselves in him, he,
Robert Winslow, had certainly seen himself in them, especially
in Cynthia's young man who was, even as he thought it, stealing
down the hall toward his daughter's bedroom.

If he had been thinking more clearly, Robert Winslow would
have realized that his sense of shame and betrayal was even fur-

ther exacerbated by the fact that since receiving his daughter's letter the week before, he had actually, in his quiet way, been looking forward to the possibility of the young men's visit. The letter had come, as always, addressed to him at the church, just as her letters to her mother always came addressed to the house, and he had liked the letter and liked his daughter for writing it, amazed as always by her instinctive blend of tact and candor.

Dear Daddy, it began, in purple ink on sorority stationery, *Just a line before I get back to work on my papers. How is everything at home? Have you met the new preacher, the one who is going to replace you? (As if anyone could replace my sweet Daddy) If not, when will he be in town, and when are we going to move? I hope we can between semesters, so I can be there to help. Won't it be nice to be in a nice new town without any grouchy old Tommy Lee Bagley to tell you how to preach? I have heard Odessa is a darling town and I am sure you will be real popular. Two of my sorority sisters are from Odessa (one lives outside of town on a ranch, and has just tons of money) and they said that they would come and hear you preach. I know that doesn't sound very exciting, but I thought I'd tell you anyway, just to let you know that I'm looking forward to moving, and that I have some friends in Odessa. Aren't I sweet?*

Oh! I have met a nice boy. Well not a nice boy, as Mother might define it, but he is sweet to me. In fact, don't you dare tell Mother this, he is quite wild, or so I've heard. But he knows that I am a "Preacher's Kid" and he also knows that I know about some of his excapades (sp.), so he goes out of his way to be extra sweet and nice with me. In fact, he's about twenty times nicer to me than the ministerial students I have been dating. And not an "Octopus" like "you know who," Mother's favorite. Well, I've just got to tell you some things about him. I met him in Seventeenth Century Poetry. He sat beside me and copied my notes, although he's not the type at all to be taking Seventeenth Century. But who is? I'm sure not. He belongs to the wildest fraternity, but, as I said, he's very sweet to me, except to kid me about my bangs. And we talked about you the other night! I told him how you got into trouble for quoting Keats and Shakespeare in a sermon, and he said he might like you because he likes Shakespeare, and Keats too, when he's not too mushy, and you said that

*too. And then he said: "I'll bet your father is a mystic." And I asked him
what he meant and he said that it was kind of hard to explain (meaning
that I am too dense to understand), but that he had a room-mate once,
who was his best friend, who was sort of a mystic.*

*We were in a parking lot overlooking the campus when he told me
this (Isn't that scandalous) but anyway he said: "I don't know but the
way Boylan explained it, it's just that sometimes when you look at things
they seem to be, well, glowing, kind of alive by themselves. Like the
campus now, if I were like, you know, mystical, it would seem bigger and
more beautiful than real." He said that he could feel like that himself
sometimes. But not about trees and flowers and stuff. He said the plains
did that to him sometimes, empty places. But then he said you have to be
careful and not let yourself get carried away. (He's very responsible. Hee
hee!) He said if you do, it can all rush in and . . . "Well, hell," he said,
"I don't know. You just have to be careful when things are too beautiful.
Like I have to be careful about you. You're much too beautiful." Now
wasn't that sweet? And then he kissed me.*

*Well Daddy, I bet you're shocked, but he really is nice, and I think
he just acts wild as a cover-up. Anyway, you might get to meet him
at Christmas, because he and one of his fraternity brothers are going
fishing at Possum Kingdom. And he said he'd like to meet somebody who
read books but wasn't a professor because they're mostly "dorks." I told
him my Daddy wasn't a "dork" for sure. So maybe you'll get to meet him.
Anyway, must go now and roll up Shirley's hair. Shirley says Hi!*

Bye now,
Cyn

†

The moment the conversation had drifted onto the subject of
books, Robert Winslow recognized Cynthia's young man as one
of the fortunate ones. He had not met many during his tenure
in the West. Mostly he had quarreled and counseled with those
who had not been so lucky, who, among the narrow options
open to them, had never come upon that *thing*, that place or
private endeavor around which their lives took on some natural
shape, and had settled instead for next best. So he knew all too

well that had young Kevin Lloyd not at some point, by happy accident, stumbled upon some book worth reading, it might just as easily have been commodities, or fast horses or violent crime that focused his attention—but not so well and never so naturally, for here was a happy convert, a sailor who had found his ship. He had stepped into their conversation with the nervy confidence of a young athlete stepping onto the field to play a game he fully intended to master—moving restlessly, speaking with a kind of accelerated, unselfconscious seriousness that Robert Winslow did not find altogether attractive.

"Keats"—he was saying—"I'll tell you the trouble with Keats: he loved nature. It's as simple as that. He loved to go out and look at it, smell it, taste it, walk in it and say, Isn't that pretty? Well, that's a town person's way, and I don't know much but I know better than that! I mean, look out there! That's a *bad* place! You only go out there to be reminded of it, and maybe get even a little."

The young man had made himself comfortable on a yellow packing box full of books. He was talking now around a cigarette, arms spread wide as if he were carrying a large load of packages, taking an occasional sip from the coffee cup he had positioned on the floor between his boots and using the saucer that rested on the corner of Robert Winslow's desk as an ashtray.

"I mean, I'm not trying to present myself as some kind of, uh, Natty Bumppo. *I'm* a town person, a city boy, in fact, through and through, but I've lived close enough to old Ma Nature to know her for the witch she is. Still," he said, pausing to take a sip of coffee, "it's so easy to forget. Like I was down in the Valley last year hunting pigs with my cousin Virgil and we were out in the brush one evening and there was this amazing sunset, I mean, spec-*tac*-ular! I said, 'Wow, Virg, that looks just like a *Turner*!' And ol' Virg just shrugged and said, 'Looks like *rain* to me, Kev.'

"I had to laugh, you know. But it really brought me up, because I realized I just wasn't looking at what was there. I was walking around with a *gun*, looking at a *painting*! I mean if you depend on the land, for your food, for your *life*, I guess you

might say, you can't love it like Keats did. At least not this country." He made a broad proprietary gesture. "You can look at it
and say it's beautiful, I guess. And it will choke you up sometimes. But you've *got* to respect it. Because, like my grandaddy
said, *it's* looking at *you* and thinking, 'Yum yum, here comes
supper!' In fact, that might of been what killed Keats, not having
sense enough to get out of the rain. On that tour of Scotland."

"You may be right about the tour," Robert Winslow had said,
smiling, "but I think Keats would've understood what your
grandfather was saying."

But that was all he said. He could have gone on at some length,
of course, citing chapter and verse, to refute what the young
man took to be Keats' "la-di-da" vision of nature; he could have
quoted, most centrally, those terrible lines in Keats' letter to
Reynolds from the seashore:

> I was at home,
> And should have been most happy—but I saw
> Too far into the sea; where every maw
> The greater on the less feeds evermore:—
> But I saw too distinct into the core
> Of an eternal fierce destruction . . .

And, without even digressing into his view that Keats' Nature
was not nature at all but the landscape of his generous heart,
Robert Winslow could have won the argument, decisively, but
he had not—first because he was Robert Winslow and not some
professor and second because he recognized that it was not an
argument at all. What young Kevin Lloyd was trying to articu-
late, however contentiously and at John Keats' expense, was, he
knew, nothing more than the homegrown version of his own disappointment. They were living in a world violently at odds with
their imagination of it. Even its malevolence was too mechanical
and impersonal to take heart from.

Those lines from Keats to Reynolds, in fact, had occurred to
Robert Winslow within the week, when he too had looked too
far into the sea and discovered, almost inadvertently, that his

doctrinal dispute with Tommy Lee Bagley—a dispute in which he had taken some small measure of pride—had been nothing more than pretext, a device to clear the pulpit for the son of Tommy Lee's closest political ally, who was, it seemed, graduating from seminary that very term. How nice for him.

"But you see what I mean, don't you?" Kevin Lloyd had said, his inflection for an instant betraying insecurity. "If not about Keats, about this country."

"I do indeed," Robert Winslow had said nodding, acknowledging to himself as he did that at least the boy was sensitive enough to know when he was on delicate ground.

Kevin Lloyd gestured toward the black windows. "In country like this," he said, "you can only afford to have your visions on weekends."

"Well, I'm lucky in that respect," Robert Winslow said quietly. "I've never had a vision anytime. But I can tell you this," he said with more emphasis. "When I was an undergraduate—I went to this little normal school just north of Champaign, that's in Illinois—when I was an undergraduate, the *only* thing that ever tested my faith was the idea that the man who wrote the 'Ode to Psyche' should not have been granted a full span of years. I remember sitting in my carrel one night. It was in the fall and I was in the library reading that poem for an exam and I suddenly found myself weeping, tears just pouring down my face without my really being aware of it, because he had written that and died so young."

"Actually," Kevin Lloyd said, "I think Rossetti or somebody said if there really was a God, John Keats would get to be alive one day every year."

"I can understand what he meant," Robert Winslow said. "I used to have the poem by heart . . . I still remember the last, I think . . ." He looked at the ceiling, reciting:

> A rosy sanctuary will I dress
> With the wreath'd trellis of a working brain,
>   With buds, and bells, and stars without a name,
> With all the gardener Fancy e'er could feign,

Who breeding flowers, will never breed the same:
And there shall be for thee all soft delight
   That shadowy thought can win,
A bright torch, and a casement ope at night,
   To let the warm Love in!

He had meant for it to come out lightly but his years in the
pulpit betrayed him and his recitation conveyed some of the
orchestral finality with which the poem concluded; it stopped
the conversation dead. They sat silently and listened to the
mixed snow and sleet clicking on the dark windowpanes. Kevin
Lloyd coughed and Robert Winslow could smell the bourbon.
The sweetness hung in the silence between them. And *that* had
gone all wrong. He could have handled *that* in a more reasonable
manner. The fifth of whiskey.

At this point the other boy, Gregory Falstaff, appeared at the
door. He was shorter than Kevin Lloyd, a little older and considerably heavier, with black, unruly hair, an open blue gaze
and, obviously, a heart without malice. He had excused himself
on the pretext of using the restroom but his cheeks were flushed
and there was snow in his hair, no doubt from a clandestine visit
to the car. They had only been in his house four hours, Robert
Winslow thought, exasperated with himself, and already he had
become involved in a moral dilemma.

Four hours ago they had appeared at his door wreathed in
snow, with watering eyes, red noses and a three days' growth
of beard, smelling of coldness and wood smoke. And he had
immediately taken to them as they stood there in heavy parkas
over sweat shirts, snow-caked blue jeans and boots rimmed with
dark lines of dampness.

"Looks like we came to dinner," Kevin Lloyd had said. "But
we brought food."

"Well, Emmy's already got dinner on the stove. Plenty for all,
but maybe we can use it tomorrow. Cynthia's had her hair rolled
up, so while she's madly brushing I'll help you unload."

Robert Winslow had grabbed his overcoat and followed them

into the snow. He had picked up a sack from between the seats of the MG and seen the fifth of whiskey; there was no mistaking what it was. *Wild Turkey Bourbon Whiskey*, it said on the label, and the boys had seen him see it.

If only he had said: "Well, I see you boys brought a little warmer-upper. Bring it on in the house and we'll have a little nip after dinner."

His father would have done that, but he hadn't spoken. He had grasped the damp sack of groceries to his chest and turned to trudge through the swirling snow back to the house, wanting to say something at every step, wondering if he wasn't becoming a Tommy Lee Bagley without even knowing what one was.

Now the two boys sat across from him in his study smelling of bourbon whiskey and his own Old Spice aftershave, and Robert Winslow, who didn't drink, who in his life had never had the opportunity to drink, would have liked one. It would have helped him talk to this young man who gazed at him so confidently and told him about John Keats.

The trouble with Keats! This boy was telling *him*, of all people, about Keats! Poor John Keats with whom Robert Winslow had journeyed for thirty years, whose words wound through his mind like roses through a trellis, to whose antic shade he had always played the role of loving older brother, admiring his high spirits and good-natured industry, pitying his awful gift. A more sympathetic older brother, he had always hoped, than George Keats who had abandoned him to go tramping about the American wilderness with Audubon, zestfully slaughtering mountains of birds in the name of art and science.

"And you, Mr. Falstaff, are you interested in poetry too?"

"Fatty doesn't read anything but the *Wall Street Journal*," Kevin Lloyd said, "and *Billboard*."

"That's not true," Gregory Falstaff said, smiling. "I read *Tortilla Flat*. Kevin gave it to me and I read it. I guess you could say I'm semi-literary."

"Semi-literate's more like it," Kevin Lloyd said. "It only took him six months."

"I read it to go to sleep. Have you read it, Mister, er, Reverend Winslow? It's by John Steinbeck."

"I think so."

"It's about these Mexicans and other guys who have great parties and don't work. I really liked it."

"No big words," Kevin Lloyd said.

"Right," said Gregory Falstaff happily, completely without shame. "It's a good book! And by the way, Lloyd, you know so damn . . . so many big words, what's 'marginal propensity to consume'?"

"Fatty wants to be a rock and roll mogul. Like Colonel Tom Parker, that's Elvis's manager. He's Fatty's ideal."

"No way! Not anymore!" Gregory Falstaff said. "Not since 'Love Me Tender.' What a dorky song! A complete sell-out. The 'E' would've never done it. Not if he hadn't had bad advice. Bad management. No. Buddy Holly was *my* hero. He'd've never done 'Love Me Tender.'"

"He did 'Words of Love,'" Kevin Lloyd said.

"Not one tenth the dork-out quotient of 'Love Me Tender,'" Gregory Falstaff said firmly, completely bewildering Robert Winslow, who suspected that like the Mexican ladies on the south side of town, they had shifted into another language to insure their privacy.

"It was a blizzard like this that brought him down, you know," Kevin Lloyd said, squinting out the window. "Buddy Holly, I mean. And the Big Bopper."

"And Ritchie Valens," Gregory Falstaff said, leaning forward with his elbows on his knees. "A major tragedy." He looked at the floor, contemplating the whims of fate, then looked up candidly at Robert Winslow. "Long way from Keats to Buddy Holly, huh, Rever'nd Winslow?"

"Perhaps not so far as one might think, Mr. Falstaff," Robert Winslow said. "John Keats was a spunky little devil. He was *not* a dork!"

They burst out laughing and Robert Winslow laughed with them. In a twinkling he felt at home as he had not felt at home for years, since he had been in the seminary. And for that moment nothing outside the study mattered. The whiskey, Tom Bagley . . . nothing! A sweet billow of happiness rose beneath Robert Winslow's ribs. He leaned forward and, unconsciously mimicking Fatty Falstaff, placed his elbows on his knees.

Kevin Lloyd was talking about his grandmother, who had come to Texas in a wagon with a canvas cover, which, according to her, was not technically a 'covered wagon', and Robert Winslow wanted unaccountably to say: "But let me tell you about Illinois . . ." He wanted to talk to these boys, to tell them the funny things his father had said and done, to tell them about rivers and trees, about tying flies and looking into green water and seeing your reflection with fish swimming under it, about spitting water through the spaces between his teeth that time . . . But his beautiful daughter, her eyes bright with cold, opened the door and leaned into the room.

"Got 'em all to their rightful owners," she said, "and nearly froze in the process. Now y'all come on in the kitchen and bring the coffee. Mother's got some hot pudding. And some pralines Mrs. Gonzales gave us."

So Robert Winslow rose to his full height, stretched and left it all unsaid, but that night, as he lay under the pleasant heaviness of blankets, he thought about the things he would have said, thought that there was nothing more beautiful than a river, a slow, wide river disappearing around a bend, turning luxuriously into a cluster of trees, carrying its streamers of sunlight. *The Tree and the Water of Life,* he thought.

The phrase rose in his mind and, as it did, he wondered if he hadn't somehow, subconsciously—at the behest of some perverse adolescent logic—exiled himself from the Garden, from the Tree and the Water of Life, for the love of Emily. Then, immediately recognizing this speculation as the product of a mind too well tuned to the homiletic analogy, he discarded the thought.

Of course, had Robert Winslow, Jr., followed the plans he developed and cherished during the first twenty-three years of his

life, such a speculation would have never come up. Had he, when
he graduated from that small seminary in Illinois, taken a little
church in a quiet midwestern town, his full talents would have
been appreciated, for his talents, he knew, were quiet ones. His
consideration for others was constant to a fault, his punctuality
frightening and, although he seemed too gentle to merit the ad-
jective *austere* (with his blooming smile that revealed small spaces
between his teeth), he was a man of dignity. And his smile, even
as it bloomed, was carefully benevolent, and his elegant locu-
tions from the pulpit, if not inspiring, positively glowed with the
reassurance of God's mercy.

If he had only followed his plan, which was not only his plan,
but his father's plan for him, and which was not only his father's
plan for him, but the plan his father himself had followed (and
his father had been rewarded with a long life full of happy
births, women in floor-length dresses in afternoon parlors dis-
cussing the orthodoxy of Robert Browning, and quiet deaths),
things might have been different. But young Bob Winslow, in
his senior year at the seminary, had fallen in love with Emily
McAllister on the campus walk beneath the wide sycamores
where many sincere and righteous lovers had fallen in love before them.

She had been a delicate girl with brown hair who was described among his classmates, Bob noticed, as either quietly
beautiful or mousy, depending upon the generosity of the de-
scriber. Robert Winslow remembered his provincial wonder at
her nasal Texas drawl—coming as it did from fragile and yet
unpainted lips; remembered how he was always seeing his reflection in her gray eyes, always falling into them; remembered
her as she described where she had come from with the hateful
love of a pretty girl without pretty things, growing up on a farm
without party dresses or parties or young men in stiff collars and
blazers; remembered thinking that she would have distrusted
those parties and party dresses and young men had she ever had
them; and remembered too that she could never quite grasp
what it was that touched him in poems written by mere men,

whose verses were, after all, not the Word Incarnate, neither
Truth nor Law, neither prophecy nor divine consolation.

"Father, I'm going to marry Emily McAllister."

"Do you love her?"

"Yes *sir!*"

The new Reverend Winslow stood before his father's ma-
hogany desk, and his father, long a widower, shifted in his
leather chair (the chair Robert Jr. was to inherit), nodding his
head solemnly. He kept nodding and pulling at his muttonchop
sideburns until young Bob cleared his throat and announced
that he was going to accept a church in Marshall, Texas. Robert
Winslow, Sr., stopped nodding then and examined his son's reflection on the polished top of his desk.

"I've decided I need to strike out and do something on my
own," his son said.

Robert Winslow, Sr., rubbed his chin, still inspecting the in-
verted image on his desk: the pale blue eyes, the blond hair
trimmed closely on the sides but still bushy on top. His only son
—looking very thin in his narrow black suit. *Texas,* the old man
thought, and saw something in the image on the desk, saw it also
in himself, like a little light flashed on the nature of their gift.

"Do you know where you're going, Son?"

"Yes sir, to a church full of small-town people and farmers,
people who believe in God and want a preacher who does too,
just like here in Illinois."

Reverend Robert Winslow, Sr., stared at his son, surprised at
the hint of rebellion in his voice, but he said nothing because he
couldn't frame the words he wanted to say quite as well as he
would have liked.

A year later Robert Winslow, Jr., stood in the middle of a
weedy path talking with an old man who leaned against a fence
post and let one arm swing idly, brushing the seeding heads of
the Johnson grass.

"I like you, Bob," the old man was saying, "and the old lady's
like to got a crush on you, but you can't use words a man can't
understand in these parts."

"Was something wrong with my sermon? I worked on it all week. What do you mean, Bass?" said Bob Winslow.

"I mean, to be blunt, that I ain't been to any school but the one they teach behind a plow, but that don't mean I don't need my religion. It probably means I need it worse. And I need it from *here!*" the old farmer said, slapping his chest where beneath his serge coat, suspenders, striped dress shirt and longhandles, he imagined his heart to be. Bass Carter had already taken off his collar, as had Bob Winslow. It was Sunday afternoon and as they had every Sunday afternoon of that year, since the Carter place was on the way to the parsonage, Bob and old Bass had walked home together.

"I try, Mr. C. I thought that's where it was coming from."

"May be, Bobby, may be. I ain't denying where your preachin' comes from, but you strain it through a dictionary before it gets to me, and it comes out so nice. God knows your preaching comes out nice, Bobby. But we ain't natural good folks down here, you know. Give us a little hellfire occasional."

Bob Winslow let himself smile at the old man. "All right, Bass. Hellfire you want? Hellfire ye shall git!" He slapped the old man on the shoulder and they smiled at each other. Bob Winslow smiled till his cheeks hurt; Bass Carter smiled so wide he loosened his upper plate and had to close his mouth into a clamping grin. The sun, unmindful of the Sabbath, burned down on the little community, heating the unpainted boards of the houses and the dirt in the fallow fields, turning the clearings amid the hackberry and pine into dens of flaming stillness.

The young minister left the old man standing by the wire gate. He raised his hand as he turned to walk down the weed-choked path toward the parsonage. He could feel the old man watching him, and almost in obeisance to that careful, unblinking gaze, young Bob Winslow thought about his heart. He searched his heart and found no hellfire there. Usually it was quiet and happy, his heart; usually it was sustained by his tacit affection for everything that walked on two legs or four, but now, this afternoon, as he walked the narrow path choked with drooping sunflowers, his heart was quiet and empty. Starchy sweat ran down inside his shirt and his palms were sticky, one of them dyed red by the end-coloring on his Bible. His heart was hot beneath his coat, but not with hellfire.

No one could deny that the people of Marshall, Texas, loved young Bob Winslow, or that he left their pulpit on the very best of terms, highly recommended. He was courteously replaced by Jamie Beavers, a freckle-faced native son who drove them to the station and stood with them on the dark platform as they waited for the Port Arthur train to squeal and steam to an unaccustomed halt beside the platform.

"I never knew *anything* could be like that!" the new minister had said, indulging in what he imagined to be the ministerial equivalent of talking shop. "When I got the call, you know. It come on me in a flash of light!"

"He hadn't even mastered the past tense," Emily Winslow said on the train. "But he hay-yud the cawl! Lord, he hay-yud the cawl!" she mimicked his country voice.

Looking up from his book, Bob Winslow forgave her for saying what the clacking wheels had been saying since the train, with a jerk, had begun to move an hour ago. *You haven't had the call,* they said. *You haven't had the call.*

It had always been taken for granted that he would be a minister, that he had had the call. He had never even considered it before. He dropped his eyes to the arching, rough-cut pages, and they glared yellowly back at him from his lap. It should have been his Bible, he knew, but he read steadily, poem after poem, turning the pages at random until at last he let his lids fall, let his lashes cushion softly together and listened to the wheels as the pines swept by and he hovered between waking and sleeping. Now they said, *But here there is no light,* and he knew in his heart that he would never have "the call," whatever it was, and that not having had it he would never be able to rise up and pass judgment with the unyielding ferocity required by the hard-bitten Christians of this country, nor would he ever be cynical or secular enough to rationalize the fact that he hadn't had it. But even so, he *was* a Christian and he was not a coward, and even as he dozed on that train to Port Arthur, in his hour of defeat, he felt confident that even if he hadn't *seen* the right thing, in a flash of light, and even if he couldn't always *say* the right thing, with proper, primitive fervor, he could be depended upon to do the right thing when the occasion arose.

Or so he had always thought, until he heard the footsteps in the hall. He had been lying in the dark listening to his wife's quiet breathing, replaying the evening in his head, and he thought at first it was just the timbers creaking or the wind gnawing something as it swept deep and relentless around the house. But it wasn't. It was footsteps, and he told himself it was one of the boys going to use the bathroom. They moved stealthily past the bathroom, though, and he moved a little. The footsteps continued. He moved again, making the bedsprings squeak, and the footsteps stopped.

He listened until his ears rang for them to begin again, and when they did, Robert Winslow breathed a sigh of relief. He decided they were returning to the guest room. Then he heard just the faintest of cracks from the hall floor outside his door, and another, and there could be no doubt about their destination. *Move!* he told himself. *Just get up and walk around and he'll go back to his room. Go into the hall, meet him there, he'll be scared to death and he'll say he's looking for the bathroom and you'll show him and that will be that.*

But Robert Winslow did not move. He thought what a crude, barbaric thing it was and wondered if he had done anything to provoke it—if these young pirates had perceived in him some weakness or falsity that had encouraged them, had justified, in their eyes, this contemptuous violation. Or perhaps it was just that he had relaxed, laughed with them, accepted them as equals. Perhaps the young man had taken *that* as a permission, he thought. Then he realized that, obviously, the young man *had* permission to be moving in the hall, but not from him—that he would have never ventured out in this situation without the invitation.

And he could not pass judgment on them, could not rise up in righteous anger. But he wanted it to stop! So he taunted himself, called up memories, visions of his daughter: baby Cynthia in her polka-dot swimsuit frolicking in the sprinkler; Cynthia at nine on the rocky beach at Port Aransas posing in her Bluebird uniform, like an awkward starling, all knees and elbows and gap-toothed grin. But he knew better—knew, as well, the tall, confident young woman waiting down the hall—the one with the direct green gaze and the hipshot stance who had, in her own way, warned him in a letter. But that didn't make it any better. It just made it impossible. Impossible for him to move, to judge, to preempt her invitation or betray her confidence.

He heard the door to his daughter's room open softly and then close, and he imagined Kevin Lloyd standing there in the darkness above his beautiful daughter, frozen in tableau, not speaking. In his distraction, as he lay frozen and trembling in his bed with this tightness spreading from his belly, he envisioned them poised, like Madeline and Porphyro, in Keats' medieval technicolor, in gorgeous chamber, bathed in the warmth of candle and stained glass, coming together, melting into one another "as the rose blendeth its odour with the violet . . ." Robert Winslow sat bolt upright, sweating and terrified, when he realized that he had aroused himself with his fantasies. He flung both arms violently around his chest and held himself as tightly as he could while colored lights dazzled before his eyes.

He must, he decided later, have lost consciousness for a moment, although he was aware only of regaining it and finding that the walls, which moments before had been translucent and seething with his colored visions, were suddenly solid again, that the room was dark and warm and he was simply himself, Robert Winslow, inside this room and not filled with, no longer imagining, the dark hall, or the other rooms in his house, or the frozen town with its snowy, silent streets, or his own lonesome flock in

their dark rooms and in their pain, or the terrible prairie surrounding them all. These things were simply not there anymore,
not in his head. And he was aware of himself as a single creature
in the midst of a wide creation—as something more than a mere
exemplar, a physical instrument, a conduit of God's mercy.

Something had happened, Robert Winslow knew, and he suspected that it was good. If he had done it himself, he thought,
he was a stronger man than he had ever imagined. If he had
not, then maybe there really was a God and so he reached over
beneath the covers to touch his wife, who believed there was.
Emily Winslow was sleeping on her stomach, her face away from
him, with both arms around her pillow and her long flannel
nightgown gathered up around her waist. Robert Winslow laid
his hand gently into the warm curve of the small of her back
and, for the first time in a long, long time, felt what he was really
feeling. And without another thought fell asleep. When the wind
died down about an hour before dawn, he was awakened by the
sudden quiet. Outside his window, a sliver of moon hung like an
empty cup over the white prairie.

†

It was a brilliant Christmas morning. The town gleamed in
frozen glory, all white and silver beneath the blue sky, and after
a breakfast of eggs, orange juice and dry-fried bacon the five of
them, the Winslows and the two young men, trooped through the
snow to church. And as the sunshine reflecting off the snow outside sparkled and flashed through the windows of the little sanc-
tuary, Robert Winslow delivered his Christmas sermon, which,
like every other Christmas sermon he had ever delivered, was
on love.

"Well, you boys drive carefully," Robert Winslow said, bending
over to peer into the little car.

"We will, sir," Kevin Lloyd said.

"Enjoyed your Christmas sermon," Gregory Falstaff said. "I
think I probably needed it."

The Winslows laughed and the white MG started with a clatter, backed up for a few feet through its own exhaust and pulled slowly away from the curb. As they walked back up the sidewalk to the house, Robert Winslow took his daughter's arm.

"Did you like him, Daddy?"

"He's perfectly charming. A perfectly charming young man. I think you have good taste, Cynthia."

"Did you get to talk to him about poetry? I told him you liked poetry. Especially Keats."

"Mr. Lloyd was much more interested in talking about my beautiful daughter than about poor John Keats."

Cynthia Winslow looked up at him skeptically and he gave her a smile.

THE AUTHENTIC LIFE AND
DEATH OF SMILEY LOGAN

Concerning the Youth & Parentage of that Notorious
Modern Desperado; how it was related to the Narrator;
and including for the First Time, the Authentic Facts
of his Daring, Daylight Robbery of the Odessa
National Bank at the Age of Twelve Years!!!!!!!

Friday evening I drove out on the El Paso highway to Leona's, which is the little honky-tonk where Smiley was killed. It was the first time I'd been there since, and when I pushed open the door the place was already loud and crowded with working cattle people, oil field people and just about everybody who wasn't at the Odessa Country Club or the Church of Christ. There was no place to sit, so I picked up a Falstaff at the bar and sidled over toward the shuffleboard. There was a silence while the jukebox changed records, and I heard this little squirt with a bow tie saying, "He was the meanest sumbitch ever drank beer along this highway. Why, when he was twelve years old he stuck up a bank. The Odessa National. Walked in there with a sawed-off shotgun and held them up for three hundred thousand. Carried it off in a paper sack!"

I walked right over to his table and told him he'd been watching too much television, that Smiley Logan was a friend of mine and if he wanted to tell a story on him, he'd better find out what the fuck really happened.

"I don't care a damn what happened to your punk friend," the little guy said, and two of his buddies got up from the table. There was a day when I would have fought all three, but I just walked over to the shuffleboard and put a quarter on the railing to get in the game.

74

"Never mind him," Jerry Clooney said. He was one of the guys playing the shuffleboard.

"I didn't," I said. "Somehow it don't seem that profoundly important."

"We're playing for halves, Hank," Jerry said, and I put down another quarter. After all, I told myself, Smiley was just this big ole West Texas boy who made a name for himself fighting in honky-tonks and finally got himself killed. It wasn't as if he was the president, or anything. I could look around me and see at least twenty guys like Smiley, wearing their wide-brimmed straws and fancy boots. You would have thought they were all stud cowmen but they hardly set a foot beyond the bob-wire fences that mark off the right-of-way. They talked about cattle prices, and land prices, and the oil allowable, but they lived on the highways, like those Chinamen you see on the television who spend their whole lives on the Yangtze River. And who's gonna get in a fight over a Chinaman? Jerry Clooney, who was standing beside me, leaning over the shuffleboard with his hat pushed back on his head, hustled quarters for a living. And there was Joe Bob Quinn, who worked at a Gulf station, sitting at the bar with Indian Vallejos, who couldn't hardly ride a horse but followed the rodeo circuit riding bulls—an occupation which takes more guts than sense.

So if that little guy wants to make Smiley into a hero, I thought, why not let him? But I knew I was making excuses. Smiley was my good friend and I should have pol'axed at least one of those guys. Then again, it had cost me two weeks in the hospital to learn the truth about Smiley's bank robbery, and I didn't plan to spend two more just because somebody told it wrong.

I could still remember the white ceiling of the hospital room where I woke up one morning about three years ago. I was trussed up like a steer in a Calcutta, and a fat, snaggle-toothed nurse was telling me that I had a fractured jaw and wrist, a bruised cheekbone, a broken nose and a lacerated palm where a beer bottle had shattered in my fist.

"They brought you in from Kermit last night," the nurse said. "Your guitar's in the closet."

"Thanks," I said through my teeth, since my jaw was wired up. The last I could remember, I was sprawled on the hood of my pickup outside the VFW Hall. A lot of guys from the rodeo dance were gathered around me and I could see cars roaring down the highway with bloody headlights. I was pretty sure my wounds were fatal.

"You play that fancy guitar in there?" the nurse said.

"I don't ride it," I said. "I got a band, Hank McGuire and his West Texas Windmillers."

"Never heard of 'em," the nurse said.

"We play lotsa dances round this part of the country," I said.

"You must have been a big hit over to Kermit last night," she said.

"We did all right," I said. "The fight was over this little barrel racer from Floydada. Don't even remember her name."

"Wonder to me you can remember anything," the nurse said, gathering up her needles and bottles and things. "Push that button if you need me. I'm going down the hall." Then, when she opened the door to leave, she said, "Oh, here comes somebody to see you!"

"Howdy, Hank," Smiley said, stepping into the room. For a second I had this fleeting notion that he had come to finish me off, then I noticed that he really did look like he was sorry—or as sorry as a guy who stands six four and weighs two thirty can look. He pushed his blond cowlick out of his face, and said he'd come to see how I was. I told him he could damn well see how I was, and he walked right up to the bed and handed me four *Man's Adventure* magazines. He looked so damn awkward and sheepish when he done it that I wanted to laugh, but my face was so mashed up I couldn't do anything. After he had given me his peace offering he sat down in a straight chair—just like he'd been ordered to—and asked me again how I felt.

"About half-dead," I said. "How's your ear?"

To this he laughed out loud and said it was very nearly tore off but otherwise okay. "Never in my life would I have thought of biting an ear," Smiley said. "But she sure gets the job done. Sure was good thinking, Hank." He might have been joshing me, but the more I thought about it, the less I thought it. Biting an ear was the kind of thing that would impress Smiley.

Anyway, he stayed there the whole three hours, picking at the tape on his ear and doing most of the talking, since my jaw was wired up. And it was on that morning that I learned everything I know about Smiley Logan. For instance, you might have thought his name was a nickname because he smiled so much. A lot of people do, but it wasn't, and his smile wasn't such a nice thing anyway. There was an acid mean streak in Smiley and when he smiled, that's what showed. He smiled like he'd just noticed a rattler coiling around your leg, or like he knew a dirty story about your sister. Now his laugh was different; it chased the demons out of him. When he laughed, his big face would light up like a lantern and he would beller like a bull on the prod. He'd slap his hat against his leg, or pound the table so's the beer bottles did a little dance. So when I want to remember him well, I remember him laughing. "Smiley" was his given name, his grandmother's maiden name, and his whole name was Albert Smiley Logan Junior.

He was born in 1936 in Palo Pinto County, and his family lived there beside the Brazos River until the Second World War. At this time his father farmed peanuts in the sandy bottoms and his mother fed the family with Brazos catfish. They were poor but Smiley had all the raw peanuts he could eat and in that country it wasn't a crime to wear hand-me-downs and have red dirt under your fingernails. The only rich people were the ones who owned the cattle land and they lived in Mineral Wells, off oil, not cattle, since these were the days of depression and the drought.

It was about this time that Smiley got his first pair of boots. Albert Logan loaded his son and his wife into their old Studebaker one day and hauled them into Mineral Wells to go to the picture show. Afterwards they walked down the street to watch the fancy tourists swimming at the old Baker Hotel. Then, as they were walking back to the car, Smiley saw this little pair of cowboy boots in a store window and he bawled and shouted until Clita Mae Logan bought them for him. From that day until the day he died, Smiley never wore anything but boots—though he never was much of a rider.

The Japanese attack on Pearl Harbor changed all this. Some ten months after the war started, Albert and Clita Mae picked up and moved to Fort Worth to work on the big bombers at Consolidated Vultee. Albert got a job deburring nuts, and Clita Mae, who was better with her hands, took up welding. They lived just outside the plant gates in a prefab shantytown called Liberator Village. In the evenings Albert and Clita Mae spent their time in the honky-tonks along the Jacksboro Highway—the "Jax-beer highway," Smiley called it. They'd never had so much money, and coming in every week, too.

In the evening, while his folks were honky-tonking, little Smiley would turn off all the lights in the house and listen to the radio. He would sit in the window, watching the colored lights flashing and twinkling on the big war plant, and the planes landing and taking off on the flight line that was just across the highway from Liberator Village, and he would listen every night to Charlie Chan, and the Green Hornet. How he used to get mad when they interrupted programs with war news, or how President Roosevelt felt that day! Then one night, just as the Green Hornet and his Filipino valet Cato were about to be drowned, the doorbell rang.

"Are you Albert Logan Junior?" the policeman said.

"Call me Smiley," he said.

"Well, all right, Smiley," the policeman said, crouching down to talk to him. "Your folks have been hurt real bad in a car accident, and I want you to tell me if you have any relatives."

"Only Uncle Sampson," the boy answered.

Four days later a welfare worker gave Smiley three dollars, bought him some western comics and put him on an overnight bus for Odessa. In his pocket he had a piece of paper with Sampson's address on it, and a letter explaining his mission "to whom it may concern." Holding these tightly, he climbed off the bus in Odessa after giving his comics to a Pfc who was riding on to Los Angeles. He settled himself down in the bus station to wait for Uncle Sampson. It turned out he was in for a long wait, and the next morning he was awakened by someone shaking his shoulder.

"Hey, pardner," a clerk said. "You been waiting here for a whole day. Who's supposed to be picking you up?"

Smiley handed the clerk his letters, and the clerk bought him a sandwich and then borrowed a car to drive Smiley out on the Kermit highway to Sampson's mailbox.

"Your uncle's house should be right up that road," the clerk said.

"Thanky, pardner," Smiley said and pulled his cardboard suitcase out of the car.

Sampson's house was an old adobe place that had been a line camp in the days when the ALZ people owned all that land and had just begun fencing it. Now it sits on the fence line where Jinx Matlock's property borders with the old ALZ, about two miles off the highway. When Smiley reached the house and lugged his suitcase up onto the porch, he found the door locked and no Uncle Sampson. He sat down to wait some more, and that night the little kid who was to grow into the meanest man in West Texas pulled his flannel pajamas on over his clothes and spent his first night in Ector County curled up on Sampson's porch looking at the stars and watching out for snakes.

Sampson arrived in the morning, unshaven and smelling like Mexican perfume. He had been in Juarez celebrating the first insurance check he got for keeping Smiley. But he didn't waste any time putting his little nephew to work. In about two weeks Smiley was a combination maid, cook, drink-mixer, beer-opener and cigarette-roller. As Smiley put it, "I tell ya, Hank, I was a goddamn Cinder Ella."

I should tell you a little bit about Uncle Sampson here, because he wasn't near as bad as this story makes him out. Sampson was just a little fellow with a straggly mustache and a receding chin who didn't take to peanut farming. As he told me once after

Smiley and I became friends, "One day that old mule just farted in my face for the last time, Hank. I dropped them reins right there in the furrow and headed for the oil fields. I was what they call a 'Boomer', which is kind of an oil field forty-niner, and I ran from one end of this state to the other at the first whiff of oil. Every major field that was brought in in Texas, I was there, but I never got so much as a finger in the oil. While the guys I played nickel-dime poker with were outfitting their wives at Neiman-Marcus and hiding from 'em in Acapulco, I was still standing around the table looking for crumbs.

"I was the man Roosevelt forgot," Sampson would tell me. "I roughnecked some, hustled a few leases and swindled some farmers who didn't have enough cash to make it worth my while. For a while I even tried doodlebugging, which is witching oil like a water witch witches water. Now you've heard people say that the doodlebugs found as much oil as the college-boy geologists ever did? Well, you'll never hear me assay that opinion. The closest I ever came to finding oil was popping these here blackheads on my chin."

So you have to understand that the money Sampson got for keeping Smiley must have seemed a long time coming. When Albert and Clita Mae drove off that curve, he had been reduced to raising fighting roosters and staging cockfights for the local 'chucos. On account of Sampson being white, he was a lot less likely to be arrested than they were. I will say this for old Sampson, however, he did put Smiley in school, and Smiley did go. "It was the lesson of two evils," Smiley told me.

I didn't know Smiley when we were in grade school, but I can remember him in our first year of junior high, about the time of the bank robbery. He was already big for his age, with shoulders like an ox and that shaggy cowlick down in his face. I remember he was dirty for his age too, and he hung around with the Mexican kids until he could talk Tex-Mex with the best of them. (In the years right before he died, he started talking about renouncing his citizenship and moving to Saltillo. But it wouldn't have made any difference. I knew Smiley well enough to know that he would have only been knifed by a Mexican rather than getting killed in such a nice, clean American way.)

Anyway, he was the biggest, dirtiest kid in our grade. That was why we all noticed when he came strutting across the schoolyard wearing a grimy purple tee shirt, faded jeans and the damnedest pair of fancy, high-heeled Mexican boots you ever saw. They stovepiped nearly to his knees and he had stuffed his jeans down inside them. Why, there wasn't a nigger cowboy, hillbilly singer nor Hollywood homo wouldn't have been proud of those boots. They had yellow toes and red tops with a giant blue-and-green eagle stiched on the front and a purple rattlesnake slithering down the back seam. They were a bootmaker's nightmare and, Lord, Smiley was proud of those boots. Every afternoon he would wear them nearly home, then climb through a fence and hide them in a box beside a pumping station. He walked on to the house in a pair of Sampson's castoffs. The irony of it is that except for some enchiladas and some comic books those boots were all Smiley got out of the money he took from the bank. Two hundred and fifty thousand dollars and Smiley got a pair of stovepipes. The reason, of course, was Uncle Sampson, and it all came to an end one day in the early summer.

That morning, since there was nothing to do around Sampson's house but work, Smiley walked to the highway and hitched a ride into town. He spent the day peeking at the old cowmen who gathered in the hotel lobby, and reading comic books at the newsstand. Then he got a ride back out to the house with the man who hauled the afternoon papers from Odessa to Kermit. He was there about an hour before Sampson would be home for his dinner, so he had time to fix him a Royal Crown Cola, roll him a cigarette with Sampson's gummed Zig-Zag papers and read the new *Batman and Robin* he'd bought in town.

"I was such a dumb kid when I come out to Odessa," Smiley told me, "that I thought Sampson and I were going to be like Batman and Robin.

"Of course I soon found out otherwise but when I got there, I had it all figgered out in my head. I'd still read *Batman* from time to time anyway, even though I knew it was crap. And anyway, I was living in no-good Odessa, not Gotham City."

When the car pulled up outside, Smiley had just settled down on the couch to find out how Batman was going to get the Joker, who was killing people with laughing gas. Smiley knew it wasn't Sampson sliding up in a cloud of dust because Sampson didn't have a car, but sure enough, it was Sampson—drunk as old Cootie Brown in a yellow Chevrolet convertible. He swaggered up to the porch carrying a cold can of Coors and grinning like he had swallowed the canary. There was a gleam in his eye and foam on his black mustache. Smiley taken one look at him and knew what had happened.

He ran out the back door and snuggled up under the house. When he pulled out the old saddlebags, they were empty. The money was gone, and Smiley sat there in the dust hitting those old saddlebags with his fists saying, "Sonufabitch. Sonufabitch." Sampson came sidling around the house and put one boot up on the step. "Howdy, Smiley," he said, and grinned just like the Joker except for his mustache. He was wearing a brand-new, twenty-dollar straw, a pair of patent leather boots and a bright fuchsia shirt with mother-of-pearl snaps. But he didn't really look so fancy. There was a three-day growth on his little chin, and at the neck of that fuchsia shirt you could still see his dirty longhandles.

"You look like you lost something," Sampson said. Then Smiley jumped up and ran past him into the house. He knew just where to look. He ran into the bedroom and peeled back the mattress on Sampson's bed. And there it was, in neat little piles, just like when you play Monopoly: ones, fives, tens, twenties and hundreds.

"Sure looks like you can afford to start paying rent, don't it?" Sampson said.

"You keep forgetting about that insurance money," Smiley said.

"That don't even keep you in comic books, squirt," Sampson said. He was leaning against the doorsill, grinning so his chin disappeared. He took a sip of his Coors and whistled. "Well, who woulda thought it?" he said, shaking his head. "I just can't imagine you holding out on your poor old uncle."

"I woulda give you some, Uncle Sampson. I woulda shared it with you."

Sampson cut him off with a snort, like he knew Smiley was lying, which he was. When Smiley got that money changed he was heading off for Montana . . . or Gotham.

"You was gonna light a shuck with that money," Sampson said. "I can't figger out why you're still here."

"I had to get it changed first," Smiley said.

Sampson squinted at him. "Changed?" he said.

"Yeah *changed*!" Smiley said. "You can't go spending that money around here. You got to change it into other money. Why, the Texas Rangers have a list of every number on every one of them bills." Smiley sat back triumphant. He knew this because the Joker got caught once, not changing the bills he stole. Sampson ran his thumb along his lips. It was pretty obvious he had never thought of that.

"I ain't changed the twenties and hundreds yet," Smiley said. "I'd have to get some fancy clothes to do that."

Sampson squinted his eyes and tried to look businesslike. "How do you change that money, squirt?" Sampson said.

"It's pretty easy," Smiley said. "Whenever you go off on a toot, I go down to Cuña. When I cross the river, I change the hot money into pesos. Then I hang around the square and eat some tacos off a cart. Then I come back across the border and change the pesos into good money."

"Well, I swan," Sampson said. "Yer a regular Jesse James!" He threw his head back and gave a big haw haw haw. "Old Albert would have been proud of you!"

"You can stop casting asperations on my pa," Smiley said.

"Ex-cuuse me!" Sampson said, "Now how about telling your old uncle how you stole that money?"

Smiley felt like he was gonna tune up and bawl but he bit his lip and didn't. He flopped the mattress back down on the money and walked into the living room. He felt like there was ten tons of ice stored in his stomach, and he couldn't think of anything else to do, so he walked into the kitchen, got one of Sampson's Zig-Zag papers and—cool as you please—started to roll a cigarette. He had the tobacco all arranged in the paper when Sampson swatted him up beside the head. The paper tore and the tobacco went all over the floor.

"You didn't have no call to do that," Smiley said.

"Hell I didn't," Sampson said. "How'd you get that money?"

Smiley just grinned, and Sampson rared back like he was gonna hit him with the Coors can. "I just took it," Smiley said, and Sampson pushed him down on the couch and shouted, "How?"

Smiley let out a long breath and told him how he happened to be in Delbert's Sandwich Shop after school one day when Del asked him if he would run some sandwiches over to the bank for a quarter. Smiley took the tuna fish sandwiches over to the bank in a wire basket, and a fellow said to bring them back here in the vault. They were clearing out some old money and getting some new money to replace it, and this teller was working overtime. The teller said they were going to burn the old money as soon as he finished his list. Smiley gave him his tuna fish and the teller went back to counting. Then, as Smiley was walking out of the vault, what should he spy but a brown paper sack full of that old money.

"So I thought right then," he told Sampson, "why burn that money when me and my uncle can sure use it? I decided we could drill us a couple of gushers with that money, so I put the paper sack in my wire basket."

When Smiley told how he walked, soft as a summer breeze, right past the guard and into the street, Uncle Sampson lost control. He crumpled up on the couch and started laughing. He snorted, and sputtered, and gasped around his mustache, and spilt Coors on his fuchsia shirt. "Eeeeehaw!" he yelled, and kept going on about how the Rangers thought it was an inside job and put lie detectors on everybody in the bank, including the president. "And all the while, my no-account nephew had two hundred and fifty grand in a pair of old saddlebags!"

Smiley had to laugh too, but pretty soon they both stopped and just stared at each other. It must have been a sight to see. Just like a showdown in the movies. On one side was Smiley, thirteen years old and trying not to cry, and on the other side was Sampson, stark drunk and dressed up like a cigarette advertisement. Sampson swatted at a fly that had been attracted by the beer on his shirt, and Smiley rubbed his palms on his jeans. Neither of them spoke, and in the silence Smiley could hear the big Sinclair rig just across the fence line sucking oil out of the ground. They were trying to stare each other down but Sampson lost his focus pretty regular and Smiley's eyes kept blurring with tears.

Finally Sampson said, "The most of that money's mine. You know that, don't you boy?"

"Ah-ha-ha," Smiley said.

"You're hot-damn right it's mine! You owe me four years room and board. And besides, you hid the money at my house, which makes me an accessory!"

Sampson kept forgetting about the insurance money and how he made Smiley work. Just lately Smiley had had to look after these seven goddamn cattle Sampson had won on the shuffleboard. As he said, he was a Cinder Ella, but now he had the golden egg and he was Montana-bound.

"I'm leavin' out," Smiley said. "I'm goin' to Montana."

Sampson just looked at him. Then he walked into the kitchen and got a Royal Crown Cola. He poured it in a jelly glass and added some Crab Orchard bourbon. Evidently he hadn't had time to buy any good whiskey. The Crab Orchard was Margie's, who was one of the women Sampson brought home to sleep in his bed and drop bobby pins in the commode.

"You ain't going nowhere, squirt," Sampson said, real soft. "Now you and your Uncle Sampson might just mosey out to Las Vegas. Just you and your Uncle Sampson, how does that sound?"

If he had known it would have been just him and Sampson,

Smiley might have gone. But it would have been him, Sampson, a bunch of women and a herd of these honky-tonk cowboys Sampson ran with, and Smiley had popped his last can of beer for those barroom bronc fighters couldn't tell a horse from a hackamore.

"It don't sound no good," Smiley said.

Sampson squished his RC and Crab Orchard around in his mouth, then lit a ready-made with a filter. "Well, it don't matter how it sounds to you. That's how it's gonna be." Sampson hooked his thumbs in his belt and stuck out his stomach, like he'd seen in a movie, no doubt. "You got too little respect for your elders, squirt," Sampson said. "And you don't know nothing about bad luck. My whole life has been a run of bad luck. There ain't no bad luck I ain't had—"

"You won those cattle," Smiley said.

"You shut your blathering mouth!" Sampson said.

"Well, you can't have that money and that's your bad luck too," Smiley said.

"Do you know what would happen if I just decided to pick up that phone and call the county sheriff? Why, they'd tote you off to Gatesville and throw away the key. You'd be a steer or a queer when you come out of there. So if you want to stay a free man, don't try to keep me from what's mine."

It was obvious then that Sampson's idea of his being a free man and Smiley's idea of being a free man were not one and the same. Sampson was walking around the room, looking out the window from time to time. Suddenly Smiley really wanted to go to jail, a good rock jail with a bunk and a blanket where nobody could get in and nobody could get out, where he could just sit in the window and watch the cars go by.

"I'm going to do the right thing," Smiley said. "I'm going to turn to states evident."

"What?" Sampson said.

"I'm turning myself in."

Sampson whirled around and Smiley grabbed the .30-.30 leaning beside the fireplace. It was kept loaded for varmints and snakes. "You just go on, Uncle Sampson," Smiley said, edging toward the phone. He put his foot on the couch and laid the barrel across his knee, then he picked up the phone.

"Who're you calling?"

"Sheriff Gunney," Smiley said.

"Now come on, Smiley. You get your toothbrush and we'll get in that little Chevy and head for California. If you call they'll just put you in jail."

"I reckon," Smiley said. Jail was looking better and better to him. It wasn't Montana, but it wasn't goddamned Odessa either.

Then Uncle Sampson did a stupid thing. He jumped at Smiley, and if it hadn't been for his new boots Smiley might have killed him. But the slick soles of his boots slipped and Sampson fell forward. His hand hit the muzzle of the .30-.30 and the rifle fired. It blew Sampson's middle finger clean off, and there was a lot of blood and noise and the smell of cordite. Sampson screamed and rolled around on the floor, holding his wounded hand between his legs, so when the ambulance arrived they thought he was shot a lot worse than he was.

"You just hold on, Uncle Sampson," Smiley said as he put through the call. "Sheriff Gunney? This is Sampson Logan's nephew, Smiley, out here on the Kermit highway. I just shot Uncle Sampson accidental, and I robbed the bank. That's right, sir, I want to turn to states evident. That's right, Sheriff, of my own free will and violation."

The nurse came in with my dinner while Smiley was still talking. He was sitting backward across one of those famously comfortable hospital chairs, still picking at the bandages on his ear.

"Cain't you knock?" Smiley said.

"'Course I could, if my hands weren't full of this tray," the nurse said. "You better not pick at that bandage, young man, if you don't want to get an infection."

"I already got an infection," Smiley said with a leer, and the nurse put down the tray and left.

When she was gone, I told Smiley that I had never heard about his being in Gatesville, and he said he never had. "That would've been the best thing that coulda happened. Man, I wanted to get to jail so bad I could taste it. I wanted to get in a cell and just sit on my ass for the rest of my life."

"What happened?" I said.

"Well, you just heard the story," Smiley said, "I'll ask you. What would have been the lousiest damn thing that could've happened to me?"

"They sent you back to Sampson?" I said.

"You goddamn right!" Smiley said, crashing his fist into his palm. "And everybody in the county got a big laugh. When I confessed to Sheriff Gunney, he turned blue and nearly had a heart attack laughing. And when they had this juvenile hearing, those damn fat cats in their black suits just sat up there and snickered! You know who was the head of that juvenile guidance shit? Gil Taylor. And you know what he did? He patted me on the head and told me not to rob any more banks! I'd've rather hung!"

"Well, you can't hold that against old Gil. That's just the way he is," I said. "Anyway, Gilbert Taylor's a good man; he was damn good to us." When we were playing basketball for Odessa High, Gil got Smiley and me a pair of the softest summer jobs in West Texas.

"He can afford it," Smiley said, and when I looked over at him, I could see that Smiley had gotten himself all heated up over not being sent to Gatesville. He held the back of the chair with both hands and glared at the floor. Smiley's world was like that: you hit and you got hit back; if you won, you were the king of the highway; if you lost, you were sent to Gatesville. Then he rested his chin down on the chairback and his face softened. "Gil's all right," he announced suddenly.

"I always thought so," I said. "He don't mind you knowing they was cowshit on his jeans once upon a time."

"No, he don't," Smiley said.

"And he don't brag about it neither," I said, "like those fat bastards that come up to you at rodeo dances. They're always the treasurer of the rodeo association or something, and they give you a slug of their fancy bourbon whether you want it or not and then start telling you how goddamn poor they used to be. If that ain't something to be proud of! Then they tell you you sure have a nice-looking guitar, and would you play some goddamn song nobody ever heard of, recorded about twenty years ago on the Bulldung label."

"And then ten minutes later," Smiley said, "you can hear them telling everybody at their table how hillbilly singers is nothing but trash."

"Yeah," I said. "How come you noticed that?"

"Oh, I'm a great noticer," Smiley said, pulling himself to his feet. He stretched, and then he said real casual, "Oh yeah, Hank, did I tell you I'd joined the army?"

"The army!" I said.

"Yeah," he said, and then I could see him getting excited again. "Here, let me show you something in one of those magazines I gave you." He picked up one of the *Man's Adventures* and flipped through it until he found this article about the jungle fighters in Viet Nam. "Looky here," he said. "That's what I'm gonna be, a Special Forces guy."

"Smiley, are you serious?" I said.

"Dead," Smiley said. And he was. Two weeks later he shipped off to some training camp in Georgia. A month later he was back in Odessa. It seems the Special Forces couldn't understand why Smiley had to wear high-heeled boots like he'd done all his life. So they issued him a pair of combat boots and told him to wear them. In three weeks both of Smiley's arches were broken and his feet began to swell. But Smiley didn't say anything. He forced his feet into those combat boots and trained every day until one morning he couldn't walk anymore. He begged them to let him stay but the army gave him a medical discharge and sent him home. That was all of the jungle fighting for Smiley. But it wasn't all the fighting.

When he could walk again, he started spending nearly all his time on the highway. He would fight anybody who looked cross-

eyed at him, and usually win. Sometimes I would go drinking
with him, and we would drive two hundred miles to find some
guy who was supposed to be tough. This was the time when
you could walk into any tonk from Big Spring to Van Horn
and say you were a friend of Smiley Logan and it would mean
something. If it didn't get you any girl in the house, it kept you
from getting killed trying. But it began to show on Smiley: he
drank too much and his face, which used to be rawboned and
angular, began to look puffy. In a fight with a pro linebacker
over in Colorado City he won the fight but lost two teeth. He got
a long scar on his cheek from a Mexican with a knife. And then
Sampson got killed.

Poor old Sampson made the mistake of trying to cheat a rodeo
cowboy out of ten dollars on the pinball machine at Leona's.
The cowboy went berserk and got a shotgun out of the trunk
of his car. When the cowboy came in the front door with the
shotgun, Sampson went out the back door with his ten dollars.
He hid under Indian Vallejos' car. But when the cowboy started
waving that scatter-gun, people started leaving Leona's pretty
fast. Indian backed out of the parking lot and ran over Sampson.
He died right there on the gravel.

I can't explain the way Smiley took it. I knew that he hated
Sampson, but I guess he was the nearest thing Smiley had to a
daddy, and he took it hard. For nearly a week after we buried
Sampson we didn't see Smiley at Leona's. He kept himself holed
up in that old house and only came out for groceries. Then one
night he walked in and acted just like nothing had happened.
He was laughing and joking with everybody—drinking like it
was going out of style. Then Indian walked in and the whole
place got quiet.

I'll have to say this for Indian, he had guts. He walked right
up to Smiley and with tears in his eyes he said, "Smiley, there's
nothing I can say but that I'm sorry. And dammit, you know
how sorry I am."

Smiley grabbed Indian around the shoulder and said it wasn't
his fault. Indian gave a big tearful grin, and everybody else

gave out a sigh of relief. After that we had a good night. I got drunk. Indian did an authentic Apache dance on the bar, and later Smiley and I stood on the bandstand and sang "The San Antonio Rose." We even had a toast to the memory of Sampson Logan, King of the Shuffleboard. Then about midnight Indian said he was going home. He had reached the door when Smiley called out to him and Indian turned around.

"You know what you are?" Smiley shouted. "You are a no-good, bead-rattling, greaser communist!"

Indian's mouth dropped open and he just stared at Smiley. Then he decided Smiley was kidding, and he was about to grin when Smiley hit him in the mouth and knocked him out the door. Smiley leapt after him like an animal. Indian picked himself up from the gravel and Smiley hit him again. This time he knocked Indian three-quarters of the way across the highway, and started after him. The cattle truck hit Smiley full tilt and knocked him some two hundred feet into a bar ditch. Indian was left standing just across the white line with blood all over his face and his shirt fluttering in the breeze.

And that's how the stories got started. There are people, like the guy with the bow tie, who say that it was poetic justice that Smiley Logan got killed by a cattle truck. And there is Jerry Clooney's brother, who goes to Texas Tech, who says the whole thing was symbolical. But Smiley was my friend and I can tell you different. It was an actual, authentic 1961 Mack Diesel pulling a load of underfed steers that killed Smiley. It wasn't poetic justice driving that truck, it was a guy named Ralph Dawson Cherry from Butte, Montana. And Smiley wasn't "taken away from us in the prime of life to live in heaven with our Lord and Saviour," like the preacher said at his funeral. Smiley Logan was killed dead. I saw them pour the blood out of his boot.

AN ESSAY ON STYLE

All morning I stood on the platform between the club car and
the Pullman and watched the country roll by, not thinking anything, just feeling the hot wind on my face and watching the bad-
lands of northern Mexico shimmer under the small, emblematic
sun. "Whatever it takes to be an expatriate," I told myself, "you
don't have it." Three years before, I had thought Mexico was
a lush green place for the alienated young; it turned out to
be a place for Mexicans—"and people from Chicago," I added
silently since there were forty of them in the club car playing
guessing games, blocking the bar and occasionally bursting into
song.

I spat into the wind and lit an American cigarette in honor
of going home. It didn't taste like much, but that was all a part
of it, I guess. Then, in a moment of resolution, I reached into
the pocket of my jeans, withdrew a handful of pale blue heart-
shaped benzedrine tablets and, resting my forearm on the edge
of the lower door, let them dribble from my hand as we rattled
along. They tumbled in the wind as they fell. "Just like Johnny
Applespeed," I thought. When they were gone, I resisted the
temptation to lick my palm. If anything happened when I was
asleep back in Texas, it would just have to happen, I would just
have to miss it. When I was a kid, of course, I was always waking
up to find that people I loved were dead. It seemed like every
time I got in a really good snooze, *ping,* somebody was gone; so
I took to fighting sleep, holding it off until the very last instant
and then sleeping lightly, like a Comanche on his blanket. It was
my way of trying to keep everybody alive, I guess, and it didn't
work very well, but for a long time, it seemed, I had continued
to try, keeping vigil.

At noon the Aztec Eagle slid through the battered suburbs of Nuevo Laredo. Baked streets flashed in the sun and burnished peons watched the train clatter by, some standing so close I could have reached out and grabbed a greasy serape. In one of the streets I saw a young whore walking to work; she couldn't have been more than seventeen. She trudged heavily through the blazing midday in her blue net formal, her makeup crumbling, her hunched shoulders sleek with sweat. I remembered one January night during my senior year in college when I had run laughing through these streets with one of my fraternity brothers. We had reeled from house to gutter toting great armloads of red, muddy snowballs. Pimp, whore, fellow reveler or policeman, we attacked without prejudice, hurling snowballs and advancing from doorway to doorway like troops investing a city—and we were not alone. Everyone was running in the streets. It was the first snow on the border in twenty years so for most of the girls it was a new experience. The neon lights dazzled in the flurries and reflected gashes of color on the freezing water in the ruts. Finally I was hit in the ear by an adobe snowball. I remembered waking up in the gray morning in a goat shed—curled next to a disconsolate billy—and seeing Bob propped against the opposite wall with straw in his hair, and dirt smeared across his wide, freckled face. We sat there in that freezing goat shed and laughed at each other.

When the border guard found me on the platform to check my visa and vaccination, I was leaning out the portal thinking about that miserable cold drive back to Dallas, and when the guard left, I leaned back out. The train was poised on the trestle high above the snaking Rio Grande. Far below I made out a tiny Mexican boy fishing in the green rushes. There was a jerk and the train began to ease into Laredo. In a twinkling we were back in Texas and in my excitement I forgot about Robert Breedlove and calculated the number of dollars I could get for my remaining pesos. It was luxurious to be back in the States.

Later that afternoon the train paused in Dilley, where my brother-in-law owns some land, and I got off, had a sandwich and stomped on the dry Texas ground. It seemed solid enough and it was good to read signs in English again. I climbed back on board and read every sign in sight. A dust devil skitted from behind the mustard yellow clapboard station and rushed toward the train; then, as we began to move, it swerved and danced along parallel to the tracks, skirling sandwich wrappers into the air and finally exploding against a black-and-white sign— SUPERIOR OIL WELL SUPPLY—which swept by and was gone. I had read that sign three years before, heading for Mexico, and at that time it stood for everything that I hated. Now I was glad to be able to read it. I had left the United States, which I didn't understand, and run to Mexico, which I couldn't; kind of a mad thing for a person like myself at that time, who wanted more than anything to understand.

My ticket, purchased in Cuernavaca, would have taken me all the way home to Fort Worth, but I changed trains at San Antonio and climbed down here in Austin—180 miles south. I was fool enough to come back to Texas. Only a damn fool would have gone back to Fort Worth. Here in Austin I have been living alone. I cultivate a few girls who live in the everyday world and, by bathing regularly and not growing a beard, maintain a degree of social invisibility. In the most transcendental sense I live off the land; but even though and perhaps because this is my country, it can be very lonely here. I seem to feel the generations dying inside me. I am losing my grandfather's eyes: I gaze at the country spreading beyond the buildings and never translate it into sections, or notice how the water drains. I am losing my father's eyes: I see thunderheads piling black and monstrous in a yellow sky and never tell myself that it will be good for the grass. And even my own world becomes lost to me. There is a university here, and sometimes at night I wander past the glowing dorms and houses, across the campus, and never notice anything. I did notice a poster. The president is coming to town next week and although I have seen a sufficiency of Boston Irishmen at family reunions, I have never seen a president; so I imagine I'll go downtown and have a look at him. Otherwise I intend to continue as usual, pausing on corners to let the bright cars whisper by, then meandering on like a friendly ghost beneath the spreading elms and chinaberries, down the warm streets registering nothing for fear of memories which in Mexico seemed pleasant—even fond. I realize now that even though I have returned, I have not come home, that I am still in-between —in a long in-between, in fact. Texas has a lot of these; they give the place scale and, compared to the points from which you depart and the places you arrive, they are not bad places to be.

In the evening I like to eat alone at the Scholzgarten at a wooden table under a cedar elm. In fair weather there is a warm breeze which carries the voices and, in the light of the bulbs strung from tree to tree, the leaves are green against the black sky. I eat each portion of food on my plate individually, taking a lot of time. This is a habit I affected or inherited from my father, who had many other traits more worthy of affectation.

Last Thursday I had just finished my baked potato and was buttering the broccoli when Ricky Hagel strode through the gate and approached the tables, evidently on his way to join a party in the corner. I have known Ricky all my life and probably saw him once a week from my ninth through my twenty-second year; we graduated from the same high school, the same college, were in the same fraternity and even, I think, at the age of seven, suffered through the same ballroom dancing class for young ladies and gentlemen—so I had never really considered whether he was my friend or not. He was still slim and pale, with his black hair slicked across his narrow forehead. His silk-and-wool jacket fell away precisely from his shoulders and his loafers flashed with every stride. We saw each other and spoke almost simultaneously, and instinctively I half rose and Ricky started to sit down. But either he realized we had nothing to say or he saw something in my face because I could tell immediately that he thought better of it. He compromised by crouching momentarily on the slatted chair across from me.

"Ricky," I said.

"Deano," he said. "I didn't know you were down here. I heard you were playing Kerouac down in Mexico."

"I was. But I came back."

"Well, what are you doing now?"

"Resting, I guess." I found myself drawling at him, at once defensive and a little impatient, as if he were one of those ubiquitous Midwesterners you meet in Mexico.

"Are you still writing those stories?" he said.

"Some," I said. "Played for twenty-five years, now I'm going to write about what a good time I had."

"Sounds reasonable," he said, smiling a little. He cocked his head to the side and waited for me to speak.

"And what have you been doing?" I asked.

"Oh, a little oil, a little politics, not too much." His tone made it clear that it was neither my oil nor my politics, and when I didn't reply, he lifted himself slowly to his feet, smiling all the way. "Well, I better run," he said, and then, "Oh, by the way, I hear old Breedlove's on the brink of receivership again after his divorce."

I don't know why, but this really ticked me off. I drawled back at him, "Why, my goodness! Has Bobby run out of people to buy jicky contracts? 'f I was you, I wouldn't worry my head about it."

Ricky grasped his lapels and settled his coat on his shoulders, then gave me a hurt little grin and turned to wind his way through the tables. I watched him join his friends with a stiff little bow and pull out a chair. They were obviously political people from the Capitol. One of them, a fat man in shirt-sleeves, bawled out for more beer, and Rick glanced quickly in my direction. I may have been a Boho and probably a communist but he wanted me to understand that he knew how to order beer, and that it was only his responsibility to his father's estate that forced him to deal with these people.

Rick takes his money seriously, I thought. Maybe a little too. Bobby, on the other hand, really understood what it was—the splendor of it. Even so, it's hard to be rude to a guy like Rick when you're not really obligated to be polite to him, but Breedlove had been my friend for four years in school and still was, for that matter, although others had deserted him (and me) with excellent reason. He was, in fact, the only Yankee I ever cared a damn about.

He came originally from Lake Placid, New York, where his grandfather, Anson Breedlove, had come to construct several resort hotels and where he had finally retired with his family to hobnob with the Pulitzers and the exclusive crowd who gathered there. It was their mountain refuge, far from the Bolshevik city where they made their money. When Bob came to Southern Methodist as a freshman, there was a discussion at the house about his origins, but it was reasoned that since he had left Lake Placid at an early age—his father was a major general in the air force—and had been raised in various private and service schools around the world, he was not, in the strictest sense of the word, a Yankee, and General Breedlove was, in the strictest sense of the word, a prominent alumnus, and an Olympic bobsled champion to boot.

So Bob was pledged—and to our fraternity's good fortune, for if he was anything, Bob was a good fraternity man. Not intimacy, but camaraderie was his element. I have never known anyone who looked more at home leaning against the fireplace with a drink in his hand during Homecoming, or kibitzing a bridge game during final exams. After he had lived in the house for a few months there were those, myself among them, who commented that unlike most Yankees, Bob was blessed with a taciturn, almost a distant, laconic manner, even when he was drunk—which he often was after his father's sled flew out of a curve and went crashing through five hundred feet of pine at 110 miles an hour.

The fat man at Ricky's table called out, "Hey! One a you niggers! More beer over here!" and I sat thinking about those times, watching Ricky gesture emphatically. I could remember too the autumn afternoon during our sophomore year when old Arch Hagel keeled over stone dead on the seventeenth tee and Rick became a millionaire like his father, and a Republican which his father had never been. I thought about old Arch, who weighed two fifty and had hair like silver, and about General Breedlove, and finally about my father. It seemed for a terrible moment as though they had all been wiped out in the same disaster—one which singled out those in the habit of risk and decision.

Once, when we were kids, Rick and I sat beside the Hagels' pool and listened to Arch talk about his days in the oil fields. Old Arch was brown as a rock and wore a flowered bathing suit. He squatted down in an old beach chair like a worldly Buddha and carried on a desultory game of gin rummy with Richard as he talked.

"Back in the thirties," he began, "me and Key—he was my brother, Deanie—we didn't have one goddamn red cent. All we had was an old beat-up LaSalle tanker, and we usta take that truck, when it would run, out to the fields where the major oil companies stored their crude. Key and I would jimmy the gates on the fences and then fill that old truck right up to the gills. Next day we'd drive up to the district office and sell those big companies back their oil, so's to get enough money to drop a well, which came a duster likely as not. I don't think we got one decent producer while Key was alive."

"What happened to your brother, Mr. Hagel?" I asked. I was down in the pool, holding onto the edge.

"Killed," Arch Hagel said. "Flat blown up. One night we were sucking crude out of a big Standard Oil tank when Key got careless and flipped a butt and *whoosh!* the whole thing blew up. Like Judgment Day. The blast knocked me about a hundred yards and blew all my clothes off—see here, look at that scar— but poor old Key wasn't so lucky. The cyclone fence around the tank caught him like a slingshot and threw him back into the fire. I can still remember. Standing out there in the mesquite burnt all to shit. Watching that goddamn tank blazing and flaring, shooting smoke and sparks all over God and everywhere. They wasn't enough left of Key to half-fill a beer cooler."

I could remember being dazzled, excited, I guess, imagining

that flaming tank, but then I saw that Ricky was sniffling and I felt embarrassed. It was *his* uncle, of course, and none of my own.

I walked inside Scholz's and played a Hank Thompson tune on the jukebox; then I returned to eat my cold broccoli. I was almost sick with remembering, but I kept thinking of things. I remembered a party at the fraternity house when Bob solemnly announced he was going to become a publisher so that I would have someone to buy my scribbling. He was going to do this out of fraternal love.

"Publishing my scribbles is the only way you'll ever get any richer," I told him, and Bob looked at me unsteadily over his glass. "O'Connell," he said, "you have to admit it. Being a beatnik is as bad as being a Yankee." I admitted that it was and Bob lifted his glass with a jerk. "Here's to the Pulitzers," he intoned, "wherever they might be."

†

This morning I found Bob's picture on the society page of the paper. I have the page spread before me now and there he is, in a photograph taken at the Jewel Charity Ball in Houston, a little stouter than I remember him but otherwise the same. He is wearing a well-cut tuxedo with an air of studied carelessness, as if it were one of twelve (which I'm sure it isn't since his mom disowned him when he married and refused to un-disown him when he was divorced). He is guiding a faintly equine debutante from the dance floor, her elbow cradled in his palm, somehow instinctively aware that his picture is being taken. His lips are tightened into a grim, Cheshire smile that cuts across his freckled face and seems to say, "I know she's a pony, but I'm being gentlemanly as hell about it." The bejeweled companion, towering a good five inches over him, looks bemused. I would guess that Bob has just bestowed one of his oblique compliments upon her: "You look nearly as lovely as your mother tonight, my dear." Something along those lines.

This photograph, coming as it does on the heels of Rick's

comment, is reassuring. It's also a little spooky, like an apparition from the past come to sprawl on my breakfast table beside my chilling eggs. But there is pain as well as reassurance for me in this picture, a general unease that would be hard to explain even to Bob himself, for he deals in hard currency while I speculate in memory, taking, it seems, one last-ditch seat-of-the-pants flyer after another in hopes of recouping ancient losses. It is a volatile market rife with clandestine trends and precipitous devaluations and I have learned a lot about its dynamics since my return from Mexico. Still, if Bob were sitting across the table from me now and I tried to explain to him how I must control this capital, he would no doubt grin at first and then favor me with a gale of his boistrous, infrequent laughter. "Come on, O'Connell," he would sputter. "You're having me on!"

I would light a cigarette, lean back and explain: "You see, Roberto, it's as simple as this: *The past*, taken as a whole, *hurts*. So, for reasons of sanity, I've sorted out the vintage seasons of my slapdash, discontinuous life, sealed them off from one another, as it were, in metaphysical bottles and stored them in the cellar of my self where, hopefully, after proper aging, they will lose some of their bitterness, mellow and mature perhaps and with luck even acquire some value worth redemption.

"The alternative is to literally give myself up to them, my memories, to let them pull me down into their toxic, high-test, 180-proof bitch's brew of incoherent distress, to let them ring bells-within-bells within me down to that stunned, blank polarity where words face off with nothingness and thoughts go zinging by at a frequency so high they hurt but can't be heard."

Bob, of course, would laugh at all this melodrama, and I, of course, gesturing away his levity with my cigarette, would try to explain just how much I envied him the sheer mathematical simplicity of his core currency. "Money," I would say, "once in your possession, is at your command—at once yours and apart from you in some marble vault or drawing interest in abstract circulation—while even with my extreme precautions, at the slightest jolt (*Ricky. A picture in the paper.*) bottles are exploding in the cellar, the fumes swirling through all my tidy rooms and corridors, fountaining up."

Now, for instance, I am driving through a fine twilit Christmas Eve and there is snow around the bricks of the street. The sky is a frozen purple, the moon a violet sliver, and a pale star falls toward the black horizon. I am on my way to meet you at Duke's and the smells of bitter Christmas and frosty beer swarm into my nostrils; phantoms flicker up before me blotting out the bright morning that gleams across this breakfast table where the paper is spread . . .

It was the Christmas vacation of our senior year, and in the late afternoon of Christmas Eve I was playing a game of solitaire on the coffee table, while my sister Sandra combed her newly platinum hair in the mirror over the mantle. Mother was sitting to one side of the fireplace wrapping my grandmother's yearly nightgown. (As you remember, Christmases at our house, or any other holiday for that matter, were inevitably calamitous. My mother is a sentimental, high-strung woman who was completely unprepared for the sudden widowhood that left her in command of three bullheaded, Irish-tempered brats who could outshout and out-argue her. Her people were from Georgia and it was completely incomprehensible to her that her offspring might argue for fun. When we were kids, she would stand frail and wavering on the sidelines with terror in her eyes and a look of disbelief on her delicate features as we brawled like roughnecks. She thought the once or twice a year the entire family was together should be perfect, and of course it never was.) The house was very warm and smelled of the large fir Christmas tree Mom and Sandra had decorated. (My little brother and I didn't decorate Christmas trees.) It was about this time that you called and said, a little mysteriously, that you were a genius. I asked you why and you said to meet you at Duke's and you would explain.

As I walked back into the living room, Sandra glanced over her cashmere shoulder and, apropos of nothing, suggested that

I get out of college, where I was obviously doing nothing but dodging the draft. I returned to my solitaire game and lost it quickly as I told Sandra in no uncertain terms to go to hell and mind her own business. Mother thrust the nightgown into her lap, lifted a scrap of wrapping tissue to her eye and began to sniffle.

"Oh goddammit, Mother," I murmured, and she leapt straight up from her chair, dropping the nightgown, and ran out of the room trailing about four feet of red ribbon from her apron pocket. Her door slammed and we heard the springs squeak as she threw herself on the bed. The dark face of the maid appeared in the kitchen door and then quickly disappeared. Sandra told me to look what I had done, which, as far as I could see, was not a damn thing. I told her this at length as I divided the cards into suits and stacked them.

"Dean, would you please go and apologize?" Sandra had her hands on her hips, looking indignant and smoothing her skirt at the same time.

"It would go on all night if I tried," I said. "I'm getting out of this madhouse." I threw the cards on the table and told Sandra I was going to meet you at Duke's.

"Are you leaving this house on Christmas Eve?" Mother called from her bedroom.

"Yes'm," I called back. "I'm just gonna go have a Christmas beer with Bob."

"Dean O'Connell, you are breaking my heart," she cried.

Sandra was crying now. I grabbed my coat off the couch and burst out the front door, kicking the screen and intending to stalk to my car, but I stepped on a loose pack of snow and went skittering down the drive.

"Dean!" Sandra called shrilly.

I turned to see her framed in the doorway with her right arm up, elbow thrust awkwardly forward and wrist cocked. She threw a green package at me. It chunked into the snow at my feet. "That's your present from me," she cried.

I picked the package out of the snow, threw it into the car before me and wished my sister an icy Merry Christmas in return. (Of course if I were living at home today and something like this were to happen I would probably pick up the package and apologize—but I am older now and marriage has civilized my sister a little. At that time she had a tendency toward the grand gesture. And I? Well, the chains which had secretly broken within me were clanking around my ankles, throwing off sparks. By June I had sold everything I could lay my hands on and caught the train for Mexico.) I slammed the door of the car just as my sister spun on her heel and disappeared. As I was backing out of the drive through a white cloud of my own exhaust, she returned to close the door against the cold.

Now again I am driving down Berry Street on my way to meet you at Duke's. The sky is brilliant and the neon lights are on— Well, not quite—not actually. Actually, I'm sitting here chatting with an imaginary friend across my breakfast table, like one of those frazzle-haired, demented old ladies on the south side who, having outlived their friends and families, sit alone in their cracker-box houses and, gazing at the sunshine on the roses outside their kitchen windows, gossip with phantoms. It was a long time ago as my heart counts, and since then, in my frenzied efforts to gain momentum, to somehow break through into the future, I have drifted down too many dark thoroughfares and traversed too many cold Mexican nights on that up-and-down handcar pumped by methamphetamine and mescal. So even the "I" in which I am speaking seems inaccurate and uncomfortable, like the brown tweed suit Mom made me wear to a funeral when I was twelve, because it was the proper thing to do, because my new suit, which was really a blazer and slacks—a blazer with a crest and brass buttons—was a little too stylish for Aunt Carrie's funeral; so that even though I have failed to find a future, the past, which a moment ago stormed into the present, has receded again. It is as if I am looking through the wrong end of a telescope. The figures are small, but clear and very delicate . . .

†

At 8:30 that Christmas Eve, Robert Breedlove and I sat together with our forearms on the bar. I was wearing a sport coat and blue jeans, and Bob wore a brown mohair suit, a striped button-down shirt and a dark reverse-rep tie. Behind us, two teenagers were playing the shuffleboard bowling machine, and before us, behind the bar, Duke loomed in the half-light like some disconsolate genie with his arms clasped about his chest. He was waiting for us to sign his petition to bring horse racing back to Texas. The wall behind the bar was cluttered with framed etchings and photographs of racing thoroughbreds—a motionless stampede. After we had signed, Duke jerked the paper away and placed two glasses of Budweiser before us; then, with sultanic grace, he withdrew to a chair beside the telephone and picked up a *Racing Form.*

"All right," I said. "Why are you a genius?"

Bob clasped his freckled hands around his glass and waited until he was sure that Duke wasn't listening. When Duke picked up a red pencil and began to mark the *Form,* Bob spoke in his discursive, emotionless monotone.

"Well, last week Marcie and I had a fight—big one—so just to get the hell out of the house I took off for the Valley. I was just gonna poke around, maybe try the whores in Matamoros, but outside of Brownsville I stopped for gas at this hick filling station and got to talking to this old farmer with a gimped leg . . ."

This was the way all of Breedlove's stories began. He had the salesman's talent, and could just "get to talking" to anyone. It seems he talked to this old farmer for a long time, standing there on the gravel apron with his foot up on the bumper of his car, smoking a cigarette and squinting off into the distance. Bob nodded and smiled at all the right times while the filling station attendant tried to eavesdrop as he wiped the windshield. "Fellow was a fruit farmer," Bob went on, "and we got to talking about how much hell the Teamsters gave him came time to haul out his produce. Seems that, some way or another, the Teamsters kept all of the interstate trucking in a bind, and consequently all the farmers. We talked for about twenty minutes, and finally I looked over at him and said: 'I might be able to help. I got two refrigerated trucks back in Fort Worth no union man ever touched, just use 'em locally.'"

"But you didn't have two refrigerated trucks," I said.

Bob shook his head and said of course he didn't have any trucks. "But this farmer didn't know that. He asked me, real casual, to drop by his house that evening and we might be able to work something out. This was beautiful, O'Connell. When I got to this farmer's house there were four other guys there and two of them still had their hats on. They had come to talk business. I said to myself, 'Bobby, you are about to make some money.'

"Anyway, we all sat around for a while talking about the unions and how they were communists, et cetera, et cetera, until finally this old guy, the one with the bad leg, asked me if I would contract to haul some of their fruit out for them at harvest time. I played it cool. I reached forward and poured me a long drink from this bottle of Jack Daniel's on the table, added some water and told them we might be able to work something out, since it was a slow time for my business, which I couldn't quite figure out what it was. Then I asked them how much the regular lines charged them and they quoted me a price."

I dropped my head and shook it unbelievingly. "You son of a bitch," I said. I had to laugh.

Bob grinned a little and held out his hand.

"This isn't the beautiful part yet," he said.

"When I asked them how much the regular lines charged and they quoted me a price, I just guessed they were quoting low on me, so I told them I would haul their fruit at the price they quoted and they would be making money." Bob lit a cigarette and then looked up from the match. "This was really fine, O'Connell," he said with the cigarette still clamped in his lips. "There I was sitting in the living room with these four goddamn farmers running a complete bluff. I didn't have money for gas, much less two refrigerated trucks!" He let out a cloud of smoke and took the cigarette from his mouth. "Finally one of the guys who still had his hat on said, 'You got yourself a deal, sonny.' The others came in with him and we made a contract the next morning in Brownsville at a notary."

"But you know nothing about trucking produce, right?"

"Don't know zip," he said. "But listen, my child, and glean wisdom from my words: In the cutting of a trucking contract, if one knows *everything* about contracts, one need know *doodly-squat* about trucking. ¿*Comprende?*"

"Breedlove, where in the hell are you going to get two refrigerated trucks?" I said.

"Got 'em," Bob Breedlove said. "Or rather I *had* 'em. I took the contract down to the Chevrolet place yesterday along with my last three hundred bucks and conned them into ordering the trucks. Told them I was waiting for a check."

"So now you're in the fruit-hauling business," I said.

"Hell no! Last night I ran into Ricky out at Riverlawn. I got to talking about this and talking about that, and then I started telling him how I was gonna screw the Teamsters. Well, you know how Ricky is when you start talking about unions. He wanted to buy into the deal. I had to argue with him for two hours before I let him convince me I should sell him the whole kit and kaboodle. He bought the contract and the titles on those trucks for *twenty . . . five . . . hundred . . . dollars!*"

I put my head down on the bar and laughed out loud. When I turned my head back to Bob, he had just taken a long swallow of beer. As he lowered his glass his face was impassive but his eyes were shining. "You son of a bitch," I said again.

"Twenty-five hundred bucks," Bob said to no one in particular. Then, suddenly, his face burst into a radiant smile. "O'Connell," he said, "when I am rich, I am going to be one good son of a bitch to my friends."

"Will you buy me a pony?"

"Christ, Dean, I'll let you manage the Breedlove Foundation. I'm going to be rich in style!" Then he glanced down the bar. Duke was taking a bet on the phone with his shoulder hunched away from us. "But listen," he continued, dropping his voice. "Don't tell anybody about this, will you?"

I said that I wouldn't and nodded in Duke's direction. "You owe him some?" I said.

"Duke? Hell no. He's chapped because I hit a daily double off him and never placed another bet."

"You gave up the horses?"

"You never give up the horses. I got a better bookie in Dallas. Nah, I don't owe Duke. He's one of the few."

"I owe you forty," I said.

"Forget that. Wouldn't make a dent," Bob said. "Ah, but look at all that lovely money." He opened his billfold and held it below the bar, flipping through the bills as if they were the pages of a book, pausing occasionally to investigate a denomination.

"Loan me twenty," I said, smiling.

"Sure," he whipped out a bill.

"Hell, Bob, I was just kidding."

"No," Bob Breedlove said. "Here, nothing's too good for my friends."

"Bob, I don't need it."

"The hell you don't. All starving beatnik writers need money. You have just won the Breedlove Prize for Literature." He folded the bill and stuffed it into my shirt pocket. "Now let's get out of here and drink up some of your prize money."

He started to turn away from the bar, but I stopped him. "I've got a goddamn date at ten. Why don't you corral the wife and we'll all go out and—"

"I'm sleeping on the pool table at the fraternity house these days," he said.

"Locked out?"

"Locked out," Robert Breedlove said, coolly. "Maybe I should join the Teamsters." He shook his head. "The woman has cost me a lot of pride and a good deal of money."

For a long moment we fell silent and turned to watch the two teenagers playing on the bowling machine. The yellow lights climbed the toteboard. Thousands of non-negotiable points were scored amid the ringing of bells. I absentmindedly placed my hand in my jacket pocket and withdrew Sandra's package wrapped in green paper. I tore the seal with my fingernail and opened the little box, dropping the cotton on the floor. It was a heavy gold ring with my initials and fraternity crest.

"What's that?" Bob said.

"Ring. My sis gave it to me for Christmas."

"Nice."

I stared at the ring for a moment, blinking my eyes. Then, solemnly and with great ceremony, I slipped it onto my finger. It glinted darkly in the flashing lights of the bowling machine and I found myself thinking about dangerous abstractions, so I looked up again and watched the teenagers who were playing for beers.

"Breedlove," I said. "Consider this: What if all those dorks who are designing pinball machines were designing spaceships? We'd be on Mars by now."

Bob slipped down off the stool and, suddenly grabbing me around the shoulder, stretched his free arm before him, grinning and squinting ironically into the distance as if he were gazing at some magnificent vision. "Yeah," he said. "Mars. But think of this, Deano! What if all those goddamn space engineers were designing *pinball machines*! *That* would be the *American* way!"

We laughed and Bob continued: "O'Connell, you are my good friend. You know why?"

"Because I owe you money."

"No, because we don't have anything in common," Bob Breedlove said.

"Except we're both poor."

"Right. And I better get the hell out of here before one of my creditors shows up and makes me poorer."

Bob turned toward the door.

"Bobby?" I said.

"Yeah?"

"Let's make it down to Laredo between semesters. Screw ourselves blind."

"Right," he said and turned again toward the door.

Maybe you're right, I thought. Maybe common interests don't
make friendships—but perhaps analogous ones do: parallel lines
that run ruthlessly into infinity without crossing. Are matters of
content really that important on that last, fast track, if the style
is the same?

I looked out into the evening and saw Bob pause to light a
cigarette. The match blazed up illuminating his self-contained,
almost oriental face. In that moment I realized a little brutally
that when it came down to the wire, Bob would destroy me as
quickly for a deal as I would destroy him for a story. But perhaps
not, perhaps there was honor among stylists at least. Maybe,
when it all came down, regardless of the consequences or the
fashion, I would award him the O'Connell Prize for Hustling
without a Net. I didn't know, but I did know that both Bob and I
had cut ourselves loose—fired ourselves like untested skyrockets
into the night sky—that we would either burst into the splendor of our imagination or plummet to earth, alone through the
darkness. As I watched Bob walk on past the window with his
springing step I knew that neither of us had made any provisions
for landing.

"You owe me four bits for the beer," Duke said.

I paid for it out of Breedlove's twenty.

As the past comes swirling back, I must admit that this picture in the paper reassures me. My friend Robert Breedlove, to
whom I still owe sixty dollars, may be on the verge of disaster,
but there he is with his silk shirt and sapphire studs, riding tri-
umphantly on the crest of that disastrous verge, even as it rolls
inevitably toward some dark promontory. In some inexplicable
way it matters a great deal to me. Although I no longer move in
those circles (and circles are what I used to move in), I have never
found sufficient cause to repudiate those friends and fools from

the long party of my youth—the ones like Ricky, clutching tena-
ciously to what they have, preparing to drink themselves quietly
to death—or those like Bob who have fired themselves into a trajectory which will reach its absolute zenith on the ledge of some
twentieth floor. I am not sure that these friends of mine are not
engaged in the sanest of enterprises, given the particulars.

But as I sit here in Austin, poised between one life and
another, in a world poised as well, I am aware that this position is going to become increasingly difficult to maintain among
people more verbally "aware" of everything. How can I convince
them that Breedlove, or Rick even, is worth the words—that no
matter where you stand, or what you stand for, when you feel it
giving way beneath your feet, or solidifying around your ankles,
the moral terror is the same? Don't we all, at some point, wake
up in panic at our first intimation of adulthood, of its sinister
glamour?

Maybe not, but this is what I consider as I wander the sweet
evening streets: We were no gang of Byronic hoodlums in con-
vertibles, nor could have been, growing up as we did between
battlefields, scrubbed and stratified, tyrannized by the heroes of
legendary conflicts already won for us—by our grandfathers on
the land, by our fathers in the Depression and in the second war
and even by our older brothers in Korea. And growing up close
enough to these heroes to learn that even the most heroic of
them was only occasionally courageous, we began by worship-
ping their courage and ended up envying them the occasion. We
were not, like graduates of another generation, given everything
we wanted (we were no "flaming youth"); quite the contrary, it
seems that no one, least of all ourselves, considered whether or
not we wanted what we had. And what did we have? I ask myself
to the cadence of my heels. What did Bob and Ricky and I and
all the rest really have? Sometimes, as I watch the day burning
itself out in the west, behind country I have never ridden, the
answer comes back: Everything, you had everything perhaps,
but grace and the occasion. But that is no answer and anyway,
given the occasion, God knows what we might do in the absence

of grace. So I watch the orange fire falling from the western sky and feel helpless, as old Arch Hagel must have felt as he watched the flames that consumed his brother flare against the night while he stood naked in the brush.

GARLAND MARLINBERG
AND THE CITY OF GOD

When the telephone rang, Garland Marlinberg was doing what he really liked to do. It was a little ritual with him. He had drawn the curtains on the desolate street and the South Texas sun, unbuttoned the jacket of his gray Glen-plaid suit and hefted his feet up onto his wide blond-wood and chrome desk; then he had yanked the orange and green paisley display handkerchief from his jacket pocket and pressed it to his nose. The silk was sprinkled with his favorite scent, Sweet Lilac, and he was inhaling its fragrance while gazing at the longhorns his predecessor had mounted over the office door; then the telephone rang. Pushing his black leather chair away from the desk, he let the heavy heels of his elevator shoes fall to the carpet. The telephone rang again and he glared at it, thrusting the handkerchief into his pocket. On the third ring he reached up with both hands and smoothed his thinning hair to his skull, and on the fourth ring he yanked the receiver from its cradle and barked into it. It was Bucky Widows in the front office.

"Now don't get riled," Widows drawled. "I'm just callin' to put in a request for a little less blood. That suicide last night? I got five complaints awready, and that's just off the switchboard. God knows what we get in the mail. Five complaints, cowboy. Make that six, if you wanta count mine—"

Garland Marlinberg wedged the receiver between his shoulder and his ear. "Now look, Bucky," he said, gesturing to the empty office, "what am I supposed to do? Right here on my desk I got the survey. Says the viewing audience is up thirty per since

I come here. That's what I was hired to do. Liven up the local news, right? Well, to do that, you gotta use a lotta film. You use a lotta film, you take a lotta pictures, and *some* pictures *some* people don't like. The sad fact is that a little death livens things up."

"Aw, fuck, Marlinberg."

"Gotta be expected. You lose the sensitive plants—so what? let 'em listen to FM—but you gain the greasers—as *you* call 'em —and that, Bucky boy, was what *I* was hired to do. You shoulda seen what we cut *out* of those suicide films. There was one—"

He listened to the dial tone for a moment and then flung himself back into his chair, pulling his hand down across a face so ravaged by the sunlamp and the television business it could have been hewn from sandstone. The weathered lines around his peeling, hawked nose were carved deeply like parentheses from his brow to his chapped, sarcastic lips. But the first thing you noticed was his eyes. They were black and set firmly in ruddy, chiseled lids, never shining but on occasion flickering coldly—as they did now as he stared at the remnants of the Old West that Gantry had mounted over the office door. The telephone call had irritated him. Now it rang again.

"News director!"

"This is the news director?" a woman's voice said.

"It ain't the janitor, lady. What can I do you for?"

"I am the chairman of the Anglo-American Committee for Constitutional Government, Miss Rose Culpepper. We want you to make an announcement on your station. We're having a Freedom Rally—"

"'Scuse me, Miss Culpepper, but we don't announce meetings for free. Especially partisan political meetings."

"Your voice sounds funny," Miss Rose Culpepper said. "What's your name, Mr. News Director?"

"Marlinberg, lady, Garland A."

"Well, if you ain't one of those dirty Jew gangsters—"

He slammed down the receiver just as Nelly Sue Blanks was venturing through the door. She jumped a foot. Nelly Sue was from Rotan, Texas, and Garland Marlinberg scared her to death.

She stood there, frozen, wobbling on her still unfamiliar high heels. Garland Marlinberg looked up at her and smiled. He rather liked her; she didn't talk back and she was pretty in a 1943, Betty Grable sort of way. She reminded him of the pinups they had had in the Pacific.

"You know what that bitch called me, Nelly? A dirty Jew gangster! A dirty Jew I am, but *gangster*! Huh, I could tell her from gangsters." He lit a cigarette and Nelly Sue's lip trembled as if to speak, but he continued, drumming his fingernails and exhaling smoke. "I thought being a Jew in Dallas was bad, but San Antonio . . . ! At least in Dallas they appreciate a sharp businessman. Friends," he said, waving the cigarette, "friends, I don't need, but respect—"

Nelly Sue blurted it out: "Mr. Marlinberg, they're ready to look at the rushes."

"Oh hell, already? Okay." He sprang to his feet, buttoning his jacket and smoothing his hair. "Nelly, you know who respects me around here? That survey! That crummy piece of paper, and it's damn cold comfort. Love, you can have, but respect— Christ, they even *respect* Khrushchev!"

He strode out of the office and down the hall, swinging his arms vigorously. His heels clicked on the terrazzo. As he walked, he laid his chin to his shoulder to catch a trailing whiff of Sweet Lilac, and twisted the worn silver band he wore on his wedding finger. The ring had belonged to his grandfather and he wore it for business purposes. It was always best to be married, although he was not, and never would be. He was the last twig on the last branch of what had been a fine old German Jewish family tree, and when he returned from the war, his mother had picked out a nice Jewish girl for him to marry. But after the war he was no longer his mother's son. He could no longer be closed in musty rooms in brownstones on the brink of respectability, or by New York streets where the sky was just a distant strip of light. He could no longer be happy, as he had been, making quaint photographs of the Little Church around the Corner, having seen men die suddenly in the Pacific. He had tried, but it hadn't worked.

And it was strange, for when he had enlisted and been made a combat photographer, he was sure that he would hate the sight of death. At eighteen he felt that he had seen enough of it in ochre rooms smelling of ether and menthol. In one year he had seen three great-aunts and his beloved grandfather choke and gag their lives away. His grandfather had shriveled into a yellow skeleton, and his great-aunts, like listing tankers, had sunk slowly into their pelvic structures and drowned in useless rolls of flesh—borne down by the relentless fact of gravity.

But in the Pacific it had been different. In the Pacific, if you died, you died young, in sudden agony in a violent green world that seemed to confirm the terrible thing that was happening to you. Your last sight was of the primeval jungle, or the gigantic sky, or the purple ocean sliding away. In the Pacific you didn't really die, you just stopped in a blaze of pain. Dying to him was ether and menthol and tubes, and a darkening glimpse of some tarnished, baroque light fixture above your bed, or a phantasmic doctor silhouetted against closed shades, or a tweedy predatory cousin. And so Garland Marlinberg stopped thinking about old age. He photographed the campaign in the Pacific in a kind of vertiginous intoxication, recording the sudden stopping of lives —the gasp, the spatter of blood, the flutter of fingers—confirming and reconfirming for himself the ferocity of the universe, the sweaty cruelty of victory and defeat. "After the first death," a poet said, "there is no other." Garland Marlinberg would have said, "After the first death, there is nothing else," and pain became a kind of awful light.

But that was only part of it; the other part was the isolation that comes from living among great distances and men about to die. What could the hot crush of New York ever be after he had stood on a flat carrier deck in the red suddenness of evening listening to the ephemeral voices of men and watching the vast impersonal ocean? Back home, New York had repelled him. The

hot-handed cultural intimacy of his business friends repelled
him, took the edge off his anger, even as their presumption
of shared values enraged him, and he had fled. He took a job
as news director for a small Dallas television station, and his
father was glad he had a nice civilian job. But his job hadn't
really changed. He was still a combat photographer watching
men dying and about to die.

Outside the screening-room lounge he lifted himself onto his
toes to look through the diamond-shaped window in the padded
door. Jim McLeod stood by the hot plate mixing some instant
coffee, and Max Staubach, the fat heinie, was lifting a smoking
tamale from a brown paper sack. Garland Marlinberg watched
Staubach maneuver the tamale into his mouth, leaving a dribble
of orange juice on his chin. There was another streak of orange
tamale juice in Staubach's thick blond hair. All of their camera
equipment was stacked on the couch.

"—ten bloody Mexicans all over the highway," Jim McLeod
was saying. "Sweet fuck. I nearly puked." He popped an ulcer
wafer into his mouth and washed it down with coffee, sucking
in his narrow cheeks.

"Thas show bishnesh," Staubach said around his tamale.

"If Gantry were here there wouldn't be any question about
using those films. We'd burn them."

"That's why Gantry is down in Laredo and Marlinberg has
his job," Staubach said. He devoured another tamale and threw
the husk in the direction of the wastebasket. "I'll tell you what,
thersh no room in the telebision bishnesh for weak stomash."

"You would have been great in the Gestapo, Staubach."

"No worrish about Marlinberg if I wash," Staubach said.

The two photographers looked up casually, not caring if they
had been overheard, as Garland Marlinberg burst into the room.
"Let's get this show on the road," Garland Marlinberg said.
Without breaking stride, he moved straight through the lounge
toward the screening room. The two photographers followed,
towering over him. The projectionist snuffed a cigarette as they
entered and the newscaster picked up a sheaf of notes.

"Evenin', Mr. Marlinberg," the newscaster said.

"Tom. How are you this night?"

"Sick. I just saw the film your two ghouls brought in."

"You don't like anything that takes you off camera, Tom. Cut the lights and let's look at 'em." Garland Marlinberg took his seat. The newscaster slumped down beside him. From the corner of his eye, Garland Marlinberg caught a glimpse of McLeod miming his revulsion, holding his stomach and figuratively losing his lunch.

"These first are from the fire over on the south side."

"My film," Max Staubach said.

Garland Marlinberg relaxed. This was the best part of his day. The screen flickered up showing a pillar of black smoke against a clear sky; then the eye of the camera dropped through the smoke toward a great torch of flame that had recently been a frame house. The flames were seemingly fed by white arcs of water. The camera followed one of the arcs and focused on a pimply young fireman managing the hose as if it were a tame python; he chewed on the wad of tobacco in his cheek and looked immaculately bored. The film cut to a cluster of bystanders in the street, both black and white. They looked bemused, almost hypnotized by the flames. One shriveled white woman was weeping and a black boy cast pebbles into the inferno.

"Hey, Staubach," Garland Marlinberg said. "Could you get those damn tamales out of here? They're stinkin' up the joint."

Then there was a shot of the occupants of the house—a Negro family sitting among a mighty tangle of their possessions on the edge of the sidewalk. The father, a very black young man with a scar on his cheek, was sprawled in an overstuffed chair with one leg hiked up over the arm. His wife, pale and thin, squatted on a footstool clutching several Elvis Presley albums to her breast while her five-year-old daughter rode a tricycle slowly around the island of salvage. The screen went dark.

"Cut the first a little, leave the last and run it," said Garland Marlinberg. "Anyone hurt?"

"Naw," Max Staubach said from the door. "Tried to convince

that pizza-face fireman there was a child perishing inside but it was no go. No esprit de corpse."

"Ha ha ha," said Jim McLeod.

"This is police headquarters," the projectionist said. "Couple of vandals caught breaking windows."

"Mine again," Max Staubach said.

The screen showed two expensively dressed teenagers with greasy hair being hustled down a corridor. One of them saw the camera and made a dirty sign at it; the other covered his face. The film showed their backs for a moment and then blacked out.

"Cut the finger business and use it," Garland Marlinberg said. "Do you have their names, Tom?"

"They ain't for public consumption," the newscaster said. "Richy, richy."

"Okay, but run the film. The kids'll get a kick out of it."

"So will their parents."

"Fuck 'em," Garland Marlinberg said.

"Wreck on Highway 81," the projectionist said. "Ten greasers, stolen car. Six dead. Three in critical, one in fair."

"Whose film?"

"Mine," Jim McLeod said.

The screen brightened to a ground-level shot down the white line of the highway. In the distance a '46 Chevrolet rested on its side. Several bodies were visible around the car. Attendants rushed feverishly around them, then an ambulance wheeled immediately in front of the camera, cutting off the shot. There was a close-up of an army blanket flaring up and settling over a form in the bar ditch. A pointed Italian shoe rested in the gravel beside the blanket, torn from its owner.

"This camera work is pretty arty," Garland Marlinberg said. "Get to the chorus. We got seconds, not hours."

"Yeah, Ingmar," Max Staubach said.

"It gets better," Jim McLeod said.

Garland Marlinberg leaned forward and watched intently as the camera panned over the rest of the debacle, pausing momentarily on each of the bodies strewn along the highway. Then it focused on the car. A twenty-year-old Mexican boy was trapped, his waist pinned and nearly severed in the crumpled window. The upper half of his body extended from the car and, silhouetted against the sky, he looked like some modern centaur. The camera closed in to show that the lower half of his shirt was soaked with blood, as was his face. He supported his torso with his hands on the side, now the top, of the car. His lips moved in silent pleas for help as he writhed and twisted violently, trying to free himself but only tearing himself more mortally. He was visibly weakening, visibly dying before their eyes. Suddenly his jaw went slack and his eyes rolled up. He pitched forward, and the camera dropped, focusing on the asphalt pavement, then on the sky. Then it went black.

"I thought I was gonna be sick," Jim McLeod said.

"Ho-leey shit," someone breathed in the darkness.

Garland Marlinberg turned and squinted in Jim McLeod's direction. There was a tingling in the tips of his fingers. "Good film, James," he said. "Fine film. Trim that up and we'll run it all."

"Re-run it," the newscaster said. "I have to get all of these names *in order of appearance.*"

The re-run began and Jim McLeod called out the names flatly: "Manuel Estarza. Rolando Gómez. Jesus, oops, Hay-*soos*, Gonzales. Juan Gonzales. Manuel Gonzales. Three brothers. Romelo Capdeville. Antonio Morales. Claude Jimenez, that's He-*meen*-ezz. The kid in the car is George, *Hor*-hay, Guzmán. Dead."

The re-run was over and the screen went white. There was a silence except for the whirring of the rewind. "All right, what's next?" Garland Marlinberg said, thinking that these films would send Bucky Widows flying up his own asshole. Then Max Staubach was talking.

"Christ, Mr. Marlinberg, you can't run those films! They're fucking brutal. Godalmighty, those are people's *kids.* What in the . . . I mean for Christ's sake, what do they have to do with the news?"

Garland Marlinberg didn't turn around. He answered staring

at the blank screen. "I'll tell you what's news. What's news is what's new. That's the entomology of the word. The kid is dead. That's new, that's news. This ain't the Sunday School, it's life, sweetheart. People die and dead is dead, just like in war, or in the concentration camps. People got a right to know who's dead and how they died. We got a duty to show 'em. What's next?"

"Down at Breckenridge Zoo. New baby hippo from Africa."

"Cut it. What's next?"

"Beauty contest in front of the Alamo."

Why do I always do things the hard way? he thought. "Run it," he said aloud. Suddenly the screen was filled with long-legged, large-toothed, pillow-breasted girls parading grandly in matching black bathing suits. He watched them slink up and down, smiling furiously on the steps of the shell-pocked old church where over a century ago 179 wild Texians were slaughtered by Santa Anna. Garland Marlinberg knew, of course, that some of those men had died for their principles, but most of them, he was sure, stood there in the flames and died out of sheer contrariness, absolute cussedness. It was the American disease. He had seen it in the Pacific. Them, he could understand: men who did things hard, who didn't strive toward goals but rose to opposition, sought it out. It was as necessary to them as food. And today, he thought, I am getting a double helping of it.

The girls paraded on for a few moments and then the camera cut to inside the Alamo, to the room where Jim Bowie was killed. A gaggle of girls crowded into the room to apply the last touches to their makeup. Garland Marlinberg felt a great kinship with Bowie, and all those men. Not with their historical heroism, but with the actual men themselves. On that day, he thought, the room had stunk of a different kind of powder, and the men who had died there had not been the sedentary natives. They were the intruders, the invaders come spoiling for a fight. And why else had he, Garland Aaron Marlinberg, come to Texas? Had he not come for the same secret reasons the very first ones had come with their buffalo robes and buckskins—as exploiters, outcasts, plunderers, careless of life? He pulled his handkerchief from his pocket and pressed it to his face.

"You are a son of a bitch," Max Staubach shouted, and stalked out of the screening room.

"Yeah, and you are a chickenshit Nazi," Garland Marlinberg said softly, almost to himself, as Staubach left the room. More in disappointment than in anger.

The next day he left his phone off the hook until three o'clock to save the front office the trouble of calling. The owners had given him a carte blanche. That was that. He opened a few letters, answered none, and wrote his father in Queens although he knew the old man would be in the Catskills. But mostly he slid his handkerchief through his fingers, watching the colors run, and occasionally he stared into the desolate yellow street. He was watching the street when Nelly Sue peeped around the door. He gestured for her to come on in.

"Oh, I see you're not on the phone!" she said.

"Well, you got good eyes."

"They's some people out there to see you. Some Miss Guzmán and her mother."

"Tell 'em to wait."

"They been waitin', Mr. Marlinberg, for an hour."

"Then tell them I went out."

"I told them that once. They said they'd wait till you got back."

"Nelly, dammit, can't you do just some of the things a secretary's supposed to do?"

Nelly Sue bit her lip and quickly wiped her eye.

"All right, dammit, send them in!"

Nelly Sue nearly tripped over her high heels in her haste to get out of the room. "You all may go in now," he heard her say.

They entered silently. Both the girl and the old woman had their hands clasped strangely before them. If he had seen the girl on the streets, he surely would have noticed her. She was a tall Mexican beauty, about twenty-seven, neatly dressed except for the horizontal wrinkles across the lap of her shift from sitting in the reception room. But he gave the girl no more than a glance because of her mother. The old woman was hardly five feet tall and pure Indian. Her shriveled face was clutched in a grimy black shawl and her black eyes were hard, inward looking. For a moment the old woman terrified him. She poised herself almost absently on a modern black leather chair, so much of a different world that she hardly seemed to touch it. She might have been floating before him. The girl stood behind her mother.

"George Guzmán fue mi hijo," the old woman said. He looked at her quizzically and there was a dull silence.

"You don't speak Spanish?" the girl said.

"No," Garland Marlinberg said. His voice broke. "No-o I don't."

"Then excuse me," the girl said. "You looked Latino. I am Guille Guzmán. This is my mother. George Guzmán, the boy who was killed yesterday? He was my brother."

He sat down and grasped his knee. "Oh, I'm so sorry, Miss Guzmán. I can understand why you would come here to see me. You must see that we have a hard decision to make when we show pictures like that. We must decide between private anguish and the public obligation to know the news. Last night I chose to let the public see, to let them know what highway tragedies were like. Now I hope you don't plan any legal action—"

The old woman was waving her hand and saying softly, "No, no, no, no." He looked at her. "Por favor," she said. "No tenemos una televisión."

"What did she say, Miss Guzmán?"

"She said that we don't have a television."

"Well then—"

"You see, all of our neighbors saw George on the television last night, and we do not have one. I know it is a great deal to ask, but could you possibly . . . could you possibly show us the pictures? Mr. Widows in the front said that you still had them. It is for my mother."

"Well . . . well, Miss Guzmán, those films are very . . . uh . . . *vivid* of George and . . ."

"Hor-hay," the old woman said, nodding her head.

He led them down the long hall in a dream. In the library he dropped five or six reels as he clambered around looking for the right one; at the projector his fingers were so sweaty he could hardly thread the film. The girl and her mother sat silently facing the blank screen.

"Miss Guzmán, are you sure your mother wants to see these? I mean her heart."

Miss Guzmán smiled over her shoulder. "My mother's heart is all right."

The old woman nodded. "Corazón," she said, patting her chest.

The lights went down and the screen was brilliant again with the long, low view down the white-line of the highway. In the distance you could see the car where young George Guzmán would be forever dying. He couldn't watch the film again. He edged down the aisle and watched the old woman. She could have been one of the squaws who stood in the distance and watched Santa Anna's army converging on the Alamo, who did not blink at the roar of the cannon, who pulled her shawl up over her mouth against the dust raised by the marching army and watched impassively. Then her face brightened like a child's when she recognized one of the dead boys. She touched her daughter and pointed. "Romelo!" she said. When the image of her son appeared on the screen she leaned forward and watched carefully, but there was no tear, not a trace of anything but intense interest on her face.

Garland Marlinberg felt a terrible elation, like a priest before his first communicant. The old woman was his perfect counterpart.

She lightly, unconsciously, touched her fingers to her cheek, her dark eyes wide and impassively getting wider. She was no communicant; she was the force toward which he offered his canticle.

The film ran through and began flapping wildly, and Garland Marlinberg floundered back up the aisle. By the time he had the machine under control the two women were standing before him.

The old woman was nodding. "Gracias, Señor Marlinberg. Gracias. Gracias."

"My mother says thank you."

"You're welcome," he said. "How do you say 'you're welcome' in Spanish?"

"De nada, Señor Marlinberg."

"De nada," he said, nodding. "De nada."

They left him there with his blood pounding in his temples and his legs shivering. He had to hold the projection table for support. Never in his life had he felt so witheringly mortal, as if something were over and done with. Garland Marlinberg put his hand to his chest and held it there for a very long time, as if not certain whether he should take out his handkerchief, or reach into his breast and quickly snuff his heart.

THREE DAYS IN A
SOUTH TEXAS SPRING

I

And now, to put aside these exalted geniuses, I can tell you the names
of plain Roman farmers from the Sabine Hills, men who are friends
and neighbors of mine, who practically never fail to be on hand when
anything of major importance is being undertaken on their land,
whether it be the planting, the reaping or the storing of crops. In respect of these activities I suppose this is not really surprising, for no
man ever gets so old that he thinks he won't live out the year.

—CICERO, *On Old Age*

The day ended at noon, when Ernest Renslaw marked a black *X*
through May 5 on the Cattleman's Association calendar hanging
above the sink. Then he sat down to the cold frijoles, pound cake
and iced tea that his grandson had laid out on the kitchen table.
The cutting and branding was finished and the boy was on his
way to pasture the last batch of calves, so the day was over—the
season too. Sitting alone in the hot kitchen, Ernest chewed each
mouthful of beans vigorously. The sunburned skin on his face
creased around his eyes and pulled down at the corners of his
mouth, making him look even older than his sixty-nine years;
but his hair was still thick—lead gray and indented with a small
wave where his hat usually clamped it to his large skull. He had
done a day's work since the first shadow of dawn, and a drop of
sweat fell from the end of his narrow blade of a nose onto the
bare table. Not a man to waste even sweat, Ernest absorbed it
with the tip of his forefinger.

After rinsing out his glass and lowering his dirty plate into the sink, he went to the kitchen closet, yanked his pighide suitcase from its shelf and hauled it up the stairs. The suitcase settled with an easy shush onto the feather mattress of his brass-framed bed, and he had thrown his dust-colored seersucker suit, a white shirt and a forest-green gabardine necktie into it before he heard the truck clatter on the cattle guard. He grabbed his dop kit from the chiffonier, and on his way to the bathroom he leaned out the upstairs hall window. The ranch's Studebaker pickup slid to a halt at the back porch and his grandson, throwing a cigarette before him, climbed down into the white skirl of dust he had raised.

"That's it!" Ernest Renslaw called from the window. "Drive it like a maniac. It'll last forever."

Billy Renslaw glanced up impassively, then disappeared under the eave of the porch.

In the bathroom Ernest packed his toilet articles with more care than he had taken with his clothes. He stood before the basin in that queer, swaybacked posture old horsemen acquire when the back muscles start to go and patiently wrapped his Old Spice shaving mug, his bottle of Barber's Choice bay rum, his small blue bottle of Phillips milk of magnesia and his tin of Polident in several layers of toilet tissue. Using more tissue, he packed them securely into the dop kit, laid his straight razor on top and snapped the kit closed.

"Ya te vas?" Billy Renslaw said. The boy slouched casually in the dark hall outside the bathroom door.

"Dammit, Billy, talk English."

"You leaving, Grampa?"

"Usually do this time of the year, don't I?"

"I guess you do."

"You get those calves into number ten 'thout killing any?"

"Yessir."

"Well, now see if you can keep the help from running wild while I'm gone."

The boy didn't answer this. He reached behind his head and

pushed the back brim of his hat upward with one finger so the front brim tilted down over his dark eyes. Turning on his heel, Billy vanished from the doorframe. When Ernest heard the heels of his grandson's boots banging on the stairs, he felt a shallow hitch of unease at his almost instinctive abruptness with the boy and paused for a moment, his hand resting absently on the edge of the basin. Not twelve hours earlier he had wanted to talk with the boy very badly. He had awakened into his dark room with a sharp pain deep in his chest and he had thought momentarily that he was going to die. When the pain had passed, he had wanted to call out—to call Billy to his bedside and talk with him, just that once, but he had not. Instead Ernest Renslaw lay there in the darkness trying to decide whether he was too polite to burden a boy with his fear, or too proud to admit that he had been frightened. Sleep had come before the decision, and when he awakened again, this time into a room filled with grey predawn light, he had reached out for his wife, Rebecca, in the bed beside him. He hadn't done that for fifteen years, since the two shallow troughs in the feather mattress had been molded into one, and he wondered if his memory was crumbling. He had seen it happen to younger men. His neighbor, Curry Shrake, could lose and gain entire decades from day to day. Again he wished he could have talked with Billy about it, but the daylight brought other considerations. His grandson was an insolent boy, hard on the equipment and familiar with the Mexican hands, and Ernest had a cattle business to run.

Back in the bedroom, the suitcase beside him on the floor, he hesitated and rubbed his sunburned cheek, worried again about his memory, trying to remember what he had forgotten. Finally he grinned, snapped his fingers and scooped a handful of Roi Tan Perfecto cigars from the box on the bed table. He stuffed the cigars into his shirt pocket, slapped his hip pocket to check his wallet, slapped his front pocket to check his keys, picked up the suitcase and followed the boy down the stairs. He took his good straw Stetson from the hall tree and then, just to check, glanced into the dim, curtained parlor where seventeen years before he had found his wife's body. There was a tangled bridle on the needlepoint cushion of her tall wing-backed chair.

"Billy, dammit."

"Sir?" The voice came from the porch.

"You leave this harness in the parlor?"

"Yessir, I was mending it."

"Well, get it out to the tack room where it belongs."

"Yessir, in a minute." The voice came without intonation.

When her heart failed, Rebecca Cody Renslaw had been reading with that chair turned to catch the watery November sunlight on the page; and, coming in from a bitter day of penning cattle, Ernest had discovered her sitting in the darkness, her head nodded politely onto her chest, her morocco-bound copy of Ruskin's *Seven Lamps of Architecture* still open on her lap. After Rebecca's funeral Ernest had left her parlor as it was. He wasn't a sentimental man but with her death the house had become a masculine institution again, centering around the back porch and the kitchen table. He had little use for a parlor, so the two gilt-framed portraits on its south wall had been allowed to darken. Rebecca's diploma from Sophie Newcomb had yellowed in its frame. The cherrywood secretary where she had made entries in her commonplace book was locked, the key misplaced, and the three framed photographs arranged on top of it were faded almost white.

The first photograph was of a younger Ernest and Rebecca Renslaw sitting in a hack; the second was a blurred snapshot of their son, Benton, rather uncomfortably astride his first Galiceño pony; the third was a posed picture of their nephew, Cody Lee Peterson, looking mock-fierce and gangling in his Cabot Springs football uniform. But to the older Ernest Renslaw the photographs might as well have been of strangers. Somehow, Ernest could remember the faces of men he had worked with, men he had fought with, a half-century ago, while the faces in those photographs seemed to have evanesced in his memory. He could remember them, certainly, only the visual memory had faded, leaving blind spots in his vision of the past. He penetrated these blind spots only occasionally, and when he did, it was rarely pleasant.

Benton had married Isabella Valdez, whose father, García Valdez, was county agent in Cabot Springs; then, six months after Billy was born, they had fled to Venezuela. Cody Lee was coaching football at Bruce College in Kansas, and for the first few years after he took the job he had come down to open the dove season with Ernest. But none of them had set foot on the ranch for seven years now and Ernest didn't understand that. He had treated them all—Rebecca, Benton, Cody, even Isabella —as honored friends, but somehow he had lost them all. They had all drawn away into death and distance, and he kept the parlor intact out of respect, not sentiment, as he had not been able to keep the family. When he finally shut down his generators and hooked into the REA line, he hadn't even put an outlet in the room.

Now he kicked the screen door open before him and, lugging the suitcase against his thigh, strode out onto the porch. Billy Renslaw was sitting on the steps peeling a peach with a Barlow knife. The vaqueros lounged in the shallow shade of the headquarters buildings. "You move that harness, heah," Ernest said and the boy nodded, leaning aside to let the old man pass. Ernest heaved the suitcase into the cab of the pickup and clambered in after it. Paco Valdez ambled over to the counterweighted aluminum gate and held it open until the old Studebaker had barrelled through, trailing blue exhaust and bouncing the pipes of the cattle guard. The vaqueros and Billy Renslaw watched the thin curtain of dust that rose in the pickup's wake.

Before he left the ranch Ernest stopped the truck on the ridge where Rebecca was buried. From the cab he could read the inscription on the gravestone, although he didn't. The inscription was a verse from Shelley he had found copied and underscored in Rebecca's commonplace book. The German stonecutter he had hired in San Angelo, an artist of the old school, had reproduced Rebecca's tall, angular handwriting on the polished face of the gray stone.

This ride was my delight. I love all waste
And solitary places; where we taste
The pleasure of believing what we see
Is boundless, as we wish our souls to be.

REBECCA CODY RENSLAW 1903–1950

Ernest had thought the verse appropriate for a tombstone at the time, but he had never been affected by it; nor was he in the habit of contemplating it during his stops at the grave site.

Today, as usual, he tugged the brim of his hat to his wife, then scanned the rolling country that the ridge commanded. There had been rain this spring, and mesquite was lime green on the ridges spreading away from him. The prickly pear bloomed white and huisache yellow among the low mesquite trees. Cenizo flared purple on bare caliche slopes and, in the distance, the green ridges faded quietly into brown, and the brown ridges dissolved into dusty violet where the land met the sky, where skeins of cloud furled like carved surf. The clouds slid silently northward and, high above, hawks rode the warm south wind that had blown the clouds up from Mexico. There would be rain again tonight. He stepped down on the clutch and pulled the gearshift into low. He hoped that Billy had sense enough to close the windows in the house.

Ernest took the ranch road into Cabot Springs and turned left at the stop sign onto the San Antonio highway. On the hard road now, he cranked down the windows and opened the wind-wings so the warm wind thundered in the cab as he picked up speed. The wind cooled his head as it rushed through the perforations in the crown of his hat, and his spirits rose with the speedometer. For fifteen miles beyond Cabot Springs he drove through Curry Shrake's property, and there was no fence on either side of Texas 85. He beeped his horn at three of Curry's hereford who had broken through the solid thicket of mesquite to graze on the short grass along the right-of-way. The cattle looked up without interest, then returned to their grazing. Holding the steering wheel steady with his knee, Ernest unwrapped a cigar, stuck it into his jaw and began salivating it into a chewable consistency. He couldn't remember the last time he had actually smoked one; usually he just charred the end a little for appearance sake. Alone in the windy cab, he didn't even bother with that.

His good spirits held until just west of Big Wells when he noticed a herd of yellow-white goats grazing on a bald ridge and, seeing the goats, looked around for their keeper. He saw the horse first—a striped dun standing free—and then, sprawled in the speckled shade of a mesquite, a Mexican with a saddle rifle across his lap scanning the empty sky with reserved interest. Something in the hard angle of the Mexican's jaw, or perhaps the carelessness of his pose, reminded Ernest of his nephew but he suppressed the thought and swung his attention back to the highway. It ran straight and empty before him like a dry vein through the green mesquite but the recollection of his nephew rose again involuntarily. Ernest could feel his stomach gathering into a fist and the skin around his eyes tightening as he remembered his awkward efforts to make Cody Peterson a son after his own son had left him. It was a humiliating memory and, as a soldier attacked by night might call up flares, Ernest called up the good times he and Curry Shrake had had in San Antonio, driving one memory out with another.

He recalled the all-night poker games he and Curry had weathered in hot, crowded rooms of the Gunter Hotel, cigar smoke eddying beneath the ceiling fan as the dealer snapped the red Bicycle cards from the deck. Those rooms had been silent except for the late-night sounds from the street below and the murmuring laconic ritual of the dealer as he sailed the cards across the blanket-covered table. "Pot right? Okay, shooting out. Queens. Two-per bets." He remembered the way Curry would run his thumb along the red hat-mark on his forehead and then throw his bet into the pot with an almost contemptuous backhanded gesture. "Two pair worth about ten to me, gentlemen." And blunt fingers, nails pared down to the quick, would poise over concealed hole cards as the betting moved around the table.

For nearly twenty years Ernest had made this drive from

Cabot Springs to San Antonio with Curry slouched down in the seat beside him, rolling one cigarette after another. And every year, sometime after they had crossed Curry's property line, they had had essentially the same conversation. Curry would look out across the desolate vista and shake his head wearily.

"Strange country, Ernest," he would say. "Lived on it all my life and I don't even know if I like it."

"Well, you can't like it much," Ernest would say, "the weather being what it is."

"That's the God's truth, Ernest, but I can't seem to get up a good hate either. It's the goddamn'dest, most impersonal son of a bitch . . ." Curry's hard tenor voice would trail off for a moment. "You know, you can *hate* a horse."

When Ernest laughed at this, Curry would lean forward anxiously, elbows on his knees.

"But it's got us, Ernest. We ain't fit for anyplace else on the green earth. Hellfire, I'd move to Dallas with my sister, shuck the whole shebang, but I ain't *fit* for it."

"Well, it's made you a passel of money, Curry," Ernest would say, knowing the reaction he would get.

"Shee-hut, it has. Whatever money I got in the bank was made by the sweat of Curry R. Shrake with very little damn help from anything. And the pity is he's too stove up to enjoy it."

"You pore soul. You should've gone into storekeeping—yard goods and such."

"I might should've," Curry would say, but he would be smiling now, amused at the vision of himself as a storekeeper, the exorcism complete. "It's gonna be drunk in San Antonya, you know that, don't you, Renslaw?"

"I know it for a fact," Ernest would say.

In those days, whenever they came to San Antonio, they had stayed in the old Gunter Hotel. It had been their safe haven in the sprawling city. The old lobby had been dark and cool, even in high August, and it was always crowded with country men who had come so recently from the isolated ranches between San Antonio and Monterrey that English tasted strangely on their tongues and had to be cut with whiskey. Ernest liked to remember the pleasant, sharp smells of old leather, sweat, tobacco, whiskey and bay rum that struck you as you stepped in off Houston Street, and the echoing shouts of recognition. That lobby had been his second home. Deep in one of the old leather chairs, with a new cigar, shined boots and a smooth barbershop shave, he had relaxed among his own kind—safe momentarily from his family, who didn't seem to be his kind at all. But most of those old cattlemen were dead now, or trapped, like Curry, in rocking chairs with blankets across their knees. And one spring in the early fifties, he and Curry had come to San Antonio and found that they had remodeled the lobby of the Gunter with blond paneling and florescent lighting. The old leather chairs were gone and in their place were couches covered with coral and chartreuse plastic. He and Curry had stood dumbfounded in the Houston Street entrance.

"I'll be goddamned," Curry had said.

So that year, and every year since, Ernest had stayed at the Menger Hotel, up on Alamo Plaza. The Menger had modernized too but they had left the old lobby intact when they built the new one. The old lobby of the Menger had a balconied mezzanine, a stained-glass skylight, dingy western panoramas and grotesque German-Victorian furniture. It lacked the intimacy and the informality of the old Gunter, but since he lacked them too, it suited the old Ernest Renslaw just fine.

On this evening, after bathing at length, Ernest dressed slowly in his high corner room, watching the tourists far below wandering in and out of the Alamo or resting on the plaza. Finally, he knotted his forest green tie into a lopsided full Windsor, wiped his boots with his dirty shirt, ran his fingers through his hair and headed downstairs for the coffee shop, where the waitresses all knew him and called him Mister Ernest. When he entered the coffee shop, Frieda ordered him a sirloin medium without asking, and brought a Hamm's over to his table. After dinner, waiting for the heat to rise off the streets, he ordered two cups of coffee and invited Frieda to join him.

"How's your boy, Frieda?" Ernest asked as she pulled up a chair and settled tentatively on it, so as not to look too much at home.

"He's in Manila now, Mister Ernest. I had a letter from him yesterday. It looks like he's gonna stay out of the fighting. We thought for a while he'd be in the thick of it, since he's in communications, but they sent him from Guam to Manila. He just has ninety days to go now, if they don't extend him."

"Well, what's he gonna do once you get him back?"

"Oh, he'll go into the shop with T. R. You know T. R., don't you? My husband?"

"Fixes televisions, don't he?"

"Yessir, that's why Larry went into communications, so he could come back and work in the shop." Frieda took a large gulp of coffee, like a woman used to eating on the run, and looked up at Ernest. "By the by, when are you going to get that Ben Renslaw back in the country? I haven't seen him since he was a tot."

"Don't think I will, Frieda. He's happy as a pig in clover down there."

"Do you hear from him, Mister Ernest?"

"Not as much as I should, but I get a card from time to time, mostly about Billy."

"Well, that's nice," Frieda said.

"You knew Ben married a Mexican girl from the Springs, didn't you?"

"I can't say that I did. I knew he was married though."

"Pretty little girl, Frieda. Nice folks, too. I got her brother working for me out at the place. That dern boy can do things with a rope that make you want to cry."

"You know, T. R. grew up down around Cotulla. He says there's nothing better than a Mexican cowhand if you can find one that's not rough on your stock."

"Anyway, I can understand why Ben wants to stay down in Caracas. I got not one thing against Mexicans, lived among them all my life, but I dern sure know how it can be in this part of the country."

"It must be a lot easier for them down there, Mister Ernest."

"One heck of a lot easier, Frieda. Ol' Ben wasn't much on ranching anyway. He always took to the big-city life."

"He'd find a friend in T. R. on that subject. But you still have your grandson, don't you?"

"Sure do, and there's a boy born to the cattle business, or what's left of it. Kid don't know whether he's Tex or Mex but he sure knows the horse and the cow."

"It must be a great comfort to you, having him there with you."

"I'll tell you what, Frieda, if I didn't have some family there, I'd sell the damned, excuse me, derned old place, move to Uvalde and buy me a television set."

"Now you ought to get you a television anyway," Frieda said. "T. R. could get you one at cost. I wouldn't let him make a cent off it. It sure would help pass the evenings out there in the lonesome."

"I thought about it. But Curry got hisself one and all he does is sleep in front of it. I figger I can sleep just as well in front of a window. Of course Curry's not as well as he once was, but ever' time I go over there, there's Curry, snoozing in front of the television while some derned fool is trying to sell him Oxydol."

Frieda laughed and got to her feet, picking up their cups. "Well, you can't teach an old dog new tricks. Twenty years with the same man I ought to know that. You have a nice visit, Mr. Ernest."

"I'll see you at breakfast, Frieda."

"Two eggs over light with dry toast and soft bacon," Frieda said.

Leaving the coffee shop, Ernest felt refreshed, more by his conversation with Frieda than by the steak which rested heavily behind his ribs. In fact, as he left the Menger, he felt exhilarated. On the ranch he spoke Spanish almost exclusively, even to Billy, but, unlike many of his friends, Ernest had never been able to think in Spanish, and after several months on the ranch he began to feel nervous and cooped in by the foreign language. So he enjoyed speaking English, even if it was only to a waitress. But it was more than that. Talking with Frieda, he had gotten to say some of the things he had wanted to tell his grandson. It was a damned shame, Ernest knew, when you could talk to strangers and not talk to your own kin, but he had held his tongue so well for sixty-nine years that he was shy as a hawk of intimate conversations. He had never had one in his life; he didn't have any idea *how* you had one.

Mentioning that Ben was married to a Mexican had taken more courage, for Ernest, than swimming a flooded arroyo, and a man like that, Ernest knew, didn't just start talking about the things he thought, even if his life depended on it—which it might have the night before when the pain had run up through his chest into his neck, shocking him into wakefulness. And when he had awakened the second time, reaching out for Rebecca, the first thing he had felt when he realized that she was gone was anger, a suffocating anger that had blurred his eyes with tears. If only she had been there asleep in the bed beside him, he could have locked his fingers into her warm sleeping hand and relieved all necessity for talk. Just by the pressure of his hand, Rebecca would have understood how he had never intended or expected to get old. But the anger had passed before it could disintegrate into self-pity and he had lain there alone in the brightening room remembering the morning he had discovered her weeping in the kitchen, her crewel work lying neglected on her lap. That had been in 1932, the day after one of their neighbors, Johnny Ray Covington, had drowned in a flash flood trying to keep a bale of new wire from washing downstream.

"It's so awful, Ernest," she had said, looking up at him with tears streaking her angular face. "Johnny was here just yesterday. He stood right there by the door and rolled one of those horrible cigarettes of his, and now he's dead. I just—"

"Now don't get yourself all tore up, honey. It won't help John
Covington where he's gone," Ernest had said. He poured himself
a cup of coffee from the pot simmering on the stove. "The way
I see it, people like John and me *ought* to get killed by accident.
It's an easy way. At least you don't have to worry about it ahead
of time."

"Ernest, that's just *terrible!*"

"Now, darlin', you know it's not. Accidents are just one way of
getting out of your life. One day you're here, the next not. You
got to do it somehow. There's sure no help for that." Balancing
the steaming cup of coffee, Ernest walked over and tousled her
long brown hair. "Seems derned practical to me."

She had stopped crying at this point and looked up at him,
smiling faintly. "You know the difference between you and me,
Ernest Renslaw?"

"Well, come on upstairs and I'll try to show you," Ernest had
said.

"There," Rebecca had said. "That's just what I mean. I am a
civilized Greek and you, sir, are a Macedonian barbarian." But
she said it with a smile and, reaching out to link her arm around
Ernest's leg, she pressed her cheek against his thigh.

"Sweet thing," Ernest had said, "I am a cattleman with work
to get done, and you are a politician's daughter who reads too
derned many books."

"That's true too," Rebecca had said.

But that had been in his prime, when he was working. Then
it had been easy to believe, like the vaqueros, that life was a
colored flower that bloomed for a while before your eyes, then
closed into darkness, that it had no more meaning than the
wildflowers that bloomed along the fence-lines. But now, when
he could work only one day in five and spent the other four
looking back over the length of his life, everything seemed to
have been arranged according to some rigorous mathematical
pattern—one that had brought him, inevitably and alone, to
San Antonio in the spring of 1967 and that now propelled him
for its own reasons across the damp grass of Alamo Plaza at

his favorite time of evening. But that was something. It *was* his favorite time of the evening. The rich purple light falling from the sky just matched the light from the newly lit mercury-vapor lamps around the plaza so the air seemed illuminated from no particular source and the buildings surrounding the plaza, the cars in the street, the sidewalks, everything seemed to glow with its own clear radiance.

Ernest strode past the Alamo (he had never been inside) and crossed the street, turning west toward Milam Plaza in the old section of town. There was a soft western breeze in his face, funneled through the long canyon of buildings, and Ernest lifted his chin to it, striding steadily westward until he approached the gritty facade of the Gunter. The sight of it and the smell of the bay rum he had splashed on after shaving called up the ghosts once more, so he stopped and bought an *Express* from the hunchbacked newsman beside the lobby door, asking him if they had had any rain. The newsman shrugged his twisted shoulders and said not much.

"We had a good deal down in Dimmit County," Ernest said, then glanced over the front page of the paper. He hoped the newsman would continue the conversation but when he didn't, Ernest folded the *Express,* tucked it under his arm and stepped off the curb against the light.

"Hey, viejo! Watch the light!"

Ernest was being yanked backward as a turquoise Oldsmobile flashed in front of him, its tires whispering by six inches from the square toes of his boots. A Mexican teenager held tightly to his arm. With his other hand he brushed off Ernest's coat as if he had fallen.

"You okay, mister?" the boy said.

"Si, compadre," Ernest said. "Y gracias, muchas gracias."

"You don't speak English?" the boy said. He looked quizzically into Ernest's face.

"Sure I do, son, and thanks a lot. I must have been daydreaming or worse."

"They'll run you down in this town," the boy said. "You gotta watch out. You sure you're okay?"

"Fine. Fine," Ernest said. He nodded his head a little too spasmodically to be convincing. "I ain't blind, just stupid. I'm okay now, right as rain."

"Okeydokey, cowboy," the boy said, patting Ernest once more on the shoulder. "You watch out now." He waved his hand and disappeared around the corner.

When the light changed, Ernest struck out again, a little unnerved that he had just missed an easy accidental death. But he felt better as he walked west past the bright windows of the Mexican stores and gradually, as the evening grew darker, the sidewalk began to fill with people. Soon he was moving through knots of dark-skinned people, excusing himself and overhearing snatches of animated Spanish conversation. Milam Plaza was deep in the Mexican section of downtown and in some ways it was as unlikely a place to look for old men from the brasada as the elegant Rathskeller in the Gunter. A man didn't come to town, Ernest thought, after looking at greasers for six months, then go right down and find some more; but maybe he did? There were not many places left in San Antonio where an old man of country habits could be comfortable. At least down around the produce market there were always the old boys who had gone into truck farming, and the men who liked to sit in Mi Tierra dawdling over coffee and listening to the out-of-work mariachis plunking on their guitars.

By the time Ernest reached the Casa Linda Restaurant, across from Milam Plaza, the sky was black above his head and scattered with a few stars. He glanced about the Casa Linda's not too antiseptic interior; then, seeing no one he knew, turned away from the dusty window. The wind was still blowing steadily out of the west as he strode across the dark unmowed expanse of the plaza toward the lights of the produce market, but now the smell of rain was on the wind and the clean smell of fresh vegetables from the market. The market was nearly two blocks long, shel-

tered by a concrete shed, and it was bright and lively even at this
hour of the evening. Mexican housewives wrangled over prices
before the stalls while farmers unloaded their produce from
pickups and three-quarter-tons parked in the wide concrete aisle
that ran the length of the shed. Neat rows of crated cantelope,
spinach, cabbage, honeydew melon and squash were arranged
on either side of the aisle, looking bright and fresh under the
overhead floodlights, and dark-haired children dodged among
them, their shouts echoing in the rafters. Ernest walked halfway down the aisle and positioned himself beside a concrete
supporting pillar, out of the way.

Skilled in waiting, he stood silently, enjoying the spectacle and
investigating each face. Once, he moved his knee to shake his
pant leg down over his boot, and occasionally he would reposi-
tion the cold cigar in his mouth, but otherwise he was still. Even
if he found another old man, Ernest knew, he wouldn't be able
to talk to him, not really. But just swapping stories and being
silent would be pleasant.

He had been waiting nearly an hour when the gas pain stabbed
through his bowels, sharp as a sliver of bone. Ernest nearly
doubled over but he grabbed the concrete pillar and clung to it
until he could pass wind. That relieved the pain a little. "You,
sir," he muttered to himself, "are going to pay for not taking
your milk of magnesia." He glanced once more up and down
the length of the shed and, seeing no one but strangers, pushed
himself away from the pillar and struck out for Mi Tierra only
a half-block away. By the time Ernest had found a booth and
ordered his coffee the pain was nearly gone but he still felt
uncomfortable, and feeling uncomfortable made him feel old.
When his coffee came, he saucered it and blew it cool, then relaxed and let the noise and the young people in the large coffee
shop cheer him up.

Across the aisle a young mariachi wearing black charro pants
and a ruffled shirt sat sideways in his booth and played a slow
fandango on his ornate Spanish guitar. A dark Mexican girl in a
nurse's uniform sat across from him, sipping coffee and watch-

ing intently. The mariachi played very well, with careless authority, reaching up to retune the strings as the melody changed modes. When he paused, Ernest leaned across the aisle and said, "Conoce 'El Abandonado'?" The nurse, startled out of her private world, dropped her coffee cup into its saucer with a bang and eyed Ernest suspiciously, making him feel, for a moment, like an interloper, but the boy seemed flattered. He smiled and nodded. Bending over the guitar and staring at his fingers, he began picking out the old border ballad.

Ernest had known the slow rhythms of the "Abandonado" for most of his life. It was a night-herding song and Ernest had heard the vaqueros singing it even before he could sit a horse. Now it reminded him of the night watches he had stood in cattle camps below the border. On those long watches, as he smoked quietly with his leg thrown up over the pommel of his old McClellan saddle, the sound of a vaquero singing it somewhere out in the night had made him more aware of the dark silence surrounding him than of the song itself, which was as much a part of the night as the snap of the cicadas or the snorting of the cattle. But now, in the bright, noisy coffee shop, Ernest found himself straining to hear the words as the young mariachi sang them softly, more for the girl than for the old man.

> Tres vicios tengo, los tres tengo adoptados:
> El ser borracho, jugador, y enamorado.
> Pues ¿qué he de hacer, si soy el abandonado?
> Pues, qué he de hacer, será por el amor de Dios.

"I have cultivated three vices: drunkenness, gambling and love. But what else am I to do, since I am the abandoned one?" Ernest almost had to smile. It was the perfect Mexican song, right down to that final shrug of the shoulders. "Well, whatever I do, it will be the will of God." How many times had he seen that shrug? It was *suerte*, luck, fate, the will of God; they were all interchangeable, but this time Ernest understood the deep sadness in that shrug, the hopelessness in it. Sitting there in the booth, sipping his coffee, he felt the loneliness of the "Abandonado" for the first time and he realized that, in those days, he had never been lonely at all—that he had actually reveled in the absolute separateness of a man high on a horse in the middle of a black Mexican night. The vaquero singing out in the darkness might have been lonely, but the young Ernest Renslaw had been alone. And although he had respected them, the Mexicans he had worked with, for all their fierce virtue and courteous brutality, he had never understood them or the world their music made. He had been too young and too sure of his power. To understand, Ernest thought, looking down into his coffee cup, you had to be old, or you had to believe in the will of God. He raised his eyes to watch the boy again. Or perhaps, he thought, you had to cultivate the vice of enamorado.

As he sang, the boy would lift his eyes slowly from the strings to stare at the nurse through lowered lashes, smiling a smile that, very carefully, meant nothing, then dropping his eyes again. That look, Ernest thought, was the secret of the vice of enamorado, but he had never been able to cultivate it. It was mighty elegant in a handsome Mexican but somehow it was damned undignified in a white man. Or so it seemed to Ernest.

When the song was finished, the mariachi leaned back and grinned.

"Gracias, señor," Ernest said, getting to his feet and bowing slightly. "Bueno!" When Ernest reached for his wallet, the boy waved his hand; so instead, Ernest grabbed the check from the boy's table and strode quickly with it toward the cash register.

"Gracias to you, señor," the mariachi called from the booth.

"De nada," Ernest said.

Out on the sidewalk Ernest looked back through the long plate-glass window and saw the boy saying something to the nurse. He was still smiling broadly but the nurse was glaring down into her coffee cup, her shoulders drawn up, her dark Indian features closed. She looked up and snapped something at the boy, and his smile transformed itself into astonished indignation. He slapped his flat palm onto the table and the nurse gave him what could only be described as a sneer. This was all the boy could take. He snarled, made an indelicate gesture under the girl's nose and scrambled to his feet. He said something else and stalked away. The mariachi didn't see Ernest standing by the window as he burst through the door. He plunged blindly across the street and out across the dark plaza, clutching his guitar by the neck so its brilliant, inlaid body jerked behind him like a free rudder. Ernest knew they had argued over his paying the bill, and he felt sick. He had ruined everything for them; and he had done this kind of thing before. The girl was still seated in the booth staring down into her coffee cup, biting her lower lip and angrily trying to hold back tears, and Ernest—upset by her tight, dark rebellion—watched helplessly through the window. He had seen that look before—on the morning Ben brought Isabella Valdez Renslaw home to the ranch—and knew there was nothing he could do. During Isabella's two years at the ranch, Ernest had had to weather her bleak, petulant silences in total impotence, never sure how he had wounded her pride but certain that he had, somehow—perhaps just by his existence. And he had respected her. His daughter-in-law had been a proud, quiet girl, but he had had to admire her from a distance as she grew big with his grandson.

Finally, unable to do anything else, Ernest slammed his fist into his palm and turned away from the window of Mi Terra. Mexican women were difficult bitches, there was no denying it, he thought as he walked back past the market. And there was no doing anything about it either.

Halfway back to the Menger, rain began to spatter around him and Ernest hailed a taxi. He dozed for a moment on the short drive back to the hotel, but that night, with the rain drumming steadily on the window, he didn't sleep well at all. Tossing among the crisp hotel sheets, he worried about the windows in the house, about his grandson, about his son in a foreign country which he imagined as mainly jungle, and then, just before sleep, he had a dream in which nothing happened: it was just a vision of his cattle standing motionless in the dark brush with the rain rushing down their rust-red flanks.

I I

Take my own case. I know the names not only of all the citizens of
Rome who are now living, but also those of their fathers and grandfathers, and I'm not a bit worried by the popular saying, "Read tomb-
stones and lose your memory." It is by reading those very stones that I
refresh my memory of the dead. And really, I have never heard of any
old man forgetting where he had buried his treasure; the old remember what is of real concern to them: their days in court, their debts
and their debtors.

—CICERO, *On Old Age*

The taproom of the Menger Hotel was always dark and clean,
and it smelled sweetly of fresh beer when Ernest came in after
lunch. It was his favorite daytime place in San Antonio and, for
the next few hours, leaning against its dark oak bar with his
boot up on the patinaed brass rail, Ernest carried on a desultory
conversation with Leroy, the black bartender, and sipped the
Guinness Stout that Leroy had put him onto. "Guinness is good
for you," the label read, and this appealed to Ernest, mitigating
somewhat the uncomfortable feeling he had at trying something
new. There had been several empty tables in the room when he
came in but he hadn't wanted to sit down alone; so now, ignoring
the wooden soreness in his legs from last night's walking, he
leaned against the bar and sipped the dark stout. Last night he
had searched; today he would wait.

"I picked up on this Guinness when I was in London during
the war," Leroy was saying. "So when I came here to the Menger,
I got Mr. Ryan to stock it. I told him, Hell, Mr. Ryan, you got
yourself an English bar, you ought to stock some English booze.
This whole place, you know, is supposed to be an exact copy of
the bar in the House of Lords in London."

Ernest knew it, had known it for forty years, but he shook his
head no. At sixty-nine, he decided, you had to resign yourself
to hearing some stories twice, and he liked Leroy. During their
conversation he had served the customers, tapped a new keg of
Michelob and was now pouring mixed nuts into a row of shal-

low bowls. His long fingers worked steadily, totally disassociated from his line of conversation.

"Now I never got to the House of Lords when I was in London, but that's what they say. I do know they hauled this bar here, and the back bar too, all the way from Galveston in a freight wagon. There's the picture of it. That was over a hundred years ago, Mr. Renslaw."

"Hell, Leroy, I was drunk at this bar twenty years before you were born," Ernest said.

"I don't doubt it, Mr. Renslaw," Leroy said with a smile. "Excuse me." He rushed off to wait on a woman who had just come in from the street loaded with shopping bags.

When he returned, Ernest asked Leroy where he was from.

"Oh, I come from around here. You probably noticed my accent. I got that in the army. When they made me sergeant, I had a whole platoon of guys from New York and Jersey. They couldn't understand a word I said. I figured I'd better straighten that out or get us all killed. So I got me some public speaking records. You ought to hear me do the Gettysburg Address."

"I bet it's something," Ernest said. "What did you do in the army?"

"Me? I had a heavy weapons platoon. Liberated France single-handed, like my daddy before me."

"Your daddy?"

"Yeah, he done it in the first war. That's what we Appletons do best of all. Liberate France. All the good it did." Leroy, it turned out, was not an admirer of French culture and particularly not an admirer of President de Gaulle. Ernest didn't have an opinion about President de Gaulle one way or the other but he was inclined to agree with Leroy. According to Leroy, he had a lot of dead friends who didn't care much more about France than General de Gaulle cared about them. He would rather live in Mississippi than in France; Frenchmen, Leroy felt, were little better than white trash, and de Gaulle himself no better than a Mexican.

"Put not your faith in princes, Leroy," Ernest said. For some reason Leroy's remark about Mexicans irritated him. But he had been shot at and that gave a man certain rights, regardless of his color, so Ernest only smiled and listened to Leroy's war stories until three o'clock, when Chub Burleson came through the outside door.

Chub whipped off his wide-brimmed straw hat and slapped it against his leg, out of habit since there were no longer clouds of dust in the streets of San Antonio. Also out of habit, Chub ran his fingers across his bald pate, smoothing golden curls long since fallen. Silhouetted against the frosted glass of the door, he looked as huge and pale as a new-shorn goat, but Chub had been a dandy in his prime—a gentleman rancher of sorts until a horse had fallen on his leg and he had retired to become a county commissioner in Hebbronville. Blinking his small, pig-like eyes accustomed to the dark, Chub fished a pair of gold-rimmed spectacles from his shirt pocket and, with one hand, carefully fitted them over his ears.

"Chub Burleson, I mighta known," Ernest said.

Chub lurched around on his bad leg, pushing his spectacles up onto his nose with his forefinger.

"Waal, Ernest Renslaw, you son of a bitch," he said. "How long, oh Lord, how long?"

"Too long, Chubby, but you're looking fit."

"Just don't ask me to dance a jig," Chub said.

Ernest stepped out from the bar to grasp Chub's enormous hand. When their eyes met, it seemed to Ernest that the walls, tables and chairs in the taproom took depth and solidity for the first time, like a picture in an old stereopticon suddenly moved into focus. Then both men fell silent for a moment, shy at feeling too much too quickly. Finally Chub grabbed Ernest's shoulder. "Shit, Renslaw, it's good to see you. I thought you was dead."

"It's hard to tell who's here and who's gone to glory, you get as old as us."

"Ain't that the awful truth. Leroy, pop me a Falstaff beer and toss me one of those Dutch Masters. I got some visiting to do with my friend Renslaw here."

"Sure thing, Mr. Burleson," Leroy said. He had already opened the beer and now he laid the cigar on the bar with a self-satisfied smile. "Y'all need anything else just holler."

"Okay, sergeant," Ernest said.

As they moved off toward a table, Ernest carrying the bottles and Chub unwrapping his cigar, they were already talking about the first dry-up they could remember. That had been in 1906 or 1907, when they were boys. Chub was saying that no one who hadn't cut sotol for cattle feed could understand the luxury of dropping seedcake from a pickup truck, or singeing prickly pear with a surplus flamethrower. Chub would have picked dollar cotton before he cut another batch of sotol. Ernest agreed; he still had scars on his hands. Chub said that he had scars on his soul and that the youngsters didn't know what it was like then. They got it all off the television. Riding and firing off your weapon and screwing dance-hall girls. Hell, the only dance-hall girl Chub had ever seen had one ear half-chewed with syphilis. If the television people wanted to do real service, Ernest said, they'd show five solid hours of some poor illiterate digging post-holes through shale with the wind whooshing in his ears. That ought to make them drugstore cowboys happy to be working at the filling station. Chub said shit if it wasn't the truth.

"I wouldn't have one of those damn things in my house, Chubby. I sit over at Curry's the other night and watched this play called 'Gunsmoke.' You ever seen it?"

"Seen it, hell! Gotta grown son thinks it's the gospel. Full growed and he goes around the streets of Hebbronville like it was Dodge City."

"Well, just tell me," Ernest said. "How long would a marshall like that have lasted in Del Rio?"

"Three days," Chub said. "If he come on a Thursday."

"Some drunk taken a short-leg shotgun and spattered him from there to Monterrey."

"Without so much as a by-your-leave," Chub said, and that reminded him of the time his schoolteacher was shotgunned climbing out of a local rancher's bedroom window. "Poor old Brixton died right there in the flower bed. You couldn't hardly blame him for what he did, either. Hell, they wasn't a single woman for fifty mile, not a single white woman for eighty. And like I said, Kathleen McCoy would flirt with a cedar fencepost. They acquitted Bert McCoy, naturally, but nobody ever forgive him, especially my ma. She used to say that Bradley Brixton's schoolteachin' ability was a hell of a lot more self-evident than Miz Kathleen McCoy's sacred virtue."

Ernest chuckled. "Schoolteachers were sure hard to come by in that country."

"Took nine months to replace Brixton," Chub said, "and *then* we got a harelip. 'Course that was fine with me, having a vacation, but it's a wonder we ever got educated at all."

"If we did," Ernest said. "You know, Chub, the only decent teacher I ever had was old Louis Ambergey. You 'member 'im?"

"Amber-gay? Sure. The little skunk bluffed me out of a full house with a pair of queens one night. Hung my head for a week."

"Well, did you ever hear how Louis got to be a schoolteacher?"

"Thought he was born one."

"Nossir. He come down from Tennessee and bought a little spread out from La Pryor which he promptly run into debt and got foreclosed on him. The banker in Uvalde—I think it was Roscoe Crawford at the time—showed a good deal of sense doing it, too. Louis just wasn't cut out to be the businessman. He was a damn good rope-hand, though, so everybody just assumed he'd hire on with somebody else in the territory. Didn't, though."

Ernest took a long swallow of his Guinness, pausing as much for effect as anything, then went on to tell Chub how Louis Ambergey had taken to saloon life. It had gotten so you couldn't go into Tad Chesser's without finding Louis backed up to the stove or bellied up to Tad's sawhorse bar. When the drink was on him,

Louis would prop himself in the corner and recite "The Charge of the Light Brigade" and "Come into the Garden, Maude," and this had given them an idea. Louis owed everyone in three counties but nobody had the heart to throw him in jail. It wasn't that he was a crook, Ernest explained, he just didn't have the least bit of sense about money. So they had a meeting and appointed Louis schoolmaster, in absentia, since Louis was down at the bar at the time. "They figured Louis would do just fine since he'd been through seven grades back in Tennessee and had all those poems by heart his grandma taught him," Ernest said.

"He had 'em, too," Chub said. "I heard him go on for four hours one night."

"He could go on for days," Ernest said, then paused. "Christ, Chub, I'll never forget that school. It wasn't much more'n an adobe hutch, and all the books we had were two primers and three volumes of an old encyclopedia. Some damn goat rancher had burned the rest of the set for kindling, and Louis told me later how much he wished the old bastard had burned the whole batch. He was okay in the primers, and with the poems, of course, you could sound 'em out. But those encyclopedias give him fits."

The climax had come, Ernest went on, the morning a little boy named Ralph Burns brought an encyclopedia volume up to Louis's desk. He had found a picture of a rhinoceros and wanted to know what it was. Well, Louis had wrinkled up his brow and run his fingers along under the words, ciphering them out as best he could. Finally, he had put down the book, risen to his feet and announced, "That, Master Burns, is the rhine-ozer-ose, a strange beast that roams the coast of Kansas!"

Chub nearly lost his cigar. "A strange beast that roams the coast of Kansas! Ooooeee, that's just *fine*," he said, slapping his knee.

"The little Burns boy fell off a windmill that very month," Ernest said. "Took that piece of wisdom to the grave, but Louis finally got to be a damn fine schoolmaster."

"Must have been his calling all along," Chub said.

"I reckon. He took correspondence courses from Baylor and the University. Finally got so he was the best educated man in the county. That wasn't saying much, but we all cared for him a lot. He used to get up at the graduation exercises and tell that story on himself."

"There is the sign of a damned unusual teacher," Chub said.

"I'll tell you," Ernest said. "Though he probably taught my boy, Ben, a little more than he needed to know."

"Now you can't blame a man for doing his job, Ernest."

"Oh, I don't. I don't a bit, Chubby. Louis was one of the finest men I ever knew, and Lord, he loved the books. When I married Rebecca and moved in all *her* books, Louis rode all the way out from Cabot Springs in a hack, just to watch. He was like a kid at a candy store. As a matter of fact, it was Louis introduced me to Rebecca in the first place."

"Now I always wondered how an old brush rat like yourself met such a high-tone lady as Rebecca," Chub said.

"Well, it wasn't a very likely way to meet your future wife," Ernest said, and he told Chub about the afternoon he had dropped into the Cabot Springs courthouse and discovered Rebecca going around from office to office telling everyone that they didn't care anything about the future of education in the State of Texas if they let their children be educated by a broken-down, stove-up cowboy. It seemed that the State Board of Education had sent Rebecca down to check on the schools in the area and she had taken one look at Louis Ambergey and decided he couldn't teach his way home in broad daylight with a tail wind. Louis, unused to educated women, much less educated women who talked back to you, had been struck dumb by her questions. The only defense he had mustered was a mumbled offer to recite "Absalom and Achitophel" for her. Two hours later when Ernest appeared on the scene, she had the entire county government treed and ready to throw Louis to the wolves. When he realized what was happening, Ernest had interrupted politely and asked Louis to introduce him to the lady from Austin. The introductions finished, Ernest had launched into an impassioned defense of Louis Ambergey which not only saved Louis's job, but ultimately won Ernest Renslaw a wife. "When I put her back on the train for Austin," Ernest said, "we had an understanding."

"Now why hadn't I heard all that before?" Chub said.

"It's the God's truth," Ernest said. "I laugh to this day when I think about old Louis, scared to death, offering to recite a poem for Miz Cody from Austin."

After that they talked for a while about Chub's grandfather, whose only claim to fame was that he had once been outsmarted by Sam Bass, and then about the government land-clearing program which neither of them knew quite what to make of. Finally their conversation trailed off and Ernest and Chub Burleson sat silent with their legs stretched out beside the table and watched the white smoke curling up from Chub's cigar. Ernest was remembering the first time he had seen Rebecca Cody in the dusty hall of the Cabot Springs courthouse. That had been in 1927 when Ernest was a bachelor rancher of twenty-nine, just beginning to look for a wife, and when he saw Rebecca standing there in the cream-colored light with her dark hair flowing down over the shoulders of her high-necked dress, Ernest decided that this was the woman he wanted to live in his house. She had been a gaunt, graceful girl of twenty-four, an old maid by country standards and not pretty by city standards, but she was exactly the woman Ernest Renslaw wanted. She carried herself with dignity and there was a neatness and an angularity in her manner that attracted him. Something about her reminded him of the fragile, decorous señoras he had met in the haciendas of Nuevo León. But after he had married her, brought her home to the ranch with her leatherbound books, her family portraits and her corset stays, he discovered that neatness and reserve, like beauty, can be only skin deep and that he had married a girl of considerably more liveliness and passion than he had expected—more, really, than he knew how to cope with. While she had been growing up in Austin and New Orleans, going to parties and hiding her Byron behind her Plutarch, Ernest had been learning to sweat a living out of the dry windy brasada between the Nueces and the Rio Grande. Simply, he was not prepared for the smothering closeness, the serious talks and personal entanglements of a marriage as Rebecca Cody had envisioned it. He was a creature of silences and distances. He *had* loved her, though, and he had done the best he could, but over the next twenty years he never really changed. He gave her chivalrous respect and an awkward passion, and in return Rebecca gave him all of herself that he would accept. Even then Ernest knew that it was much less than she had to give.

It is not a pleasant thing for a young man to realize suddenly that there are strict boundaries to his capacity for feeling, but Ernest did realize it and lived with it. There was no denying it and no doing anything about it; it was a fact that would not go away, and did not go away even after Rebecca was dead. The irrevocable nature of this fact, which had made him a stranger to his wife, did not make it any easier to live with; his thoughts would always have to flow around it, as a river flows around a granite boulder, until they stopped flowing altogether. The terrible thing, Ernest thought, about Rebecca's death was that all of those things she had thought and seen in the privacy of her parlor and on her solitary rides to the ridge where she was buried now were lost; like a lantern slide left too long in the projector, they had crackled and flared into smoke and empty white light. Ernest knew, as he sat here staring at the toes of his boots, that he had lost something valuable, something worth the sadness that he felt.

He glanced up to say something and saw that Chub was drowsing slightly across the table, with his hands clasped beneath his enormous belly. His eyelids drooped irregularly, and he had lowered his chin onto the cushion of flesh that hung beneath it. For some reason Ernest felt a wave of revulsion toward the huge old man across from him. He was dirty and fat and smelled faintly of sour milk, but that wasn't all of it. The sleep had drained the life and individuality from him, and he wasn't Chub Burleson anymore; he looked for all the world like a carcass.

"Wake up, Chubby," Ernest said. "Dinnertime." He poked

Chub in the belly with one finger and waited tentatively for the life to return.

That evening after a walk around the plaza Ernest and Chub Burleson ate the blue-plate special in the coffee shop of the Menger Hotel and afterwards, over coffee, they brought Frieda up to date on the sorry state of the cattle market, thanks to the feedlots, the supermarket Jews and the politicians who let the Jews import cheap Australian beef. Chub started to explain how the market might hold if the war went on in Viet Nam but Ernest kicked him under the table and he shut up. Then, as they were paying the check at the counter, Frieda called out, "Oh, Mister Ernest, I have something to show you."

"Okay, sugar," Ernest said, then turning to Chub, "See you on the plaza in the morning, right?"

"About ten," Chub said. "You take care." He turned and lumbered out into the lobby.

When Ernest turned back to Frieda, she was standing before him fumbling in the pockets beneath her apron.

"Now," he said. "Whatcha got?"

"Here you go," Frieda said. She smilingly produced a photograph from her pocket and handed it to Ernest. "That's Larry. He sent it from Guam."

The photograph was of a stocky, bland-faced young man in army fatigues standing under a palm tree. In the background you could see the wide horizon of the Pacific.

"Don't look like they starved him none," Ernest said, holding the picture out so he could see it more clearly.

Frieda laughed. "Oh, it'd take wild horses to starve that boy, I tell you."

"You know, Frieda, with his hair cut off he's a handsome boy. But that's to be expected, having a pretty mother like he does."

Frieda blushed and looked down at the floor. "Now, Mister Ernest."

" 'Course I wouldn't want T. R. to hear me saying it, but it's the God's truth," Ernest said. He extended the photograph to give it back to Frieda.

"Oh, you can keep it, Mister Ernest. He sent twenty of—"
Then she realized that she had done the wrong thing, that there
was no reason for an old man she saw once a year to need a
picture of her boy. She blushed again, embarrassed this time. "I
mean . . ." She gave a nervous laugh. "I mean, there's no reason
for you . . ."

"Why, I'd be proud to have it," Ernest said. He took out his
wallet and tucked the photograph neatly into it. "You sure you
can spare it now?"

"Oh, yes. He sent twenty of them. I been giving them to
every . . ." She paused and stammered again, even more acutely
embarrassed, staring at the floor.

Then Ernest became embarrassed too and tried to smile. He
patted her on the shoulder and thanked her again. "I'll see you
at breakfast, Frieda," Ernest said.

"Thank you, Mister Ernest," Frieda said. She turned and scur-
ried back to her post.

In his room Ernest stood at the window and lit a cigar. For a
change he drew the smoke into his lungs and blew it out into the
night. He didn't know whether he had hurt Frieda or not, but
he didn't see how he could have handled it better. If she'd only
taken it back without getting so upset. Hell, he didn't want the
thing. He was tempted to take the photograph out and inspect
it more closely, as if it contained some cipher, but he didn't want
to see it again. It was just a snapshot of a dumb Bohunk kid he'd
only seen once and hadn't liked when he did. But he did like
Frieda and you didn't refuse a woman who offered you a picture
of her son. Then Ernest saw why Frieda had been embarrassed.
He hadn't even thought of it, but it must have seemed to Frieda
that by giving him the picture she was somehow loaning her
son to a poor old man who had lost his. She had pitied him,
instinctively, then realized that you can't pity old men like Ernest
Renslaw.

Ernest felt his face getting hot. It was humiliating, but he
couldn't get angry at Frieda. She was a simple woman and a good
one, and that was the trouble. That was the whole goddamned

thing about women. They were rude, there was no other word for it. When they saw where you were hurt, they couldn't keep it to themselves. A woman could always see where you were wounded, but she could never see that you had learned to live with it. She couldn't see that you had more blood to spare than dignity, and she would treat the wound even if it killed you. She would slice you open from crotch to gullet and drain your blood if she thought it would cure the wart on your thumb. Ernest realized that he was holding his breath. He let it out in a rush.

It was his fault anyway, Ernest thought. He had *wanted* Frieda to understand how he had lost his son, but he hadn't wanted her to make a spectacle out of it. He had an urge to take the snapshot out and burn it—or drop it out the window. But you didn't do that regardless. You didn't burn a picture of a woman's son after she had trusted you with it. He decided that he would leave the picture in his wallet until it rotted, but never look at it again; that was a decent compromise but it didn't make him feel any better. It had been his fault—blabbering like a sewing-circle gossip about Ben and his Mexican wife—and it had been stupid. Now he had embarrassed Frieda, who was only acting like the poor simple Bohunk that she was, and made himself feel like a fool. Ernest threw his cigar out of the window and watched it fall like a star, trailing red sparks. Before he climbed in bed he took a double dose of milk of magnesia.

III

There had to be some kind of terminus; there had to be, as with the fruits of the tree and the crops of the land, some point, so to speak, at which things shrivel up and fall away, and this must be taken in good part by any man who calls himself a philosopher. For to fight against nature is no different from battling the gods. . . .

—CICERO, *On Old Age*

Ernest Renslaw didn't eat breakfast in the hotel coffee shop; he had coffee and toast at a diner down on Houston Street, and although he didn't plan to start back to the ranch until after lunch, he was already beginning to feel restless when he met Chub on the plaza. He couldn't think of much to say as they waited for the young Mexican who was going to drive Chub back to Hebbronville. The morning was hot and glaring and Chub seemed a little abstracted as well, running the edge of his boot along a crack in the sidewalk and occasionally remarking on the hereditary slowness of Mexicans. When the car arrived, Ernest took Chub's hand.

"Chubby, it's been good talking to you. You made my trip."

"Dammit, Ernest, you drive that old Studebaker all over the state. Point it down toward Hebbronville sometime."

"I might do it," Ernest said. "You take care."

Ernest slapped the door of the car as it pulled away from the curb, then stepped back and watched it nose its way into the glittering traffic. Every year the friends he met in San Antonio became fewer and the conversations with the remaining few more difficult, so he felt a little sad to see Chub go. Someday, he knew, if he lived long enough, he would come to San Antonio and see no one at all; that year he would speak to no one but the desk clerk, Frieda, Leroy and perhaps the crippled newsman, but even so he wouldn't consider the trip wasted. There was always the luxury of the long drive back into his own country; and that afternoon, as the hamburger stands, the honky-tonks and drive-in movies began to fall away, Ernest's eyes began to rest more comfortably on the landscape. The horizon retreated and the sky became a dome again, free from its rectangular margins.

For sixty-nine years Ernest had reduced everything which took unnecessary contemplation to habit. He had smoked Roi Tan Perfectos for thirty years and drunk Hill & Hill whiskey for nearly as long. He had driven Studebaker trucks since the first Studebaker wagon he had bought from a nearsighted German in Del Rio. The habits had freed his mind to consider fallen fence, screwworm and burned pastures, but now that there were others who considered those things, he found himself with an empty sequence of rituals. So he enjoyed the drive back through the wild country between the Balcones and the Rio Grande. Away from the enclosure of the city he allowed himself to become totally preoccupied with driving and seeing. The horizon was a circle now, with the highway bisecting it, and Ernest Renslaw at its center doing seventy miles an hour.

But too soon he found himself slowing down to make the turn at Cabot Springs. Ricky Avalos, the constable, was lounging on the courthouse steps sipping a Coca-Cola. He sat squarely in the center of the lone patch of shade cast by the scraggly palm that stood on the courthouse lawn. Ernest honked at him and rolled through the stop sign. Ricky scrambled to his feet and made a mock charge in the direction of his patrol car as Ernest gunned the pickup through the flashing red light on the next corner. In the side mirror Ernest could see Ricky feigning despair. Fifteen minutes later Ernest parked the truck on the ridge beside Rebecca's grave and climbed down out of it. He didn't want to go to the house just yet so he leaned against the fender and looked out across the spreading country below him. Most of it was his and it sprawled for thousands of square miles without a single man-made mark except for an occasional twist of road that snaked up over a rise then disappeared.

Gradually he was overtaken by a terrible unease, a feeling that when he died, he would not be buried here beside Rebecca at all, that he would just drop into the soil somewhere out there, like a sailor drowned at sea, just disappear into that wild expanse of country like an Apache who had never slept on the same ground twice. His bootheel snagged a clod as he turned back toward the truck. He stumbled three or four steps, surprised to find that he was frightened again, and, as he climbed into the cab, his body felt very heavy. He jammed his foot down on the starter. At the last moment he remembered to touch his hat to Rebecca, which he did without looking back, banking the truck down into the arroyo and gunning it up the opposite slope. Once the truck was moving he felt better. Soon he was barreling down the rutted road, swerving occasionally up onto the shoulder to avoid the high center and humming to himself.

When he was young, though, it had been fine. He'd geared his life to the rhythms of the brasada, to the rising and falling of the light and the turn of the seasons, but he had been separate from them. He had something to do, raise beef cattle, and the country did not. Ernest had been the country's adversary then; now he moved more and more unresistingly with the sun and fled when he could not fight, driving the empty highways with a cold cigar clamped in his teeth. But he always had to return to the house, as he was doing now, to its sensuous comforts and warm memories. As he topped a rise he saw the roof of the house for a moment, bright in the falling sun, and nearly stepped on the brake, but he knew it was silly and stepped down on the accelerator again.

He would live his life right out to the end. In the morning he would get up when the sun hit the west ridge turning it the color of peaches. He would prowl around till noon, looking for things left undone or done sloppily, and then, when the sun was white and pale above him, he would retreat into the shade of the porch and sip iced tea from a quart glass. When it was dark, sleep would come over him like a drug and he would climb the stairs to bed and go to sleep with the rock and roll music from Billy's radio faint in his ears. If that was what an old cattleman did in the Year of Our Lord 1967, then that, by God, was what Ernest would do. He didn't care a damn about dying, about the pain, but he hated the idea of being dead—especially the thought of having been dead for a while, say, ten years. Any goddamned thing was better than that. He rebelled at the thought of it much as he had rebelled at the thought of marriage. It was going to rob him of his separateness; he was going to lose himself—forever. He bumped the aluminum gate open and drove up to the house, honking his horn. He sat in the cab until Billy appeared from behind the stable, walking slowly toward him.

"Take this damn suitcase in, will you?" he shouted. "I'm a tired old man."

Later that evening Ernest sat at the kitchen table and read through the mail while Billy set the table. Billy forked the chicken-fried steaks out of the skillet onto the plates, filled the coffee cups and finally brought the pan of beans from the stove and set it down on a ragged hot-pad in the center of the table. Each of them ladled some beans onto his plate and they began to eat in silence. Ernest found he wasn't hungry; he pushed his plate aside and brooded over his coffee while Billy continued to eat silently across from him. The shiver of the truck was still in Ernest's bones and for some reason he found himself thinking about his nephew; he didn't know why. He looked up at Billy, who was methodically shoveling beans into his mouth, his eyes downcast.

"Goddamn, I'd like to see ol' Cody," Ernest said. "I wonder if I called him up there in Kansas, if he'd come down on his summer holidays?"

Billy raised his eyes and gazed at Ernest without expression. Brushing his cowlick out of his eyes and swallowing a mouthful of beans, he said, "Cody Lee? El no vendria." He stood up and walked quietly out onto the porch to light a cigarette.

"Well, I'd like to see that boy again," Ernest said to the empty kitchen.

There was a thump as Billy jumped off the porch and walked out to talk with the vaqueros.

You couldn't expect much from a half-breed, Ernest knew. Then he remembered he hadn't told the boy about meeting Chub Burleson and talking about the old times. He leaned forward, his elbows on the table, his chin cupped in his hands, and stared into his half-eaten dinner. It was dark outside the screen door and he was tired, but he didn't rise and climb the stairs. He stared at the dirty plate and said to himself, "Ernest Renslaw, you are an *old* son of a bitch."

Finally, still leaning on his elbows, he drifted off into a hot, drowsing dream.

In the dream Ernest walked across his number four pasture in high August. The sky was bone white and dry grass crackled under his boots. As he strode over the top of a small rise and down into a coulee, the chaparral rose high over his head, blocking his vision and smothering the stale wind. The dusty gray-

green mesquite was all around him, leaves shriveled back revealing thorns, and the blossoms on the yellow cactus had been
burned and dried into parchment. A sound made Ernest stop
dead in his tracks: a covey of brown Mexican dove broke at his
feet. In a flutter like small flags the tiny birds scattered, swoop-
ing and banking steeply, weaving intricate patterns in the brush
as they skimmed magically through the thorns and spines. Then
a sluggish rattlesnake, invisible in the mottled shade, sputtered
dryly and retreated, since he was a snake and not a man, but
even the whirring of the snake was muted in the windless isolation of the brush. Staring down at the white dust on the toes
of his boots, Ernest realized he was in a dream but kept on
dreaming. The collar of his shirt was heavy with sweat and cold
droplets trickled down over his ribs.

Suddenly Ernest decided to sing "The Streets of Laredo."
Somehow he knew that if he could get one word of the song out,
it would wake him up and he could climb the stairs to bed. But
when he tried to open his mouth, his jaw seemed frozen and the
effort made him dizzy. His whole body seemed sluggish and un-
controllable, as if it were filled with water, and far down inside
him he felt a chill. Then, with a frantic effort that wrenched his
whole body, he broke his jaws open and his loud, hoarse voice
burst out into the empty kitchen.

"As I walked out in the streets of Lare . . ."

When he was sure he was awake, Ernest Renslaw stopped
singing. Feeling a little foolish, he poured himself another cup
of coffee and carried it with him out onto the porch.

PROOF THROUGH THE NIGHT

An Essay on Morals

Stay awake, don't rest your head;
Don't lie down upon your bed;
While the moon drifts in the skies,
Stay awake, don't close your eyes.

Though the world is fast asleep,
Though your pillow's soft and deep,
You're not sleepy as you seem;
Stay awake, don't nod and dream.

—RICHARD M. SHERMAN/ROBERT B.
SHERMAN, "Stay Awake" (© 1963
WONDERLAND MUSIC CO., INC.)

He had not liked the dreaming. That's what he would have told
you eighteen years ago, if you had asked him why he stopped
writing fiction. He had come to dread that narcoleptic state of
reverie into which he would retreat to write, and from which
he had such a difficult time returning. So it didn't surprise him
now, rereading the text of these stories, to discover that he had
written not a book of dreams, but a book of awakenings—that he
had imagined a whole procession of characters either fighting
their way out of dreams, or being summoned or shocked back
into consciousness after having let themselves drift away.

He had never noticed it before, but it made sense; and he liked
to think, as he read back through these litanies of dreaming
and waking, that he had been trying to tell himself something
all along—something which, in the last pages of the last story

161

he wrote, he finally understood—because that final dream and awakening *had* been a self-conscious and personal gesture. He had meant it to conclude his career as a fiction writer, and now, realizing that the first story in this collection, which was also the earliest one, began with a dream and an awakening as well, gave him a sense of resolution. He liked it when personal decisions had formal ramifications; it was much preferable to the other way around.

The leaving, of course, had always been easy for him; it was a genetic proclivity, a family trait. He would just *go away* to write these stories and not return, not really, until whatever he was writing was completed—a week, two weeks, or two months hence. His wife had come to refer to it as "going off to fiction-land," and, in fact, it had been like going off to camp when he was a kid—diving into this green, swimming world, structured out of time, and then returning, two momentary weeks later, to find his own room dusty, sepia-toned and odd—familiar yet somehow changed. He could still remember the sense of irretrievable loss he felt on these homecomings: the world had drifted on without him, things had changed in the neighborhood, on the baseball diamond, in the standings, on his radio serials—even his dog had new rituals in which he swung no censer and new hideouts he knew not where.

After returning from camp, of course, its green hallucination had soon dissipated into friendly recollection and the everyday world of dogs, records, maps and explorer books quickly reasserted its intimacy and familiarity. Coming back from "fictionland," however, had never been such an easy transit. He had come back, as often as not, with his "vision" still intact—with the net of words he had so carefully structured for his dream still tidily knotted together. And softly, almost imperceptibly, over a period of time, he could feel that net casting itself over the world into which he was returning, altering and revising his primary reality, editing his life. And that had not been a good feeling at all.

It was one thing, he began to feel, to "realize a fiction," and quite another to "fictionalize reality" in its reflection—one thing, as well, to convince someone else (who had more or less agreed to be convinced) of the justice and integrity of one's imaginings, and quite another to convince one's self. Madness, he knew, lay in that direction and, for a long time, he thought he was crazy, regarded his difficulties negotiating the shadow line between life and his own letters as symptoms of a sickness—as an attention disorder (which, no doubt, to an extent, it was) or a figment of some childhood trauma (which it doubtless was as well). But by that time he had tried his hand at other kinds of writing which, although they were not regarded as seriously as fiction, did not leave him nearly so unrequited. So, gradually, and partially in self-defense, he had begun to suspect that his "disease," whatever it was, had some broader artistic, cultural and moral ramifications. At least he hoped like hell it did.

He had been taught, of course, that "modern art of the highest order" was intimately related to a condition of suffering, alienation and mental dysfunction. He didn't doubt it. He did, however, begin to wonder about the causation—about the possibility that this suffering, madness and alienation arose *out of* these "high orders" of "modern art" rather than the other way around. It seemed, to him at least, that the artistic materials he was working in possessed a degree of toxicity that had little to do with the cultural conditions out of which he was operating.

Further, he suspected that this toxicity was related to something else he had been taught: which was that he didn't understand Coleridge. Perhaps he didn't, but he had always assumed, on account of having read a lot of him, that when old Sam proposed the "willing suspension of disbelief," he was suggesting that if you could suspend your quibbles about the improbability of imaginary narratives as "stories," you could experience them as a form of speculative discourse, as imaginative arguments. *Wrong*, he was told. You suspended your disbelief in order to disengage your critical faculties; you just stepped on the clutch and disengaged the language from the friction of public experi-

ence so you could participate in the illusion, empathize with
the characters, and feel the meaning—whatever in the hell that
might have meant. He hadn't the faintest idea. (Except for dirty
books, Chuck Berry songs and movies about beagles, he never
suspended his disbelief, not willingly.) He *did* know, however,
that writing the kinds of stories he was learning how to write
seemed to encourage that sort of disassociation and that, however pleasant its effect on the reader, it was having some rather
unpleasant side effects on him.

But, probably, he just didn't understand. Probably, he had just
dozed off during the lecture where all of this was being quite rea-
sonably explained and some professor would eventually—very
slowly and very patiently—explain it all to him again. But not
one ever had—not to his satisfaction and, for him, the bottom
line had become his moral certainty that any sane man would
seriously reconsider an endeavor that so totally filled his head
with sights and sounds, with webs of words, that he could lie in
bed in the sweet darkness next to a beautiful woman, between
cool sheets, amidst the warm breezes, and not be able to break
through into all that wonder for staring at the ceiling and fretting over the syntax, tempo and decor that empowered some
imaginary engine of his own device. Moreover, it was clear to
him that these engines—if he continued to devise them at the
expense of women and music and the magical inconclusiveness
of everyday life—would soon enough be running on empty.

†

He could see now, of course, that all of these problems derived
from his not having encountered literature within its proper
middle-class cultural context. As a result, he had never been
imbued with the proper institutional and attitudinal disclaimers
as to its pleasures and powers. He had come upon it very young,
in nomadic transit—as a Tuareg child might find a weapon in
the dust—and applied it to his own urgent and unaesthetic ends,
ends that derived not from "culture," but from the perpetual
state of anguish and drift in which he was growing up.

When he was very small, when his dad was still playing gigs

and his mom was still painting paintings, before his sister and brother were born, they had made cradles for him in hotel chests of drawers. Then, as the demands of the world came down upon them and the music and the paintings gradually stopped, the moving had not. And the quarrels, once they started, had not either; so, in tiny incremental stages, the constants of his youth had been reduced to an endless procession of schoolyards and the ongoing drama of his mom and dad's doomed romance.

He had taken his consolations where he found them, in dogs and music and public libraries. (The television, when they got one, had been too public. Watching it in the living room, you were a sitting duck, visible and therefore vulnerable. And he had never liked the movies. They took away the top, bottom, back and sides of his world, and left him sitting in the dark.) The dogs, of course, deserved a book of their own, as did the music —except to note that the first thing he remembered remembering was Lorenz Hart's lyric to "Mountain Greenery." He had known all the words when he was six, and, although he hadn't the faintest idea what most of them meant, he could still remember sitting in the crotch of a chinaberry tree beside their house in Oklahoma City chanting them, like an American mantra— giving special emphasis to the euphony echoing from the head line of the chorus—

> *In a mountain greenery where God paints the scenery . . .*
> *Beans could get no keener reception in a beanery . . .*
> *We could find no cleaner retreat from life's machinery . . .*

The library cards had been more crucial. They amounted to real transportation and, by the time he was out of junior high, he had a neat bundle of them from the places they had lived, bound up with a dirty red rubber band, like little tickets. He had gotten his first card in fifth grade—from the Highland Park library in North Dallas—and had immediately set off rationalizing his own transience by reading books about more intrepid and hardpressed travelers than himself—boys' books about explorers to begin with: *I Sailed with Magellan, Cabin Boy to Columbus, Captain Cook: Navigator, Two Years before the Mast,* et cetera. But he soon moved on to any book that appeared, even vaguely, to be about square-riggers. In the process he had fallen upon *Captains Courageous, Typee* and *Omoo*—stronger stuff for him. Cannibals. Yum yum. He knew about that.

Then, soon after they moved to California, he had checked out *The Adventures of Huckleberry Finn* (probably because it said "Adventures") and formulated out of it a little metaphor for his life. He and his family were "river people," he decided, floating along down this endless highway, adventurers who lived in space and time. The people who lived in the places where they touched down were "bank people," affixed to the earth and living in time alone. Then, about six months later, on a brilliant Southern California morning, prowling around among the redneck bums and elderly Jews who populated the Santa Monica public library, he had stumbled upon the Mother Lode—an entire shelf of these dusty, dark green books with silhouettes of square-riggers stamped in dark orange on their spines. He checked out two to start with: *The Nigger of the Narcissus*, because of its sinister title (his dad was a jazz musician so they couldn't use the word "nigger" at home), and one called *Youth*, because he was a youth. (He was in sixth grade at the time.) And if one's life could ever be said to begin at any moment beyond birth, his, at that moment, had.

He read as many and as much of those dark green books as he could, understanding maybe one-tenth of what was happening but reading them nevertheless, as he had memorized "Mountain Greenery," because he really didn't have a choice, and because kids are more tolerant of not understanding. He didn't understand Joseph Conrad, he knew, but he didn't understand the telephone or the television either, and that didn't stop him from using them. But he had not used these books to escape. Escape was easy. It was what his family did. He had *consulted* Conrad on how best to behave in unstable circumstances. He knew the books were "just stories," of course, but he never thought of "suspending his disbelief," rather the reverse. He tested every line against the world as he knew it and found Conrad, on the whole, to be a fairly reliable old guy.

Even so, he had given up on *Lord Jim* and *Nostromo*, and *Victory*—which he never *had* got through. But *Youth*, and *The Nigger of the Narcissus*, and *The Shadow Line*, and *The Secret Sharer*, and *Typhoon*, and *Almayer's Folly*—they were everything he wanted to know and how he wanted to know it. And even today, if he listened for the qualities of any "good" writer in his own writing, the music he heard, most prominently, came echoing from those pages he had read on the beach beneath the Palisades —fugitive remnants of those dark green books and of Conrad's skeptical, recursive manner.

In early 1970 he had gathered up all the fiction he had written during the previous decade and executed one final, valedictory swoop through it—making extensive revisions. He did everything he could for those stories, because, by then, they had done all they could for him. Then he packed the manuscripts up in a blue cardboard carton where, along with some old song lyrics and a few packets of canceled checks, they were to remain for the next fifteen years. But he had not packed them away with any sense of disappointment or failure or rejection, nor had he, during the intervening years, despaired for their privacy. Rather the reverse. He thought they were good stories—and that he could get along without them. Packing them away had been a gesture of confidence and a symbol of his disdain.

The truth was, if he had written the story of his life up until that moment, it would have had a happy ending. (He would have never done so, of course; he was too determined that *his* American life, Scott Fitzgerald notwithstanding, was going to have a second act.) He had found a home for his manners and morals in the mean streets and gorgeous salons of Pop America, and a touchstone for his writing, as well, in the flexible imaginative prose of nineteenth-century writers like De Quincey and Ruskin. That was all he needed—a past and a present—so he left, taking these stories with him, feeling at the time that their existence had less to do with his having written them than with their having taught him how to write, and having taught him as well—by contrary example—how he wanted to write and how he wanted to live and how he did not.

He had known by then, for instance, that it was important for him to do for a living what he did to live, for no more complex reason than that his parents had not been able to. So he could never be one of those writers who lived to write, who could teach to support their habit and take consolation in the prospect of posterity's garland and comfortable retirement benefits. He wrote to live and so should write for a living. He cared fuck-all for posterity—its garlands or its deferred benefits—and higher education had rendered him profoundly unsuited for academic life. Moreover, he had been then, as he remained now, a fool so beguiled by the dazzle and friction of the life "out there" that he would gladly type long hours into the night—writing prose with the shelf life of milk—for the privilege of living as much as possible in the private, untidy midst of it.

And he had known then that he was not going to win that privilege writing short fiction. And long fiction was out of the question. First, his life to date had been too episodic for him to have had any experience of sustained behavior (if, indeed, such a thing existed). Second, he had no intention of "going off to fictionland" for a long enough time to write a novel. (He would have come back chattering like a chipmunk.) And finally, he was too much a musician to write anything that took more than one sitting to read. He was a sprinter (a hurdler, really) and what mattered most to him in writing (assuming, of course, the integrity of what was being said) had always been the mental music of the language rushing by, from start to finish, as a single occasion.

So if you had asked him, when he was writing these stories, what he wanted them to *do*, he would have told you that he wanted them to move along like dark and silent machines, without pings or clatters. He always visualized it in a high-angle view: a sweeping expanse of the starlit high plains bisected by a blade-thin, steel gray ribbon of highway along which, as effortlessly and as invisibly as a thought, this black coupe de ville ran without

lights between two towns whose lights, scattered out like hand-
fuls of diamond dust, you could just make out, glowing in the
opposite distances of the dark, receding plain.

That was the idea he had. And even though nothing he wrote
at the time achieved anything like that kind of clandestine swift-
ness, that intellectual alacrity, that *was* the image up against
which he tested his decisions. And for a writer like that, one for
whom the order in which things happened on the page and the
relative speed at which they took place mattered as much as the
events themselves, the idea of writing at length, of a reader starting and stopping, and starting again wherever, whenever, was
simply unthinkable. (Which meant that he knew it happened; he
simply couldn't think about it.) It put his entire machinery of decision out of whack. He could never write anything in "pieces."
He always went straight through, first to last, every time, because
the last words only occurred, he felt, as a temporal consequence
of the first.

He hadn't known why. That was just the way the language
came alive for him. And this meant that for him, compared to the
issue of length, the issue of fiction or nonfiction became a moot
one. In fact, strictly speaking (and he could be a strict speaker),
it disappeared altogether. If you were listening to the music
with your faculties engaged, all narrative became argument and
all argument, narration—neither more or less "rational" than
the other, nor more or less "imaginative"—and the difference
between "characters" and "concepts" was that you gave them
different kinds of names.

But *nobody* (excepting Coleridge and some Frenchmen he was
reading) was *that* strict, and at the time he had cared very urgently about the world his words portrayed, and about the integrity with which they portrayed it. So there had been an issue. It
had to do with "showing" and "telling"—with whether you were
looking or listening, and with what you were looking at and what
you were listening to. He suspected, for instance, that in the kind
of fiction he had learned to write, everyone was looking at the
pictures and nobody was listening to the words, so that the men-

tal music, which *made* whatever magic there was, remained, by the conventions of the genre, unheard, subliminal. Everyone, he suspected, was disengaging the clutch and "participating" in the illusion—and he did not wish it so. It was too covert. It smacked of seduction, which he hated, and made flirtation, which he really enjoyed, all but impossible. He would always opt for the risk-taking of the latter over the manipulation of the former.

But it was more complicated than that. It wasn't simply that the "showing" masked the "telling." It was that the things he wanted to "tell" could *not* be "shown," because the change from "telling" to "showing" altered their essential character. It took him long enough but he finally figured out that the world he had learned to live in and the ways he had been taught to describe it just did not fit, period, end of report. He lived in the invisible West, in a world of words not pictures, in an America whose aural and ideological nature simply could not be portrayed within the visual and psychological parameters of modern fiction, not without infecting it with the framed, sensory materiality of "modern art" and abandoning all felicity to what he felt to be its primary virtue: its acquiescence to the dry and quiet flow of real time in negative space and the elaborate dance of language and behavior created by the people who lived in that space—people for whom, in the absence of anything else, language and behavior were everything.

He had paid a price to learn this. Early in the sixties he had written a story called "I'm Bound to Follow the Longhorn Cows." It had been based on a news item from the Austin paper and written as a solution to the sort of cinematic problem Michelangelo Antonioni might have conjured up for a film class: *Rather than telling your story by moving a character through the world, hold your character stationary and tell a story by moving the world around him.*

He had further intended, in the process of solving this problem, to give people some idea of what a sensible and likable man his grandfather had been, and some idea, as well, of what his grandfather's world must have been like. Rereading the story, however, two years after the fact, he found that the cinematic conditions and point-of-view conventions he had set into place had subverted not only his intentions but his imagination as well. First, by placing the reader in his grandfather's head, he had not only invaded the old man's privacy but, by encouraging the reader to "identify" with him and see through his eyes, he had generalized the old man's character and shifted the focus from his individuality to whatever of his "feelings" the reader might share.

And what was even worse, in the process of translating "telling" into "showing" he had mythologized the whole environment, making it blunt and stupid and "archetypal." That bathtub, which in his mind had been the actual bathtub, the one in his grandparents' house, had been transformed by method into this resonant, all-purpose *declivity*—a combination womb, deluge and baptismal font. And around this inadvertently resonant symbol the story had arranged itself as a mythical folktale about Death and Rebirth, about Man Born Again Washed in the Water of Life, about Temptation, Baptism and Redemption. So that even the "meaningful" pictures he had intentionally employed to imply the old man's sense of his own impotence (cows losing legs, cowboys sans noses) took on anagogic overtones. *A fucking Jungian gumbo!* he thought to himself. It even had a sacrificial virgin.

He was able to see, then, that the trendy, "cinematic," formal agenda he had implemented to translate what he meant to "tell" into what he thought he should "show" was, in practice, not too dissimilar from the agenda a medieval artisan might have employed to translate some Aquinian theological point into a stained-glass window. And however stunningly beautiful the resulting window might have been, however powerfully accessible it might have been to the peasants kneeling beneath it in the colored light, Aquinas it wasn't gonna be. And neither was he a medieval artisan.

He was simply dismayed, profoundly so—and not a little ter-

rified. Had he, in fact, been brainwashed by graduate school?
Was this, at last, his retribution for dodging the draft: that, in his
effort to honor a single man, a plain citizen of the republic, he
would end up writing a fantasy of *salvation*? And a "successful"
one to boot! Because there was the rub. He *did* want to write
"successful" stories, and he thought "I'm Bound to Follow the
Longhorn Cows" was one of them. But it was hard to measure
the success of an endeavor which had failed so miserably in its
human task and somehow exploited his grampaw in the process.

Further, he was genuinely surprised to find he felt so strongly
about it. Up until that time he had more or less assumed that he
agreed with Faulkner's dictum that one "Ode on a Grecian Urn"
was worth any number of little old ladies. Now, he wasn't so sure.
And so, a few years later, to make amends with the memory of
his grandfather and to restore some integrity to the world he felt
he had misportrayed, he tried again. In "Three Days in a South
Texas Spring," though, he abandoned the "cinema," and tried to
make a plainer, less "successful" style for that plainer and less
successful world, and to pour into it as much talk and music, as
much memory and decent behavior as he could, because it was
that invisible filigree, and nothing you could "show" or "identify
with," that filled up that empty country and made it beautiful
for him.

†

At the time, however, his rudimentary insights into the perils
of "modernizing" the West had only served to move his stock
rather precipitously downward in the eyes of his contemporaries.
In the early sixties, around the time he wrote "I'm Bound to
Follow the Longhorn Cows," he had written a number of other
historical romances, based on stories his grandparents had told
him about West Texas. They were not "horse operas" exactly,
but "pony epiphanies" for sure, and his friends had liked them a
lot. In fact, years later, after he had exhausted that material and
begun trying to write about subjects a little closer to his heart
and life, they *still* liked them. "I still like the cowboy stories,"

they would say after reading one of his recent efforts. This had distressed him. He worried about his stories. He worried about whether he'd lost it before he ever had it. But, finally, since he did have *some* confidence, he just worried about his friends.

Also, he really wasn't much of a cowperson at all. He had grown up around jazz and, if the truth were told, he knew a good deal more about The Bird than he did about the horse. Probably as a result of this, he had begun to feel that there were whole dimensions of everyday experience whose complexity and depths he could not even find a way to hint at in his stories. Somehow, he began to feel, the content of his writing was becoming less and less indicative of his own experience and more and more indicative of the kind of experience that kind of writing could best portray (guns and guys, death and landscape, explosions and existential weather), which was the kind of writing his peers and professors were reading—and the kind of subject matter they approved of. And he found himself floundering around, more and more desperately, for some handhold on what he was doing, or some explanation for his being so far out to sea.

Then, in 1964, he had had one of those wonderful years that everyone deserves at least one of—one of those moments when you realize that you might be crazy, but at least you're not crazy alone. First, he had gotten married and gotten fired from his teaching assistantship. Then he had gone to New York and to Europe and come home with his head full of rock and roll and his eyes popping out: he had seen his first Warhols and Lichtensteins, his first Rosenquists and Ruschas. And finally, he had read two books which, if they did not change his life, at least confirmed its direction and reassured him that all his fretting about "showing" and "telling," about the word and the world, had not been in vain.

The first book had been *The Horse Knows the Way* by John O'Hara, whose books he had sought out for the same reason he sought out the paintings of John Everett Millais: everybody he hated hated them, so there *had* to be something there. And there was. The first story in the book, "All Tied Up," was about a bank teller in a small Pennsylvania town who decides one day that since he stands behind a counter at work, it would certainly be all right for him to wear his slip-on loafers to work rather than his lace-up bank-friendly shoes. The ultimate consequence of this small indiscretion is that another young man's life is nearly destroyed.

And that one story, when he read it, felt, sounded, looked and tasted more like the world he lived in than anything he had read in three years of literature classes where John O'Hara's books would never appear—because there were no pictures in them, nor myths, nor metaphors—neither generalized experience nor invitations to empathy. There was just that plain-style American world told in O'Hara's voice and in the American voices of his characters, who stayed life-size—no high-angle shots, no low-angle pan; in fact, no cinema anywhere.

By the time he finished the book he was a little stunned and very excited. O'Hara had figured out how to do something he didn't think could be done: he had figured out a way to write about *everybody*, about *anybody*, anywhere in America, and seemed delighted to do it. All the other writers he knew at that time (excepting his beach buddies, of course) had "specialized" styles to write about their "special" people. There were Hemingway people, Fitzgerald people, Joyce people, Beckett people, Mailer people, Bellow people. O'Hara just wrote about people, passed his judgment clearly and never blinked.

The second book couldn't have been more different. But it had been equally amazing to him, and equally acute in portraying the elaborately mediated world he lived in. Donald Barthelme's *Come Back, Dr. Caligari* simply dispensed with atmospheric reality and made a world of words and fiction, loosely pegged down here and there by proper nouns—like a great, tethered balloon —to the "real fiction" of American culture. Again there were no pictures of any consequence, just wonderful talk, extravagant exposition and long, amusing conversations as often as not (and again like O'Hara) set nowhere but in the reader's mind. There was none of the operatic machinery of "atmosphere" that set one to hauling flora, fauna and architecture on and off stage. There was no "gripping human drama," no "experience," no "character development," no "point of view"—nothing but the actual experience of reading "stories" made by words written in a row —by the mental music. (Later, Barthelme would write a junk-sculpture novel made up of menus, newscasts, job applications and recipes. It was called *Snow White* and was, indeed, about that breathless virgin and her diminutive cronies. But the title made more sense than that: Barthelme's writing proved about fiction what Walt Disney's film had proved about movies—that you didn't need to make it look like the "real thing" to make the real energy that makes real people care.)

Barthelme, he recognized, had done something just as liberating as O'Hara. He had figured out a way to write about *everything* and *anything*, in any idiom he wanted to appropriate ("Kierkegaard Unfair to Schlegel"!!), which couldn't be done within the reductive, psychological canon of mod lit. And both Barthelme and O'Hara had done what they had by divorcing the word from its duty as a provider of a metaphorical picture of the world which "involved" the reader. O'Hara had dispensed with the metaphor and Barthelme had dispensed with the world, but they both made real stories with real arguments in which the mental music remained audible and human life remained perceptible.

At that time, for the first time, as a third alternative to what O'Hara and Barthelme had done, he considered dispensing with fiction altogether. Perhaps, he thought, by simply ditching the mystification of imagined narrative, he might be able to retain both the ornament of language and the intransigent asymmetry of life and thought in real time—and generate considerably more intensity at their point of intersection. He had been inspired in this by reading Thomas De Quincey's *The English Mail Coach* (1849)—a long, apocalyptic essay which began with a memoir of De Quincey's ecstatic student excursions on mail coaches, moved on to a discussion of the importance of

rapid communication to the Maintenance of Empire and concluded, spectacularly, with a long eschatological vision—a blazing emblem of the heartless damage done to the populace by
foreign wars of empire—taking as its instance the ruthless effi-
ciency with which these mail coaches delivered the news of dead
sons, killed abroad, to the citizens of remote English villages.

It was a timely topic for the Decade of the Body Bag and
the most wonderful way of writing in prose he had yet come
across. But it would be a long time, he knew, before he could
do anything like what De Quincy had done; and so, for the moment, he settled for a serious reexamination of the tyrants of his
young manhood—the Modern Masters of American Literature
—most specifically the main master and principal tyrant, Ernest
Hemingway, to whom he now returned in possession of what he
had learned from Warhol, Barthelme, O'Hara, De Quincey and
the Rolling Stones.

Hemingway had died for him, he knew, back in July of '61.
But it took the intervening years and, finally, these other artists,
to give him the confidence to sit down and try to grasp the full
implications of that death. Its personal implications had been
driven home by the sting of vomit at the back of his throat. He
had been writing when he heard the news, faintly, on the radio
in the next room (*Nobel laureate Ernest Hemingway . . . Idaho today
. . . shotgun*), and a sickening wave of anger and betrayal had just
swept over him, forcing him to acknowledge how much more he
had invested in Hemingway than he had ever imagined—and
not in his writing, but in his *survival* by writing. Somehow he
had depended a good deal of hope from this fragile branch—
which was his *idea* of Hemingway, as another son of a suicide
who had filled that emptiness with language and redeemed that
sense of guilt and abandonment by his behavior—and not killed
himself. And now he had. And so he felt betrayed (boo hoo) and
by his own idea at that—which was hardly fair to the old man
who had written so well about the sensuality of fear and had, in
the end, only done what he thought needed doing.

Because the fact was, he had not cherished Hemingway at all, neither the man (who acted like a jerk) nor the writer (who wrote like an angel). At some level he had always known this—because he had not *believed* Hemingway, not in the way he believed Scott Fitzgerald, for instance, as one might believe a brave but flaky big brother, or Conrad, or even strung-out De Quincey. He had believed Hemingway the way he believed his rambling Uncle Harper, who wore tweed jackets and carried a railroad watch —because he had *wanted* to, because Harper's tall tales made the world a more colorful place. And he had wanted to believe Hemingway; and to believe in him, and in those hallucinated rituals of redemption by danger his writing portrayed.

And he had *still* wanted to believe—even after he had taken some really stupid risks himself and confirmed to his own satisfaction that the state of "grace" under pressure Hemingway so assiduously courted was, for him at least, indistinguishable from his nervous system's last, dreamy, narcotic defense in the face of its final extinction—rather like the swoon of a dying impala in the jaws of a lion. It took Hemingway's brains spattered all over Idaho, and three years of fretting over them, to awaken him to what he should have known all along—that the style and the lifestyle were inseparable—that it was *all* about narcotics, that swoon, and the triumph of hallucination.

He had been fooled in part, he decided, by Hemingway's citation from Conrad (the secret sharer of his youth). But he understood now that when Hemingway quoted that passage from the introduction to *The Nigger of the Narcissus*—about wanting to "make you see"—he intended something other than Conrad had. Conrad had been talking about "vision," about making you see it *all*. Hemingway had been talking about "sight"—about making you *only* see, do nothing *but* see—about formalizing in prose that hallucinatory visual spectacle that bloomed up in the presence of violence and simply blotted out the whole aggravating complex of invisible cultural and linguistic anomalies that, in everyday life, we struggle in the painful midst of. Learning to see that way was learning to forget.

So it was by this route, gradually, that he had come into the

knowledge of what Hemingway's writing had *done* for him. And
what (at least in part) it must have done for Hemingway: it had
made a safe place—a tidy, tastefully appointed linguistic sani-
tarium—a room with a view where you sat pre-positioned by
Hemingway's elegant, prepositional style at arm's length before
this bright, post-cubist world of general nouns, from which all
the specificity, all the music, all the cultural, social, political,
familial and sexual anxieties that plague our existence had been
purged or sublimated into hallucination. It was a world from
which all those things that hurt you had been expunged by the
prospect of those things that killed you, which, even if they
didn't *actually* kill you, for the moment, at least, killed the pain.

It had taken Hemingway's suicide to teach him that private
lesson—that killing the pain wouldn't cure his disease—that no
matter how well he blotted it out, with words that made pictures,
in fiction that made metaphors, it would not heal itself, and no
matter how cozily he might snuggle up to the edge of death
itself, in fact or fiction, his daddy, and Hemingway's daddy, and
even old Hemingstein himself, were going to stay dead, and no
amount of derring-do was going to alter the fact. As Lowry's
M. Laurelle observed, "Let such love strike you dumb, blind,
mad, dead—your fate would not be altered by your simile."

(*On a winter's night ten years later, in a loft on the Bowery, he had
seen it all very clearly, after injecting himself with his first speedball.
He still had the needle in his hand when the world lit up, the pain
stopped and the past and future excused themselves from his consciousness, leaving him high—feeling remote and splendid—and circling in
on death like some great vulture riding the wind, banking on its elegant
wings, falling imperceptibly through the warm air in ever decreasing circles toward this speck of darkness on the veldt below. He had recognized it
instantly: he was in Hemingway's universe, aloft in its ravishing visual
spectacle. And it was so beautiful, this world without sex, or family, or
politics, or society or any of the anxieties that attend upon them, with
nothing but floating and color and warmth and agape and thanatos—
style as narcotic—narcotic as style. Momentary refuge, perhaps, but no
real proof through the night.*)

In 1964, however, he had been less self-indulgent. He decided then that for him, at that moment, the best way forward led back—back before he had ever thought of becoming a writer —back before "history" and "stylistic development" and everything "streamlined," new and improved, with shorter words, brighter pictures and existential heroes—back, in fact, to his little bundle of library cards. If he could reclaim something of what he had first discovered, cast up on the beach with Conrad and Twain and Melville and Kipling, he thought he would be okay. It had not, in retrospect, been such a bad place to be.

Certainly his childish obsession with adult behavior made more sense to him than the adult obsession with childish behavior that he saw around him. He had no sympathy at all with "styling." Style, for him, was a vehicle, not a grail; it was supposed to take you where you wanted to go, not just sit there looking pretty. And all he saw around him were guys customizing their writing like lowriders styling '49 Merks. The whole business seemed to have been reduced to selecting a syntax and a vocabulary that would so delimit what you could say, and whom you could say it about, that these impedimenta could not possibly deflect any attention from what? Why, from the "writing," the "pure style."

In response to all this, he set out to write a Christmas Story— for no other reason than that, by being so self-evidently "wrong," it seemed the right thing to do. It would, he decided, be a generous, Dickensian tale about decent people whom he really liked and it would have a genuinely nice man for its hero and a genuinely happy ending at its end. And, further, since he was feeling a little weird about spending all day talking about women and books, and spending all night writing about boys and the weather, this story would have them all—boys, books, women and the weather, together for the first time in the same narrative universe. Singing and dancing their way into your hearts.

"A Winter's Tale" grew up at the confluence of these profoundly unfashionable agendas and it turned out to be as profoundly unpopular among his contemporaries as he had suspected it would be—confirming, at least to his satisfaction, his
growing suspicion that his pals were, indeed, whacking off to
cowboy stories. He took some comfort in that.

Several months earlier he had written "The Passion of Saint
Darrell," about a couple of fraternity guys concerned about their
souls. His pals had hated that one too. There were no horses, for
starters. And besides, in the sixties, fraternity guys didn't have
souls, and people took soul-full-ness more seriously back then.
So seriously, in fact, that one of his professors (who had been to
Harvard, my dear) had even suggested that the young man was
"abandoning his western *heritage*," don'cha know, by writing this
sort of slick bourgeois trash.

This had been his first encounter with the academic proclivity
for treating anyone over six feet tall with a Texas accent like
some kind of mouth breather who wipes his nose on his sleeve,
and, to his credit, he responded with stratospheric pretension.
He drew himself up into a high Ruskinian snit and announced
to this cosmopolitan bumpkin that his *heritage*, insofar as he had
one, had to do with a nineteenth-century intellectual tradition
grounded in the literature of Latin antiquity, and not with a
bunch of farm animals!

"Indeed!" his professor had murmured, sinking back into his
chair and gazing at him through his granny glasses over steepled
fingers.

"*Jeez*," the young man had muttered, stalking out the door,
driving yet another stake into the heart of his academic career.

After this, he became more concerned about the extent to
which the people who were reading what he was writing were
actually reading what he was actually writing, and about the uses
to which fiction was put by those who used it—himself included.
He had been taught that a poem should not mean but be. He
didn't believe it. And now, having set out, innocently enough, to

write good stories, he began to wonder what they were good for, and for whom. These concerns were part of the texture of the times—like the Edwin Starr song—*"War! Good God, y'all. What is it good for? Absolutely nothin'!"*—as was the war itself.

In the spring of 1966, a high school friend of his went down in a chopper in Viet Nam and, when he heard the news, he felt a shudder of loss and guilt, but felt it remotely—a door slammed in another part of the house. Then, two days later, he found himself strolling down the street, enjoying the sunshine and tinkering with an idea for a story about his friend's death—just dreaming along, you know, "putting himself in the character" and trying to get the picture of the jungle rushing up. He nearly threw up when he realized what he was doing. He had written that scene, in "A Winter's Tale," when the preacher punishes himself into excitement with visions of his daughter's tryst, and now here he was, the writer writ, indulging himself in exactly the same brand of frictionless emotional aviation. And to what end? For whom? Old granny-glasses?

He was, at this point, on the verge of agreeing with E. M. Forster, who suspected that the affection we feel for fictional characters, whom we "understand," has no real analogy in the world, that the affect doesn't transfer over to our actual, opaque companions in time on this planet—that what we "feel" for characters in fiction is really our own sly complicity in the author's narcissistic pretense to "understanding" them. He wasn't sure if Forster was right or not, or even if it mattered; but right or wrong, he was going to have to climb down off the cross and stop dying for other people (and loving it).

His friend was dead—and what he had done with that hard truth was no different than what he did with dirty books. He had *titillated* himself with it, made it into pornography, of a very highbrow, liberal sort, of course ("the pornography of literary affect," they might call it in a learned journal), but exciting nevertheless, and pretty sleazy, he thought. So, standing there stupid but alive on the sidewalk, he rather glumly discarded the residuals of his fantasy and headed home. Then, later that night, needing to write *something*, he chastened his imagination with a terse little sonnet:

> The black man dead, clenched among scruffs of dead
>   grass, open eyes powdered with yellow dirt,
>   near Capetown, is, regardless of what's said,
>   not my dying. Nor can the quick blunt hurt
>   of knowledge touch me as the private flies
> from near Phu Bai right through the door of light.
>   Surprised, robbed of his privacy, he dies
>   too far away. The dreams he won last night
>   are really lost; ruined in the quiet flare
>   of shorting circuitry, they really end
>   and I remain unravaged, quite aware
>   it does not toll for me and still pretend—
>   so like a savage in my vanity
>   I call affected death humanity.

After this he had returned to "An Essay on Style"—which he had written initially the weekend after Kennedy was shot—and tried to tease it, somehow, into the area of human relevance by not pretending to understand, by adopting a more discursive manner, a more diffuse "story" and a more aural style. He had adopted, as well, a reflexive narrative situation: that is, the "essay on style," the story itself, was, pretty obviously, the narrator's way of awarding his friend the Prize for Hustling without a Net. But even so it remained a fiction. And the characters remained "characters" and only metaphorically related to their actual names and places. And without that real, rough friction of the actual world in real time pushing the language at every step, it became a self-referenced, recursive literary exercise—a snake eating its own tail.

(John Updike had a book of essays called *Hugging the Shore*, and he loved that title and that idea, but in a way he was sure Updike never intended. Updike was comparing the relative safety of "coasting" in nonfiction to the more adventurous challenges of fictional deep-water sailing. The writer wasn't ready to accept this blarney. He had charted too many coastlines as cabin boy to Captain Cook. He knew how much tougher it was to sail that ominous lee shore that the wind blows upon—as words blow upon the world—than it was to cruise the fictional, frictionless deep where you could change the wind or weather with a word.)

So, in a sense, all it would have taken for "An Essay on Style" to court that lee shore would have been, first, a little more cold fidelity to the characters and, second, his not *calling* it fiction; because it was not the *idea* of fiction that bothered him: everything from the Congressional Record to the menu at Lutèce was fiction. It was that glass wall of moral isolation you slid into place by *calling* it fiction, and the idea of depending his little theatrical fictions from the greater invisible fiction of culture itself that left him unrequited and sitting so far back from the screen. Finally, it was the absence of friction. Sex and language may have been "all in the head," but, for him, they worked best in close proximity with the objects of their affection.

Further, he decided, not only was everything fiction, but everything fiction had "a moral" as well. Whether you acknowledged it or not, approval and disapproval were being dispensed simply by the decision to include or exclude varieties of language and experience. And so, as he began to understand "the moral" of his own stories, he began to realize that no matter how earnestly their style and content might extol or exemplify attentiveness, their generic message as "fiction" was always going to invite disengagement and reverie.

Quite inadvertently, it seemed, his errant sermonettes had been devised to say one thing and do another—like that little lullaby Julie Andrews sang in *Mary Poppins*. The lyric might have been saying, "Stay awake," but the formal message of the lullaby was whispering, "Dream away," in the children's ears. And, as Ms. Poppins' application of the song had so aptly demonstrated, it was the generic message of the form and the formal message of the music that was going to be heard, every time, always, hands down and going away. No matter how hard you were listening to what the words meant, if the form said "snooze," snooze you did. And, however unaesthetic and moralistic and totally unmentionable such concerns might have been, he felt he had the right to worry about them. The decisions he made writing stories were "yes-no," "right-wrong" decisions and they had their roots in his character as well as his heart.

So, at the end of "Three Days in a South Texas Spring," he had awakened old Ernest Renslaw from his dream, rescued him from a death that seemed preordained for him, not by his imagined life, but by the relentless, ineluctable logic of the language and the narrative rolling toward completion. He could still remember it. He had written his way through the final pages of that final scene with rising dread—a sense of increasingly suffocating enclosure. Everything that had come before those moments in the story—from the symmetrical limits of the title, to the quotations from Cicero, to the circular nature of the old man's journey—seemed to say: "This is it; this is the natural ending; the old man dies . . . right . . . *now!*"

But, of course, as he had realized at that non-fictional moment, waking up to find himself sitting in front of his old Smith-Corona on a quiet evening with Mary Jane humming "Love Is Blue" in the other room, that was *not* the "natural" ending. It was the "formal" ending, the "fictional" ending for the story. And there was no reason that he could see, beyond the logic of closure, for the old man to end along with his story; it would have been an artistically satisfactory demise, he knew, but art and life are not the same, and in life there was every reason that the old man should survive his own tale.

So he had given the old man that little dying dream about the snake and the wonderful birds and let him awaken himself from it with a little scrap of song (as he, the writer, had awakened himself a thousand times). And he let the old man find the world, when he awakened, much as he had left it. And at this point, more or less on his own, the old man had picked up his cup of coffee and carried it with him out onto the porch.

For the old man, he assumed, this was characteristic behavior, what he would normally do in the evening after supper; for the reader, he hoped, this was an appropriately sotto voce ending to a rather self-consciously prosaic narrative; for another writer, he supposed, this would have been an everyday artistic decision, to let the story end like that, with a nice, quiet diminuendo—a Scott Fitzgerald "dying fall." But for him it was a valedictory to fiction. He had written himself right up to the point of killing a person—albeit an imaginary one—for effect and affect and in the service of mathematical elegance. And he hadn't done it; and that, for him, was that.

He had picked up his cup of coffee, carried it with him out onto the porch and looked at the actual evening. After a while his actual wife came out and looked at it with him. He knew then that he had awakened himself, finally, from the kind of aesthetic dreaming that put you in a cork-lined room and let you consider killing off old men for formal reasons—and knew further that, having done so, he had, in his own private way, stepped once and for all out of the mighty, emotional, historical flow of modern culture and into a world more modest and private—a world less "significant," though to his eye no less glamorous. And that had been all right with him. That mighty, emotional, historical flow of modern culture had built death camps, for formal reasons, and killed other old men, *real* old men, in the name of artistic purity. It had composed its cities like cartographic Mondrians with tastefully isolated areas of color, and blighted the horizon with geometry. And now, looking back on that moment from the distance of eighteen years, he found no reason to fault its primary insight—that formal decisions have their moral impli-cations. But what he remembered most was the tingling in his feet. Standing there with his wife on that concrete porch in the purple evening, he had felt so light he could have flown.

Dave Hickey is a free-lance writer and critic now living in San Diego.

✝

Jacket collage is by Terry Allen, using images from
Jacques-Louis David's *The Death of Marat* (1793).
Allen is an artist and songwriter from Lubbock,
Texas, who presently lives in New Mexico.